The Adventure of the
Castle Thief

AND OTHER EXPEDITIONS AND INDISCRETIONS

Art Taylor

D1572028

The Adventure of the
Castle Thief

AND OTHER EXPEDITIONS AND INDISCRETIONS

Art Taylor

CRIPPEN & LANDRU PUBLISHERS
Cincinnati, Ohio
2023

For information contact:
Crippen & Landru, Publishers
P. O. Box 532057
Cincinnati, OH 45253 USA

Web: www.crippenlandru.com
E-mail: Orders@crippenlandru.com

ISBN (softcover): 978-1-936363-73-5
ISBN (clothbound): 978-1-936363-73-5

First Edition: February 2023
10 9 8 7 6 5 4 3 2 1

To my students
at George Mason University,
who keep me grounded and
also open the world in fresh ways

CONTENTS

Introduction: The Art of the Short Story
By Martin Edwards

The short story form has been a cornerstone of the mystery genre since the days of Poe, Conan Doyle, Chesterton, and Austin Freeman. Chandler and Hammett honed their skills by writing short stories for pulp magazines before producing their outstanding novels. In more recent times, authors as different as Ruth Rendell and Ross Macdonald wrote short stories which were just as impressive in quality and range as their wonderful full-length fictions. Today, members of a new generation of crime writers are demonstrating the potential of the short form for first-rate entertainment and one of the leaders of the pack is the multi-award-winning Art Taylor.

The Adventure of the Castle Thief is Art's second collection, following the publication in 2020 (also by Crippen & Landru) of *The Boy Detective & The Summer of '74 and Other Tales of Suspense*. In an author's note to the earlier book, Art pointed out that although his first published short story appeared in *Ellery Queen's Mystery Magazine* in 1995, there was a ten-year gap before he next published a short mystery. He mused:

> "So will this collection here be my first or my only?
> Give me a few years, and I'll get back to you on that."

This book gives a positive and very welcome answer to that question. I'm glad to have been invited to introduce Art's second collection, since I've been an enthusiastic reader of his work for years. The noted critic Jon L. Breen opined that Art is "one of the finest short-story writers to come to prominence in the twenty-first century" and I concur.

A few years ago, Art said that he believed there had been no finer short story writer than the late Stanley Ellin, and again I find this persuasive. One of the gifts that Art and Ellin share is the ability to use the flexibility of the short form so as to achieve stunning effects. We witness this in such Ellin stories as "The

Question," "The Specialty of the House," and "The Moment of Decision" and we see it again in Art's work. Examples from his first collection include "Mastering the Art of French Cooking" – a truly delicious example of murder-by-recipe – and "The Care & Feeding of Houseplants," while "English 398: Fiction Workshop" won a coveted Edgar Award from the Mystery Writers of America in 2019.

This new collection offers further evidence of his powers of invention as well as of the roaming, curious nature of his imagination. One story that I'm especially familiar with is "Love Me or Leave Me: A Fugue in G Minor," which I included in a recent Crime Writers' Association music-focused anthology, *Music of the Night*. The piece is written in four sections, each including the same series of elements, but aiming to provide some variation on the common theme.

Art has, to date, published a solitary crime novel (*On the Road with Del and Louise*, which has the telling sub-title *A Novel in Stories*) and his fans hope that more will appear in years to come. Unusually among contemporary authors, he has established a reputation as a high-caliber specialist in the field of the short story. The same was true of the exceptionally prolific Edward D. Hoch, who explained in an essay for the MWA's *Mystery Writers' Handbook* the appeal of the short form: ". . . the formal detective story, with its puzzle and resolution, is perfectly comfortable in twenty or thirty pages. . . Another factor is the unity of the author's mood in the writing of short stories that is impossible in the creation of longer works—unless you're one of those rare writers who can turn out a novel in two weeks' time." It is significant that when Lee Child and Laurie R. King put together an updated version of the MWA handbook, *How to Write a Mystery*, it was Art who was asked to contribute on the subject of the short story. He says modestly that Ed Hoch's were "big shoes to fill," but given the quality of his work, he was the obvious choice.

Some of his stories make playful and ingenious reference to classics of various kinds in the crime genre. "Murder on the Orient Express" in his previous collection is an obvious example and so is "Mrs Marple and the Hit & Run," which opens this volume. In an online interview with Mark Stevens, Art pointed out that David Goodis and Raymond Chandler were influences when he came to write "The Odds are Against Us," while Mike Hodges' marvelous thriller movie *Get Carter* provided inspiration for "Ithaca 37." Fans of the Velvet Underground will recognize the origins of "Sunday Morning, Saturday Night" [the bonus pamphlet with the numbered clothbound edition] and "All Tomorrow's Parties." In each case, the source material provides a spark for Art's imagination in such a way that the resultant story is fresh and distinctive.

Talking to Mark Stevens, Art said that he often begins stories with the idea of "an experiment or a challenge." This is a method well suited to the short form and helps to explain why he is so adept at concocting storylines which confound his readers' expectations. At one point he considered giving this collection the sub-title "Stories Light and Dark" and the title story is notable for its lightness of touch. "The Adventure of the Castle Thief" is a more traditional mystery than many of the entries in this book, with clues and a satisfying resolution; the situation, involving college students in Ireland derives from a real life study trip which Art led to that country a few years ago. Other tales, such as "A Blanket of Snow," for which he drew inspiration from the story of Hansel and Gretel, are much darker.

An interesting—and possibly unexpected—feature of some of Art's fiction is its speculative nature. This reflects one of his long-term interests; he has read Philip K. Dick, and says that aspects of Dick's fiction have, on occasion, acted as a prompt. We find characters encountering their younger selves, and people who are dislocated from themselves in some way, as in "Premonition," a tale about a young woman home alone on Halloween. "Restoration" is a chilling story of a sales pitch that begins with a prospective customer asking the question: "So basically, this is just cloning, right?" Presented with such a tantalizing start, one finds it impossible not to read on.

Art Taylor hails from Richlands in North Carolina and is a graduate of Yale University. He also holds an M.A. in English/Creative Writing from North Carolina State University and an

M.F.A. in Fiction from George Mason University, where he now teaches creative writing, literature, and composition and works as assistant director of Mason's Creative Writing Program.

It is all too common for academics to find that teaching literature and analysing how other writers achieve their effects inhibits their own creative efforts. With Art, thankfully, the opposite seems to be the case. His versatility and breadth of interests as an author of mystery fiction are such that it isn't easy to predict what he will come up with next. I am confident, however, that it will prove as enjoyable to read as the stories in this collection.

Martin Edwards
www.martinedwardsbooks.com

Mrs. Marple and the Hit & Run

Stealing through the stranger's yard, Virginia Marple regretted once more how she'd lost her temper at the Elysian Fields rest home earlier, the way she'd lashed out at the three women around the table—her oldest friends, now a twice-weekly bridge club.

"I am *not* Miss *Jane* Marple," she had declared when Cass compared Virginia's recent concerns to those of her "namesake"—stiffening sharply. "And don't any of you *dare* . . ." Some small breaking point reached, her proud composure gone.

But even now, with her eyesight already strained and the branches overhead muddying the scant moonlight, Virginia pictured ever more clearly—and with renewed astonishment—the spinster detective's pink cheeks and blue eyes, her hair fixed up in a bun, the way the old woman had been content to knit by the fire, watch birds through her binoculars, tend to her garden . . . so sunnily tranquil. The comparison had been enough to make Virginia want to forsake the pink and white vincas, the lush marigolds soon to emerge, the red and purple salvia set to carry her through to fall.

And yet hadn't her friends' comparison been accurate? Wasn't that why she was here tonight, dressed head-to-toe in black, her frail joints aching as she squatted in the shadows of first one oak tree and then the next, her knobby fingers pressed against their hides? Didn't she hope to prove that she was indeed as keen as Agatha Christie's old maid?

Virginia couldn't bear the thought of being shut up in the Elysian herself, of Preston taking away her license, stripping her of what freedom she did have. And after all, she hadn't read *all* of the clues wrong.

***

Four clues:
- The driver had wide shoulders, a fierce expression, short blond hair, an earring. (Even in the rearview mirror, that gold hoop had been vivid, winking nastily in the morning sun. Virginia had never gotten used to earrings on men . . .)

- The passenger had a thin face, wide eyes, an open mouth, a ponytail. (Virginia had seen her from two angles, once in the mirror and then in profile as the driver swerved around Virginia's Cadillac and sped away.)
- The truck was a silver Toyota SUV. (Virginia heard the television jingle dancing through her head—*Oh, what a feeling!*—even as she had emphasized to the policeman that it was an "SUV," careful to use the right term.)
- The license plate was MSW 1158. (Martin Senour White: the color her husband had used for each of their rooms, declaring, "Where paint is concerned, Gin, this house is a patriarchy." November 1958: The birth month and year of her only son, Preston.)

Three extraneous details:
- Moments before the accident, staring into the rearview mirror, Virginia saw that the trees along the street were thick with caterpillar nests, densely meshed and angular, reminding her of the first time she'd seen them more than sixty years before and of the rusting rake in her father's hand, the flaming rag balanced at its tip, and her relief that the web and the small life writhing incandescently within seemed to be just out of her father's reach.
- Virginia's knuckles had turned white as her hands locked around the steering wheel, preparing for the impact.
- Drivers get younger every year.

Assessments from two of Virginia's friends at the Elysian Fields:
- "Issues of personal responsibility are a foreign notion to young people in this day and age," Margaret said, adjusting the gauzy scarf tied tight around her long, thin neck, picking a speck of lint from the white linen suit she often wore for Wednesday church. "It's the culture they were brought up in, the world we live in today. They've become vermin. They've become slugs."

- "It's the same old story: teenaged sweethearts out all night playing lovey-dovey, and then 'Oops! What light through yonder window breaks,' and 'Wake up, little Susie, we gotta get *you* home.'" Cass, a former English teacher, cinched the belt of her silk kimono, smoothed the flamestich lapels, secured the copy of *True Detective* magazine in her pocket. "Today's morals are no different from ancient times. Young boys just don't know what to do with all that testosterone. Their little peckers start growing and their brains cut off."

The components of one camouflage outfit, pieced together from various corners of Virginia's home:

- Donna Karan slacks in the perfect shade of flat black.
- A black St. John knit sweater generally too warm for August, but pulled out of winter storage early for the occasion.
- A black beret picked up years before in Paris with her late husband. Worn only once, to a theme party at the neighbors.
- A large black handbag containing a wallet, a cell phone, and a scrap of paper with the numbers for the police and the hospital. Also hiding an orange flare gun her husband had kept for the boat they'd once owned. Found in a shoebox in the top of the hall closet with a trio of flares. Unloaded, for safety.

***

As she eased across the yard toward the lighted window on the west side of the house, Virginia tried not to notice how the boxwoods looked like sentries or how the streetlights cast ominous shadows on the yard. She tried not to think about the phone call she'd received from James Hildred, the man who owned this house, the man she now found herself stalking, and not think either about what the policeman had told her when he finally phoned to follow up on the incident. But she could not avoid recognizing that she was now closer in age to Jane Marple than to the younger women who turned up in Christie's romantic subplots, the ones she had always identified with the first time she'd read the books. She could not entirely avoid pretending that the girl inside the house—Jill was her name, Virginia had learned—that Jill was one of those innocent young women, waiting for some slim salvation. And throughout these thoughts drifted images of the Elysian Fields rest home: women who stared idly at the parlor television all day, their parade of walkers, wheelchairs, and ailments. And then Nell too, her third friend at the Elysian Fields, squat and plump in a frayed terrycloth robe, her long gray hair rolling in ringlets around her face, her hands motionless as they clutched along the edge of the table, that thickening glaze of her eyes, that silence.

The branches of the bushes scraped against Virginia's sweater as she pushed through the shrubbery. Pine needles crunched beneath her feet. Keeping her eyes focused on the sinister glow from the window farther down the wall, Virginia stopped in her tracks, waiting for another light to shine suddenly or a door to open—for some voice to cry out, "Who's there? What are you doing in my yard? What do you want, old woman?"

***

Excerpts from four conversations, mainly one-sided, that Virginia couldn't entirely untwine anymore:

- "What has gotten into you, Ginny? Don't you know burning is the only way to get rid of them? Those caterpillars would destroy the crops. Now don't you ask me about it again, you hear, girl?"
- "Mrs. Marple, this is Jim Hildred. I just got in from out-of-town and heard from my wife that you and my daughter, Jill, were involved in a little fender-bender this morning. Instead of you filing on the insurance, I'd like to pay the repairs myself."
- "Yes, ma'am, that's right: a girl. I can see how you might've thought otherwise with those big, slumped-over shoulders of hers, but it was her all right, right down to those gold hoop earrings you mentioned. 'Course, she tried to say it hadn't been her, but the badge goes a long ways toward persuading folks, and I twisted her arm enough

that she finally fessed up to what she'd done. The mother came home soon after that and told me that they'd been having trouble with their daughter lately—trouble at school, trouble at home. And to tell the truth, the mother looked about as wrung-out as the girl did."

- "So the driver was a girl. Well, I guess that shoots my testosterone theory all to hell. And worse, Margaret was right all along: Just some irresponsible little twit behind the wheel. But mark my words: I wouldn't have gotten it wrong myself if *you'd* just gotten it right in the first place. "

- "Don't you dare grab at this rake again, you hear me? You best learn your place, young lady, or I'm gonna tan your hide for real. And don't you be cryin' now. I barely touched you, and you know it."

- "No, my wife did *not* tell me that Jill had just driven off like that, and I had no idea the police had come by my home. Mrs. Marple, I don't tolerate lying in my household, and I won't tolerate my daughter's behavior toward you this morning. Let me assure you that I take discipline very seriously, and there's a good many lessons to be learned by everyone here. My daughter will sorely regret having been so careless and irresponsible, and as for my wife . . ."

- "Yes, ma'am, I ended up not putting the hit-and-run on the official report. Just listed it as an accident with the girl at fault. I've seen enough of these cases to know that some of these parents . . . Well, ma'am, you know how young'uns are. You have somebody snatch a knot in your tail—excuse my language, ma'am—but if you do, you won't make the same mistake again."

- "Anger and arrogance. That's right—it was all anger and arrogance when you had some little peckerhead pegged for swerving into you with that gas-guzzling deathtrap. Then you find out it was a girl behind the wheel and now you're chock full of compassion. But listen up: Whether it was an accident or not, she all but ran over you, Gin, and would've left you there without a second thought for *your* safety."

Three persistent images, one imagined:
- Caterpillars falling like shards of sunlight to the ground—wriggling, wrestling, pop pop pop.
- James Hildred doubling his belt in his hands, snapping it tight, seething in the hallway as he waits for wife and daughter to emerge from their hiding place in the bathroom.
- Nell's gaze drifting around the parlor at the Elysian Fields, her focus never clearer than when her eyes settle on some empty spot on the wall or some vacant corner of the room.

Questions for two of the men from Virginia's past—never asked:
- Why can we not paint the walls in the living room yellow, or have green in the bathroom? What's wrong with a nice mauve when we lie down for bed?
- But what about the butterflies?

One series of questions from her son, Preston, asked on the phone:
- "Mama, are you sure that you were already stopped when that truck hit you? Are you sure you had your foot on the brake? Did the policeman seem at all skeptical that the accident was the other driver's fault?"

***

Wedged behind the boxwoods, pressed tight against the brick, Virginia leaned her head back to stare up at the open window above her, its frame covered only by a lightweight screen. Voices murmured inside, but she could barely hear them over the clatter of Preston's questions in her memory.

"One foot off the pedal, one foot closer to the grave," said another voice—one of her friends at the Elysian Fields—and though Virginia couldn't recall which one had said it, she knew it was true. The years passed so quickly. Inevitability bred consent, and soon consent became its own inevitability. We chose a path, bided our days, slowly disappeared.

All too soon, Preston would ask again for her license. She pictured herself moving away from the Martin Senour White walls she had learned to love. She saw her lawn falling prey to leafspot and mildew, aphids and Japanese beetles, caterpillars and slugs. She imagined her hands clutched around the edge of a card table, struggling for some balance in what was left of her life. Her gaze too might drift off from disuse.

But now there was still time to see. She hadn't gotten *all* of the clues wrong, and she felt certain that the new clues were trying to tell her something. Margaret had called the driver of the truck a *slug*, but now Virginia wondered if there might instead be something else behind these walls, struggling to be born.

Once more, Virginia tried to make out the voices through the window, recognized the deep bass of the man who'd called her on the phone. Once more came the echoes of other words in her memory: *I don't tolerate . . . I take discipline very seriously . . . my daughter will sorely regret . . . you best learn your place, young lady . . . you best or . . . tan your hide . . . snatch a knot in your tail . . .* And what would she herself say when it was all over? *Look here, Preston. I can see things well. I can see things that you* don't *see, that no one saw but me. I can take care of myself. I can take care of other people. And if I can do all that, then surely I can drive myself around town, can't I?*

Virginia fumbled in her handbag and shifted through its contents. As she removed the orange gun, she smiled to consider how she suddenly envied old Jane Marple.

And when I'm done here, I'll drive down to the paint store. I'll drive down to the paint store, license in hand, and buy myself a gallon or two of paint.

She loaded the flare, shifted her weight, rose to her knees.

Monarch yellow, she thought, as she gripped her fingers around the windowsill and hefted the flare gun in her other hand.

"Swallowtail blue," she said aloud, to catch the man's attention before she pulled herself up and set her sights inside.

The Adventure of the Castle Thief

First-Class Coach, Erwin Conroy thought, thrown once more against the armrest, *Luxury Seating*, as the bus shimmied and shook along another winding stretch of their trek from Galway toward Sligo.

Toward the castle *south* of Sligo, Erwin corrected, hopefully fewer miles to travel, and the promotional materials had promised a treasure at the end of the journey: "Grand accommodations on a majestic 14th-century estate south of Sligo"—remembering those lines because he'd quoted them himself each time he'd pitched the program to prospective students. Winter Study Abroad: Creative Writing in Ireland. Three credits in just three weeks, a winter getaway, adventure—that's what the Global Education Office sold. "Around the World with GEO!" And Professor Erwin Conroy of the English Department as spokesman, salesman, emissary, escort, and educator.

"I wonder if there'll be a moat," Baxter said.

"It'll be magical, I know." Sarah's voice glowed.

Baxter and Sarah—blond and blue-eyed both of them, like something out of a J. Crew catalogue. They were the fiction writers on the trip, both of them writing short stories about college parties, impossibly idealistic relationships, unexpected infidelities, and lots of angst. Baxter had already proven the better writer of the two—a sharp, even Fitzgeraldian wit about class, society, and ethics—but his focus seemed regularly derailed by Sarah, whose own writing rarely rose above sophomoric jokes. Like something out of their stories, their own romance had moved whiplash-quickly from not knowing one another to fast friendship to flirting to undying devotion—with Sarah having to ditch a boyfriend back home to pursue this new one.

Lots of relationship drama, and Baxter and Sarah's was one of *two* romances that had started on the trip. What were the odds with only eight students in all?

Erwin glanced back toward Baxter and Sarah, but they were directly behind him—out of view unless he peered awkwardly around the seat. Instead, the twins across the aisle caught his eye, sorting through photos, letters, newspapers, and maps in the cardboard accordion file that Ainsley (or was it Carson?) had brought—"Organization is key," she said—even though Carson (or Ainsley?) had complained it was "too fussy, too business-like." They had family in Ireland and had spent most of their free time reconnecting with their roots, gathering research, and then funneling it into collaborative writing: part memoir, part personal essay, part reportage, part travelogue.

In the next row, Laurel's hiking boots crossed on an arm-rest, another massive novel in their hands—always a novel even though they themselves wrote flash nonfiction essays. (*They, them, their*, Erwin reminded himself each time, trying to get the personal pronouns to stick in his head.)

Further back, he could hear a low murmur from David, the words indistinguishable, and Mathilda's giggle—the other couple that had blossomed. David, tall and athletic, the only African American student on the trip, had been working on personal essays about race and sports. Mathilda was one of the two poets—a red-haired wisp of a girl who always seemed to be fighting a series of blushes. Her work was prose poems mostly, short lyrical pieces about teenage girls struggling to find love, to find themselves. The opposite of Sarah, Mathilda had been on the receiving end of a break-up just days into the trip, leaving her despondent until David turned his attentions her way.

Pierce, the eighth of the crew and the other poet, was quiet in the farthest seat back—brooding in some direction, Erwin felt sure.

Had there been a moat in the picture on the GEO website? Erwin couldn't remember, but he suddenly found himself hoping for one, for their sake and for himself too, even as another part of him kept expectations in check. "First-Class Coach" was a step up from a school bus, thanks only to that strip of nylon carpeting and the dingy bathroom in the back. A few days earlier, the "luxury ferry to the Aran Islands" had been little more than a gray hull and stark cabin with rows of hard plastic seats. All of the GEO's photos had been lit with holiday wonder and wintry magic: baubly Christmas trees on a Galway streetscape, gas lanterns along Dublin's Temple Bar, a swirl of nighttime snow above the Ha'Penny Bridge. (*Falling faintly*, Professor Erwin Conroy had thought, and *faintly falling*—a nod to Joyce in the spirit of their studies.) But when they arrived, workers seemed to be already dismantling holiday decorations at every turn—airport, hotels, along the streets. The weather had been drab and dreary. No magic. No wonder.

And so—Erwin sighed—the castle would probably be dank and musty, something out of an old B-movie. Or worse, an actual movie-set castle—cardboard fronts masking a ramshackle motel.

Erwin glanced down at the notebook in his lap, a green leather notebook that his wife Helena had given him at Christmas, less than a week before the trip. Opening it, he'd immediately begun dreaming of the *potential* in all those blank pages.

"Who knows?" he'd told Helena over their Christmas dinner. "Maybe I'll come back with a finished story myself—or even two?" The whole course was about writing, after all. Shouldn't he be writing too?

"A bunch of college kids to chaperone?" Helena had patted his hand, smiled. "You'll come back with stories for sure, but don't count on getting any writing done, not while you're there."

He stared at the notebook now, willing his imagination into gear. It was a kind of *New Yorker*ish story he had in mind. Portrait of existential crisis, the dailiness of life, a special afternoon that opened his protagonist's eyes. But like his own character, Erwin didn't seem to be getting anywhere. As he finally touched pen to paper, the bus swerved again, and a wild mark careened across the page.

That scrawl wasn't exactly what he'd meant when he told his students to "overcome the anxiety of the blank page by putting *something* down, and *anything* will do."

"Professor?" Pierce took the empty seat across the aisle, unselfconsciously his own portrait of the artist as a young man: Joyce-worthy spectacles, jet-black hair shooting out in ever-surprising angularities, an ever-present notebook and pen in hand—and usually an Irish whiskey in the other. "I was thinking about the castle and about our final portfolio"—his brow furrowed—

"and I wondered about writing a crown of sonnets that worked from the medieval through the modern."

"Inspired by your time at the castle?"

"Hopefully."

Beneath the *artiste* posturing, Erwin saw, was an actual artist coming into his own.

"An ambitious idea, especially with only five days left, but . . . want to wait and see if the castle *does* inspire first?"

"Getting ahead of myself." Pierce ran his fingers through his hair. "Don't put the forging in the smithy of the soul before the reality of the experience, right?"

"So to speak," Erwin said. "But what I really meant was . . . A lot of excitement about the castle, understandably, and . . ." He lowered his voice. "I hope it's not a disappointment in any way."

Pierce nodded, sagely. "*Man of Aran*," he said.

Which had been one of Erwin's own blunders. A classic of silent cinema and a vivid portrait of life on the Western Coast of Ireland, and what an opportunity for the students to see it on the Aran Islands, right at the source. Even though Erwin had never watched it himself, he'd jumped at the opportunity for a screening, adding it to the itinerary.

"It's considered a masterpiece," Erwin said now. "And plenty to discuss. Imagery, the pattern of motifs, the lines between fact and fiction."

Pierce laughed. "If only we'd stayed awake."

But Pierce had. While the other students had settled into their pints and then settled into a slumber, Pierce had sipped his way through the whole film—attentive and appreciative—and had talked about it later as an ode to the island's landscapes.

Focus on the highpoints, Helena had texted one evening when Erwin felt particularly down. Glass half full.

And she'd been right, in all directions. Maybe the kids hadn't appreciated the Cliffs of Moher as "the birthplace of Irish legends" (more of the GEO's language), but they'd enjoyed snapping selfies and posting them online. Galway's promise as "the Cultural Heart of Ireland" had been sidelined by a pub crawl, but despite too much Guinness, too much Jameson, too much too much, they'd still shown up for class the next morning ready to go. And even if Yeats and Joyce and Bowen and O'Brien had gotten lost as ever-present muses, the kids were still writing, weren't they? And all of them having a good time?

Pierce had returned to his seat. Erwin had been left with his notebook, that lone scrawl. *Not* writing.

Soon, the bus geared down and took a slower turn, passing through two stone gates. Erwin held his breath as the castle came into view—and then released it with a great sigh of relief.

***

Twin turrets rose grand and majestic, a stream of smoke drifted up from a back chimney, and all of it seemed like a fairy tale pulled into real life—as if a knight might go racing across the ramparts at any moment or a damsel might unfurl her hair from a high window. Erwin could imagine ghosts too, materializing at midnight, or maybe elves and dwarves, orcs and trolls and giants, and a dragon rearing its head over a tower. Or maybe the students themselves would prove to be the magical creatures, a whole school of them, the setting suddenly awakening unknown powers.

"Wow"—Mathilda's voice from the back.

"There's a moat, there is," Baxter said.

"O . . . M . . . G . . ." Sarah emphasized each letter. Erwin heard her shuffling in the seat behind him, then the click from her phone— destined for Instagram and surely another OMG there.

In their conversations, he and Helena had called the students "kids," but suddenly they did seem like children, excited and enthusiastic and giddy. They hustled out, crowding in front of the portcullis for pictures, as hotel bellmen unloaded the bags. Baxter nearly knocked over an older couple as he darted inside the castle and then rushed back out to urge everyone along. "You have *got* to see *this!*"

"Professor Conroy, I presume?" A man in a charcoal suit stepped forward, hand outstretched. "I'm Dara Moffett, the manager. Welcome."

Mr. Moffett —he struck Erwin as too formal to be called Dara—asked about the trip as he ushered Erwin through a short entranceway and into the Great Hall.

The soaring ceilings and vaulted windows seemed not only magnificent but even magical—nothing dark or musty or cardboard-ish. And here—finally—*here* the spirit of the holidays still reigned supreme. The smell of cinnamon and orange zest filled the air. Red, gold, and green garlands trimmed the handrails and the mantel above the fireplace. A massive fir stood fourteen feet high or even more, hundreds of lights twinkling throughout its branches, a silver star radiant at the top.

"We generally remove the decorations by Twelfth Night," Mr. Moffett said. "Tradition, of course, and considered bad luck not to, but with your group joining us, we . . . wanted to make it special."

"Special is the word." Erwin grinned, watching the kids rushing in all directions.

David checked out the enormous fireplace. "Take a video," he told Mathilda as he jumped to touch the mantel.

Sarah and Baxter had ascended a grand staircase draped in greenery and waved down from the mezzanine as if toward an adoring audience, though the guests outside their group merely looked perplexed.

"I feel like royalty." Sarah swung her scarf over her shoulder.

"Milady." Baxter gave a short bow.

Ainsley and Carson giggled as they plopped down in a pair of leather armchairs—one of several seating areas throughout the room. Laurel zeroed in on a velvet-cushioned window seat, flanked by poinsettias and with a panoramic view of the gardens. Two women shared a pot of tea on the couch near the same window. Closer to the center of the room, a beefy man in an argyle sweater peered over his paper.

Beside a suit of armor, Pierce somehow discovered a hidden door and behind it a tiny room: a thin counter bisecting the opening, enough space for one person to stand inside, and shelves of whiskies beyond. Pierce did have a nose for alcohol.

Quickly, Mr. Moffett stepped toward Pierce. "The bar will be open at four-thirty," he said, closing the secret door.

"Sorry about that," Erwin told him when he returned. "They're . . . intrigued."

"Admittedly, most of our patrons are more advanced in years." Mr. Moffett leaned toward Erwin. "It's not often these halls experience the vibrancy of youth."

Mr. Moffett plucked the chain of his pocket watch. Hotel staff members, dressed uniformly in gray shirts and black slacks, passed through, stealing looks at the fun.

For a moment, Erwin felt something he hadn't expected: warmth and gratitude and some brand of parental pride.

"But the castle does require some measure of reverence," Mr. Moffett continued. "I trust your charges understand that we have other guests in residence as well."

And with that, Erwin saw Mr. Moffett's pocket watch and the staff's careful eyes differently—and the couple that Baxter jostled and the man peering over his paper. Impatience, cautiousness, suspicion, irritation.

Parental pride vanished. Self-consciousness rushed in.

"The students won't cause any trouble," Erwin said—though even as he spoke, other images of the trip so far sprang to mind: the late party nights and hungover mornings, the histrionic relationship drama, the intense focus on selfies and social media. "I'll talk to them tomorrow, make sure we're all on the same page."

***

The evening was a festive one. Happy Hour around that hidden bar, everyone in high spirits. Pierce made friends with Conor, the barman, who served him a pour of Green Spot in a fancy tulip glass that Pierce had bought in Dublin the first week. (Sadly, Pierce had already chipped the edge of it—and then composed a mock-epic, "Tippled, Toppled," which rhymed lines like "my soul in sudden desperation" with "tragically irrepressible adoration.")

An elegant meal followed, with glasses of wine for everyone compliments of Mr. Moffett.

"Cheers to castle living!" David said, raising a toast—and even the twins, regular abstainers, had sips.

It was a surprisingly warm evening too, and many of the students stepped out after dinner for pictures of the castle in moonlight.

"Gothic dreaminess," Erwin heard Pierce tell Laurel as the group headed out the door. Pierce stumbled on a step, almost knocking over a second suit of armor.

Five more days, Erwin texted Helena from his room, a suite in one of the towers flanking the main entrance. But the message stalled, the Internet connection in his room too weak. He had to step down to the lobby again to send it, adding Good night, much love, talk to you tomorrow before returning upstairs.

Despite everyone's enthusiasm, Erwin struggled to regain the good feeling he'd had when they'd arrived.

Mr. Moffett's caution, Pierce's stumble, the flagging Internet. *These are not omens*, he tried to tell himself as he went to bed, and he convinced himself enough to get a good night's sleep and wake with a fresh view of the day ahead.

At least until breakfast, when Sarah wandered dazed and troubled into the dining room.

"My scarf," she said, between tears. "It's been stolen."

***

Erwin had splurged on breakfast that morning, skipping his regular steel-cut oats for the full Irish from the buffet—save the black pudding, ignored by everyone on the trip except David.

"Potassium, calcium, magnesium, iron, zinc." David ticked off the benefits, same as he had regularly at breakfast through the trip. Fork still in hand, he flexed one of his muscular arms. "High protein and low carb too."

"Ick," said one of the twins. The other shook her head. Ainsley? Carson? Vice versa?

"Y'all scared of the black pudding or the Black man himself?" David glared—another part of his routine. And then: "All these people talking about the Black Irish, but I'm the only brother I've seen this whole trip."

Self-consciousness as the only African American student? A strategic pricking of other people's racial self-awareness?

Ainsley or Carson nudged David's shoulder, laughing.

David and the twins were among the early risers. Laurel often showed up at the same time, sometimes sitting with the group, other times opting for a side table, nose deep in notebook or novel.

Today Laurel had joined them at the table, the five of them all sitting together when Sarah burst into the room—nearly sobbing.

"Did you say *stolen?*" one of the twins said.

"How awful!" the other added.

"You sure you didn't lose it?" David hadn't stopped eating.

"I'm certain it will turn up," Laurel said.

"I thought you hated that thing." David again.

One of the dining attendants from the kitchen had overheard.

"Not to worry, miss," she said. *Maria* read the nameplate at the top of her uniform. "Only misplaced somewhere, I'm sure."

Maria's smile was encouraging, but Erwin could feel the tension behind her smile, and he suddenly found himself keenly aware of everyone around them. The women who'd been having tea in the Great Hall—listening but trying to appear like they weren't. The couple that Baxter had nearly knocked down—glaring openly.

"Tell us what happened, Sarah." Erwin tried to keep his voice low. "Here, sit down."

What happened came out in sentence fragments and between sobs. The scarf "was there . . . I think." And "Had it—then didn't." And "Who would've . . . ?" And "Why?" And "I loved it, even though . . ." Throughout, she let out a small refrain of "Gone, gone . . ."

Everyone's attention was riveted on Sarah—which, Erwin would reflect later, was exactly how she enjoyed things best.

Sarah's break-up with the boyfriend back home had been a rollercoaster ride for everyone early in the trip. "A necessary move," Sarah had stressed to Baxter, all earnestness, "necessary for me to feel good about the direction of *our* relationship"—but that had quickly prompted a barrage of emails from that ex. How could she do this? Right after spending Christmas with his family? After the Burberry scarf he'd given her?

That scarf became a totem for the relationship. "It's fashion blackmail!" Sarah had said, and she'd tried to rip it in half—"to symbolize it's over, really over!"— until Mathilda rushed in.

"Sarah! What are you doing? Do you know how much that scarf is worth?"

Before long, everyone knew, but the small tear Sarah *did* manage had left it worth a bit less, which then led Sarah into a bout of mortal regret.

After that, she'd swiftly reversed course again and wore it every day, everywhere. "Even though *he* gave it to me, it has *nothing* to do with *him* now"—declaration, line in the sand. And since it was damaged, no chance of giving it back anyway.

And now: stolen.

Supposedly, Erwin thought, his attention pulled in several directions: the two women listening more openly, the older couple griping about the noise, the dining attendant trying to soothe and settle. Maria cut her eyes toward another attendant, replacing a cheese tray at the buffet.

Across the table, David rolled his eyes. "C'mon, Sarah. You're always losing stuff, right?"

"Sarah lost something again?" Pierce said, shambling in.

"No, no, it's not like that," Sarah said. But the way glances were darting around the table, it seemed clear that others were wondering the same thing.

Already on the trip, Sarah had misplaced a set of earrings (later discovered in her shoes), the assigned anthology of Irish short stories (never found, presumably left on a bus), and her passport, which had briefly seemed far more urgent and prompted an email from Erwin to his GEO rep, until Sarah found it wedged inside the arm of a wool sweater she'd bought during a Galway "shopping therapy" spree.

"*Stolen* seems a strong accusation, Sarah," Erwin said. "Maybe *misplaced* might indeed be a better word?"

"But it's not like that," Sarah said again, with deep, trembling breaths. "We checked everywhere"—sniff—"Baxter and me. Every corner of my room. And"—snuffle—"he's out by the pond now."

"The pond?" Laurel asked. They had fetched a cup of tea

for Sarah.

Sarah looked startled. "The pond, yes. The benches by the pond. It was so warm last night, we went out, Baxter and me."

"You're sure you took the scarf with you?" Laurel asked.

"I did," Sarah said. "I started not to, but before we went, I opened the window and stuck my hand out to see if it was warm enough to . . ." Her voice trailed.

"To what?" David smirked.

Baxter came in the dining room then, a sheepish expression, his cheeks reddening from the morning crispness.

Sarah whipped around.

"I tried." Baxter held his arms out in a hopeless gesture. Sarah began to weep softly.

Poor Sarah. And poor Baxter too, swept up again in Sarah's drama.

Laurel shot a small side-eye in Erwin's direction. Their own disdain for Sarah's reaction? Some message about what was happening? A prompt for Erwin to do something?

Another face at the door of the kitchen, peeking out. The weight of the other guests in the room. Pressure from all sides.

Despite Erwin's efforts, that word *stolen* kept echoing through the air.

***

"No inch of the estate unturned," Mr. Moffett promised when he arrived. "I have foremost trust in my staff to find this."

"Hyperbole," Pierce murmured. But Mathilda was already leading the students on a fresh search of their own.

"We've got a few minutes before class," Mathilda had said. "You lost it at the pond?"

"Yes. Baxter and I were . . ." Sarah blushed. "Such a beautiful night, and the moon out, and the castle . . . It felt so romantic, and I'd wanted . . ." Sarah sent a cautious glance Erwin's way. Behind her, Laurel's eyes widened.

Between the ellipses and the blush and the glance, Erwin had a pretty clear idea what Sarah had wanted to do in the moonlight.

He pretended ignorance. David did not.

"So, the scarf came off"—he grinned—"among other things. Are you sure what you put back on afterwards?"

"I"—more blushing—"don't remember."

Mathilda turned to David. "Your run this morning. Did you go past the pond?"

"Right past," David said. "But why would I have been looking for a scarf?"

Still, they'd retraced the path Sarah sketched: from her room door to the castle's back entrance, the stroll around the grounds, that spot by the pond, and then not only the walk back to the castle but various smaller steps inside. Baxter and Sarah had both returned to her room to use the bathroom. ("You must have taken off the scarf in the room," Laurel said. "I don't remember," Sarah said, and Mathilda, her roommate, was already in David's room at that point.) Then back down to the Great Hall, checking the dining room for a late-night bowl of cereal, "and Sarah took me on a search for hidden staircases," Baxter added—which left everyone exchanging another round of odd looks.

Inside, the search revisited all the nooks the students had discovered the day before. They pulled up the cushions of the chairs and the pillows on the window seat, rummaged through the presents under the tree. Empty boxes, Erwin assumed, and he was glad they didn't ask about opening them.

Laurel examined the garlands across the mantelpiece and along the bannisters, as if Sarah's scarf might've entwined itself there.

"Poe's 'Purloined Letter,'" they said. "It *could* be hiding in plain sight."

Pierce opened the hidden door to the bar again but closed it quickly when Erwin shot him a cautioning look.

Meanwhile, staff members crisscrossed the activity—actively searching themselves or only going about their regular duties?

Erwin's watch read 9:20. Still no luck, still no scarf.

"I think"—Erwin took a deep breath—"we should start class."

***

The castle library had been refitted into a makeshift classroom—tables in a semi-circle, everyone facing everyone else.

Oak bookshelves stretched floor to ceiling on three sides of the room, and Erwin pulled the smell deep into his lungs, drawing in the rich history of the place and its literature in one breath.

Windows spanned the length of the fourth wall, offering a view of the castle's back gardens and the lake off to the left. Garlands hung from the sill, rhododendron and eucalyptus, red and gold ribbons.

"Epiphany" was the subject of the day—Joyce's "Araby" and O'Brien's "Irish Revel"—but Erwin struggled to get them to talk about how epiphanies worked, how resolutions should be shaped.

Sarah was inattentive at best—inward-looking sometimes, staring into some middle distance at others or out the window at that pond. Several students seemed more aware of Sarah than anything Erwin was saying. Baxter stayed distracted, of course—worries trumping any writing.

It was—Erwin kept reminding himself—a scarf.

An expensive scarf, yes, but one that Sarah had disavowed—had even attempted to destroy.

And yet that word "stolen" kept a constant echo. Was Sarah right about that? And if so, who could've taken it? The hotel staff? A guest?

Slowly, the focus on the Irish literary tradition slipped away. Gone too were those images of knights and dragons and midnight ghosts. Instead, another storyline stepped to the forefront of Erwin's mind: some *Masterpiece Mystery!* episode or Agatha Christie novel, a country house whodunit and everyone a suspect . . . including the students around the room.

Baxter *seemed* the supportive boyfriend, but wouldn't he be the one most ready to be done with that scarf? All Sarah's histrionics. The fact that it was from her ex. Erwin wouldn't have blamed him for wanting to throw it away.

Or couldn't *Sarah herself* have hidden it? She did like to stay in the spotlight.

But then David's phrasing about his morning run had stood out. Not *I didn't see it* but *Why would I have been looking for a scarf?*

Before Baxter and Sarah had become an item, David had

flirted regularly with her. Some remnant of jealousy there? Revenge after having been pushed aside? The scarf an easy target?

Mathilda had led the search, but possible jealousy on her part too? Sarah in that spotlight, Mathilda in the shadows, and leading the search a good way to cover your own guilt? When Sarah had been breaking up with her boyfriend back home, Mathilda had been blindsided by an email from *her* boyfriend—admitting his own indiscretions with a woman he'd met on a separate study abroad in Barcelona. Had there been tension between Mathilda and Sarah then? Judgment?

If it *was* one of them, what should the next steps be? A search of their rooms? In his head, Erwin was already drafting another email to his GEO contact, girding himself for accusations, disruptions, worse.

Stop it. This was clearly his imagination running away with him, wasn't it?

And the truth was, if they were in an Agatha Christie tale, then the chief suspects wouldn't be the students Erwin was considering. Look to the twins, he told himself, or Pierce or Laurel—all of them working more diligently through the morning's exercises, relatively less perturbed by all the scarf business.

After all, wasn't it always the one you least suspected?

***

"One good thing," Erwin heard David saying at lunch, "y'all being more like 'The butler did it' than the Black man. On the street, I'd be suspect numero uno."

Everyone laughed—everyone but Erwin, hit by a twinge of self-consciousness about his brief suspicion of David earlier and then wider self-consciousness: the dining staff ferrying out trays of food, the guests working studiously at their own meals, all of them listening again.

Erwin leaned close to Baxter, who'd sat next to him. "How's the story you're working on? Did last week's workshopping help?"

"Still need more drama." Baxter frowned. "Like I don't have enough in real life."

Halfway through the meal, Mr. Moffett appeared at the

doorway, heading Erwin's way.

"Our search has failed to find the missing item." He toyed nervously with his pocket watch chain. "I feel confident that it will turn up, and our staff remains highly concerned—"

"I want to stress"—Sarah waved her hand—"when I said *stolen*, not at all was I thinking that the butler did it." A gesture toward David.

David gave a thumbs-up.

Sarah nodded. "I'm not one of *those* American tourists, that's what I mean."

A loud sigh from the corner, the beefy guest folding his napkin roughly.

Mr. Moffett gave a grim smile. "We did not, of course, search any private rooms, beyond our policy. But I wonder if perhaps someone among your own cohort borrowed it? And perhaps forgot . . ."

A flurry of looks flitted from student to student. Surprise? Denial? Discomfort?

"Wait . . ." Sarah said. "You think one of . . .them . . ." Her brow furrowed, then lifted. " . . .us . . ." Her eyes narrowed, then widened. " . . .borrowed it?" Her mouth opened slightly, jaw suddenly slack—the finale of some odd cascading of her own epiphanies at play. And then another of her about-faces. "No, no one here . . . No one would've . . ."

She shook her head, like shaking away a cloud of thoughts that had descended around her.

"It was a stupid, stupid scarf," she said. "Just another reminder about him." A swift chop in the air. "Better that it's gone."

"Ma'am?" Mr. Moffett squinted his eyes.

"But Sarah." Mathilda looked heartbroken. "It was Burberry."

Sarah held up her hand, and then with the sweetest of her smiles said, "Mr. Moffett, please tell your lovely staff not to worry. I didn't mean to cause trouble."

Baxter let out a long, low breath.

***

And that, surprisingly to Erwin, seemed to settle it.

No more searching, not another word about the scarf, at least not one that Erwin heard.

Back in the library, Erwin gave them free time to write, and they seemed attentive, engaged. Baxter and Sarah huddled together, comparing drafts, hopefully with Baxter's skills uplifting Sarah instead of her slowing him down. The twins worked together too—examining some photos from a visit with an uncle in Galway. Everyone else focused on their own writing.

Afternoon was a falconry expedition—the outing like a step back in time, the lords and ladies of the manor, but with each student getting a photo with a hawk on their gloved arm.

A pre-dinner concert in front of the glowing tree brought flute, fiddle, mandolin, and piano echoing through the Great Hall. Most people sat by the roaring fire, listening at a distance—students and other guests as well—but David and Mathilda stepped up to dance, everyone clapping them on. Slumped in a leather chair, even Pierce tapped his foot, a swig of Green Spot in his chipped glass, a notebook on his lap.

Another fine dinner, another easy night.

And a better start to the next morning's lessons, with a brainstorming of the different types of epiphanies.

"Emotional," said Mathilda.

"Intellectual," said Pierce.

"Personal awakening," added one of the twins—Ainsley, Erwin suddenly felt sure, an epiphany of his own.

"An encounter with the divine," Laurel added.

"Which is the root of the word *epiphany*, of course," Erwin said, pleased with the return to normalcy. And then a more relaxing lunch. And an afternoon hike.

Everything seemed . . . good.

***

Around four-thirty, Conor lit a fresh fire in the hearth, then opened his small alcove bar. Sarah ordered a glass of wine, Baxter a pint of Beamish. Others followed. Only the two older women from the rest of the guests had come to the Great Hall. "Two glasses of Chablis."

Erwin himself indulged in a Jameson's, settled in by the fireplace with his notebook, watching the lights of the Christmas tree, thinking again about his story. Perhaps he should move it to Christmas. A holiday epiphany? Renewal? Setting could be everything.

But before he could begin writing, Pierce wandered past, something off-kilter in his manner. Could he possibly be even more brooding than usual? Or no, nothing intense there. Instead, anxiety, confusion.

"Another Green Spot, young sir?" Conor asked.

Pierce nodded, leaned on the counter.

"And in your personal glass like yestereve, will it be?"

In the short silence that followed, Erwin could hear hesitancy and discomfort, a tightening in the air.

"The art of losing things, isn't that how Bishop put it?" Pierce said. "I seem to have misplaced it. Must be contagious."

***

Despite six or seven attempts, the Wi-Fi signal still wasn't strong enough in Erwin's room for FaceTime, so he found himself in the Great Hall, his computer at a guarded angle, IM'ing Helena instead. He watched the next bubble of dots, waiting for her insights.

OK. How about this? The scarf was torn and the glass was chipped. So what kind of thief wants *broken* things?

Great minds. I'd wondered that myself.

And . . . ?

No idea.

And few answers to the flurry of other questions from earlier in the evening.

When did Pierce realize the glass was gone? When had he last seen it? Maybe it had fallen somewhere? He'd dropped it before, of course—that chip, so maybe . . . ? (No one had explicitly mentioned Pierce's drinking as a possible factor in losing it.)

Mathilda had led the questions—same as the search earlier—but Sarah was sidelined this time, standing on the edge of the conversation, quiet and subdued, watchful in a different way. On the further edges, the two older women put down their Chablis and rummaged through their purses, as if they might be missing something too.

"It was on the windowsill last night," Pierce said. "'The moonlight sparks and dances on the rim.' I wrote that down. Iambs, part of a sonnet. The glass was there then, not this afternoon." A shrug. "Or maybe that was the night before."

But Erwin had seen it the previous night himself—at the concert.

"So, one of the housekeepers maybe?" Mathilda again. (Erwin cringed.) "They might've picked it up to wash it?" (A slight save.)

"Easy to check," said Conor, picking up an extension.

Two calls—housekeeping, kitchen staff—two searches, plus the students' own, up in Pierce's room.

No scarf before, no glass now.

That night's dinner felt subdued. Erwin found himself watching the students watch each other. Furtive looks? Secretive? Suspicious? Or only his imagination? A head shake here, another there. Something being telegraphed, something—some *things*—unsaid, some disappointment and unease, and renewed concern and awkwardness from the staff, worse maybe with Mr. Moffett already gone for the day.

At least nothing dramatic for the other guests to be reacting to—or against—with Erwin's group being quieter than normal.

"Dude, we'll get you another one—with a castle logo," Baxter said. Pierce gave a wry nod.

A bonfire on the castle's events calendar was scheduled for after dinner, and staff members had already headed past with skewers and bags of marshmallows and chocolate, boxes of Graham crackers. Several students had followed that way.

Now, as Erwin messaged Helena, the bonfire's orange glow played against the Great Hall's windows.

Across from Erwin, Conor stood in his alcove, reading a magazine, and David and Mathilda drank hot cider near the fireplace, their silhouettes leaning in toward one another.

Laurel was curled up on the chaise longue—one of her normal spots, but—

Erwin gave himself a mental kick—*their* normal spot. Someday it would come more naturally for him, it would.

But normal spot or not, something odd about the way they sat, something not right.

Another of Helena's messages popped up.

`Kids are irresponsible. They lose things. It's a scarf and a glass.`

`An expensive scarf, don't forget,` Erwin texted back. `But it's more than that. It's things these kids *care* about. And then everything with the hotel staff, like *my* kids are calling *them* thieves. Or the guests.`

`But the kids are thinking it's one of them too. Or is that just you?`

Erwin stared at Helena's question, finally keyed in his response.

`Yes. Maybe? I don't know.`

(Hell, he was beginning to sound like Sarah.)

He typed again:

`No matter what, not good.`

Erwin had emailed his GEO contact about searching the students' rooms and already received a resounding no. Privacy concerns, university liability, Erwin's own liability, FERPA guidelines. No search unless the police required, and Erwin had no desire to get them involved and couldn't imagine Mr. Moffett would either.

But Erwin had already, informally at least, been snooping himself. Several students had friended him on Facebook, and he scanned through their pages for potential clues. The only thing he'd found, though, was Pierce's post from that evening—a photo of his hand with a different glass in it. "Things change. The whiskey remains the same."

Helena's next message bubbled, disappeared, bubbled again, disappeared again. Finally, her message appeared.

`If they've let it go, maybe you should too?`

`Sounds like a plan. Meanwhile, I'll 1) Build a pillow fort in my room. 2) Hide inside, trying not to tremble or drool.`

LOL!!

Seriously . . . I'll sleep on it. Counting the days til I'm home.

Counting here too. Sleep tight!! ♡

***

Erwin stepped to the bar. "Still possible to get a whiskey?"

"Will it be conviviality you're after?" Conor asked. "Or something more reflective?"

Erwin gestured toward his laptop. "Hoping to write a bit."

Conor winked. "I know the thing."

Erwin leaned against the small counter, turned again toward Laurel—who seemed to turn away. Had they been watching him? David and Mathilda had left. He hadn't noticed when.

Conor set down a tumbler of whiskey, a single large square of ice.

"Writer's Tears," he said.

"Is that a traditional greeting?"

"The brand, sir. Vanilla and caramel. Good of an evening. And appropriate for your crew, methinks." Another wink.

"Too true," Erwin said. Writers and their tears.

Erwin had barely opened his laptop again when Laurel took the chair opposite.

"Professor? I hope I'm not interrupting."

A furrowed brow and worried eyes under their short brown hair.

"Office hours round-the-clock." Erwin smiled. "I hope *you're* not missing something too."

"Well . . ." Laurel drew out the word. "It's my notebook." They dropped their voice, and Erwin realized what had seemed odd about Laurel before: no notebook to write on, no thick book to read, only a single sheet of paper in their hands.

At the bar, Conor was tidying up, wiping down the counter. He hadn't heard.

"Actually, two of my books," Laurel went on. "My notebook and the novel I've been reading—the only one I hadn't finished."

They spoke with a matter-of-factness, as if deliberately understating the loss. But more than the scarf or the glass, this one hit home for Erwin. A scarf or a glass could be replaced, even the novel Laurel was reading. But the notebook? Words that had found their way from someplace inside onto the page? Ideas, notes, sentences, paragraphs, drafts. . .

Laurel was the quietest of the students (unsociable? shy? introspective? Erwin still wondered), but their writing had been daring and thoughtful in equal measure: flash nonfiction devoted to their childhood, their troubled relations with their family, their emerging bisexuality, their intermittent vegetarianism, their ambitions as a writer, and then their ambivalence about those very abilities.

They had no need for concern on that last count. Laurel immersed themself in their work, a notebook as ever-present as Pierce's but without the *artiste* posturing, and what emerged each time was, frankly, brilliant.

The loss of the notebook, something so central to everything Erwin knew about Laurel—this one pained even him.

"Your work there," Erwin said. "How much do you rewrite onto your laptop?" Erwin had often taken that approach himself.

Laurel's mouth twisted, half a smile, rueful somehow. "I'm an old soul," they said. "I like the feel of a pencil." A shrug—reminiscent of Pierce's but more poignant. "I'd been spending too much time reading anyway, too much time in my books."

"You're sure you haven't misplaced them somewhere?"

"Professor." Another half a smile. "Misplaced? I'm not Sarah."

"Of course." Erwin rubbed the rim of his glass. Writer's Tears. With Sarah, it would've been real tears, dramatic—melodramatic. More unsettling here with no tears at all.

"I'm sorry," Erwin said again, invested more now, differently. "We'll figure this out, I promise."

"About that . . ." Laurel bit their lip, glanced toward Conor. "The staff thinks everyone's accusing them, but . . ." They offered up the sheet of paper. "It's one of *us*, I *know* it, and it's something about the castle itself, and—"

"Wait, wait. Slow down." Erwin took the sheet of paper.

A grid had been drawn on it, student names along the top, and along the left margin a time chart in hour increments; blanks in some grids but in others small notations: "at the pond,"

"on a run," "at breakfast," "drinking Baxter's/David's room,"
"watching a movie," "Great Hall concert," "bonfire."

Pierce and the twins were marked "bonfire."

David & Mathilda had recently moved from "Great Hall" to
"Mathilda's/Sarah's Room."

Laurel's handwriting was precise, same as always, even on
the quickest exercises, and the page was crisp along the tear—a
small pleasure in class where everyone else ripped pages from
their notebooks, ragged edges and all, and handed them across.
He appreciated their methodicalness—at every turn.

"You've charted where everyone's been? And when? This is
extraordinary."

Laurel shook their head. "Not really. It's basically Clue—but
Sarah instead of Miss Scarlett and Pierce instead of Professor
Plum and the Great Hall instead of . . . And anyway, it's not
complete."

"It's a strong start." Erwin searched the grid for patterns—
and for the blank spaces that needed to be filled in. Were those
spots where the thefts happened? "But why are you so certain
it's a student?"

"That's the other thing I was going to say." A deep breath,
the same small pause Laurel always made, gathering their
thoughts before joining class discussion. "If I can't tell you *who's*
stealing things, I do know *how* they're doing it, and it's not like
we were trying to hide it, but . . . Really, it seems like the people
who work here would know too, but . . ."

Erwin had been right. There *was* something secretive in all
those looks the students had been exchanging. "Laurel, please,
tell me."

"It would work better to show you." They stood up. "If
you're game, that is."

***

Past the glow of the Christmas tree, up the staircase—Laurel
took the lead.

No sounds from the Great Hall below, empty now, but
through the door to Mathilda's and Sarah's room, Erwin heard
swords clanging against one another, a roar of music, and a
loud "Ouch!" A male voice, then laughter.

David and Mathilda. And Baxter and Sarah too? Laurel probably had it marked on their grid.

At the next door, Laurel took out a room key. Erwin stopped short.

"Whoa, whoa." He kept his voice low. "I'm not sure it's appropriate for—"

Laurel crossed their arms. "Professor," they said. "This isn't *that* kind of story, okay?" They opened the door. "Now *in*, before someone *does* see."

Despite Laurel's insistence, Erwin couldn't shake his discomfort. Laurel had a small single, the bed taking up far too much space, no roommate as chaperone. What would his GEO contact say?

"Back here," Laurel said.

The room's single window was high, the sill almost level with Erwin's chest, Laurel's suitcase and backpack stacked beneath it. The window was inset on each side, ledges inside and out, a view of the front lawn and the stone drive.

"Not the window." Laurel pushed the suitcase and backpack to the side. "Down here."

A pattern of raised and overlaid panels decorated the dark wood walls. Slowly, Laurel ran their fingers down one panel's beveled edge, pressed lightly. Erwin heard a small click, saw the lightest tremor of movement at one of the joints, and then a short, hidden door opened, letting in a burst of cool air.

"Ta da," Laurel said. "Enter if you dare."

"What in the world?" Erwin asked.

He stooped down and leaned forward into the hidden space, short and tight, the air thick and musty.

"Hard to see much," he said, leaning back into the room.

"Okay, Boomer." Laurel snorted, pulled out their phone, and flicked at it. A burst of light. "The magic of technology."

Gen X, Erwin started to say. *Not Boomer.* Instead, he simply took the phone.

Stooping again, he flashed the beam inside. A passageway led right and left. On the interior wall, open beams stood stark and uneven—no finished woodwork here—and the exterior wall was a span of raw, unpolished stone. Erwin half waited for a ghost to drift into view, and he pictured once more a damsel in distress, sneaking inside this hollowness in a flight from danger.

"How far does it go?" Erwin heard his voice echo.

"All the rooms are connected."

And with that, another picture: the castle thief, skulking, watching, waiting, striking.

Erwin came back into the room. "How'd you find this?"

"Aren't college students *supposed* to be inquisitive? Explorers and critical thinkers?" Laurel smiled. "Actually, Pierce found it. That boy's got a nose for trouble."

That first day, Pierce opening the hidden bar. If there was one secret door, why *not* others?

Other comments stood out clearer too. Baxter saying he and Sarah had looked for hidden staircases. And with Mr. Moffett, Sarah's sudden realization that a student might be involved.

"So, you think Pierce has been—"

"No," Laurel said. "I mean, I wasn't suggesting that. I know the rabbits have been using it, sneaking between rooms."

"Rabbits?"

Another of Laurel's impatient looks. "Our new couples? Doing it like . . . ?"

"Got it." Erwin waved away the image. "But wait, there's no reason to sneak around. They're adults."

Laurel tilted their head. "Have some imagination, Professor. A castle, secret tunnels, brand-new romance . . . . What fun is it walking down the hallway when you can . . . ?" They gestured toward the open door—the darkness and the freezing air inside suddenly less uncomfortable than mysterious, less foreboding than inviting.

"And in addition to these romantic. . . "

"Shenanigans."

" . . . you're saying that someone else is using it—"

"For different ends."

"For stealing." Erwin stared again into the open panel. "The doors to each room, they definitely open from the tunnel side as well? Or only from inside? Does someone sneaking through need to . . . to knock?"

"Ahead of you, Professor," Laurel said. "I tested it myself. The trigger is only on the room side, but it's not securely designed. Other side, it's like popping a lock with a credit card. Shoddy workmanship, but I guess they didn't have credit cards back in days of yore."

"And *all* the students know?"

"Not sure about the twins," Laurel said. "They keep to themselves a bit."

Pot meet kettle, Erwin thought, but again he didn't say anything.

"No one wants to believe one of us would do this kind of thing," Laurel went on. "And no one wants to get anyone in trouble. But unless you *do* think it's someone from the hotel, or one of the old folks stealing things from college kids . . . ?"

Erwin couldn't see it.

"I'm glad you told me. But I'm sorry that you had to have something stolen yourself before . . ." Something nagged at him—the bags Laurel had pushed aside to open the panel. "Your suitcase and backpack. You had them stacked up. How did someone get in here?"

Laurel's cheeks flushed. A sharp glance at the luggage—or away from Erwin?

"That was a slip," they said, almost to themself. "You can't let your guard down for a minute, can you?"

And doubling up on precautions now, Erwin saw, as Laurel moved the suitcase and backpack back into place.

"So . . . what should I do with this information now?"

Laurel's face brightened. "That's the other thing . . . I have a plan."

***

Erwin slumped against the wall of the hidden passageway, shivering despite both a sweater and a jacket. Without the flashlight, the darkness in the tunnel seemed nearly complete.

Seemed, Erwin thought, and *nearly* because he caught his mind finding stray glints of light within that darkness. Chinks in the masonry? Bits of moonbeam poking through? Or maybe light seeping around the edges of those hidden doors?

Once he heard the click of a latch—but nothing moved in the passageway. Another time, a small cough broke the silence, its direction and distance unclear.

Your imagination again, he told himself, and his imagination working in other directions too—a stakeout leading toward more suspicions.

"We have to keep watch," Laurel had told him—sketching the layout of rooms, two sides of the castle's second floor. "I'll set up in the passageway outside my room, here between Mathilda's and Sarah's and the twins. If you keep in position outside your room, you'll have line-of-sight if anyone comes out of one of the boys' rooms."

"Or goes into," Erwin added.

"Exactly. David and Baxter have the room two down from yours. One of them or the twins or Mathilda seem to be the ones to keep an eye on. One of them is probably the next victim."

"Or," Erwin stressed, "the thief, right?"

"Yes." Laurel took a deep breath.

"What if we *do* see someone?" Erwin had asked. "They could be moving through the passageway for . . . adventure, right?"

"I wasn't thinking we'd confront anybody, only . . . keep track of who moves where." Laurel gestured toward the grid of students. "More information. If someone comes past me, I'll say I'm on my way to . . . Pierce's room. Believable enough. I'm closest to him in the friend group. And you can keep watch without anyone coming all the way to your room."

It still rattled Erwin to realize his own room had a hidden door too—the same wainscoting as in Laurel's and a similar catch. It had opened easily—too easily—when he'd tried it later.

"You seem confident that no one would steal anything from me."

"Professor," Laurel said. "I don't think anyone would dare to break into your room."

"A principled thief? Or afraid of authority?"

Laurel thought about that. "Good point. *Are* you missing anything?"

Erwin made a mental note to check—but found nothing missing when he did.

"We can't stay up all night, though. What if the thief comes *after* our stakeout?"

Laurel's eyes lit up. "Ahead of you again, Professor." They stepped into their bathroom, came back with a small container of talcum powder. "I'll go through the full tunnel later and sprinkle this on the floor, trace the footprints."

Until then, here he was, sitting in the darkness, cupping his hand around his phone to check the time. Past eleven-thirty, then past midnight, then heading toward one in the morning.

The darkness gave him time to think—maybe too much. Jealousy seemed a possible motive with Sarah's scarf, but why would anyone have taken Pierce's glass? Or Laurel's notebook and novel? Really, what reason for anyone to steal such a strange array of items?

Or was it not about the items but the person who owned them? Had David or Mathilda had any trouble with Sarah, Pierce, *and* Laurel? Or could it be the twins behind it?

The perpetrator is always the least likely suspect. Perpetrators plural perhaps.

It made his head hurt—and the late hour wasn't helping. He felt himself dozing off a couple of times.

When his phone buzzed, the sudden light startled him awake.

anything your end?

He and Laurel had exchanged numbers to keep in touch. The message still seemed out of the blue.

1:14 a.m. he saw in the corner of the screen.

All quiet.

Small bubbling on the screen, a new message coming through.

everyone could have turned in even kids gotta snooze.

Professors too.

calling it quits?

Class is early.

i'll probly head in too hold a sec.

A scuffling then from the far end of the tunnel, a light pointed to the floor, then slowly Laurel's face in the glow.

"Stage two," they whispered, tilting the bottle of powder like a champagne toast. "G'night."

The powder Laurel sprinkled on the floor glistened as the beam of light faded from view.

Erwin felt for the edges of the secret door he'd left cracked behind him—grateful to return to the warmth inside his room, to have a soft bed waiting, but still disappointed. Hours spent, for nothing.

He stacked his luggage against the panel before turning in.

***

No time for a shower the next morning and then no full breakfast either. Erwin had forgotten his alarm, slept late. A brief text to Helena—Last day, last class, running late, much love, more soon—though with the time difference, she was still asleep, he knew, wouldn't respond til hours later. Rushing down the stairs, he'd almost literally run into Mr. Moffett.

"I trust that yesterday proved a better day," Mr. Moffett said, with a fixed smile.

"Actually," Erwin said, "I'm afraid we discovered two more thefts last night."

"Oh, dear. We've never had anything like this at the castle"—a slight narrowing of the eyes—"that is to say, not before the arrival of your students."

"Yes. Yes, I recognize that. But it was a night of discoveries, and we—" Erwin hesitated, thinking of Laurel. "The students seem to have found a . . . hidden passageway connecting the rooms."

Mr. Moffett crossed his arms. "That service access is for emergency maintenance only. I would've assumed most guests would recognize when they had stumbled into an area that was off-limits."

"They are an inquisitive bunch."

"Have they been unscrewing the ductwork as well?"

"Mr. Moffett," Erwin said. "The students—"

Mr. Moffett held up a hand. "The castle welcomed the opportunity of hosting an educational program. I'm sure it's been a learning experience for both of us. If tonight wasn't your final night, I would suggest different accommodations. But in the meantime—"

"I *am* trying to take care of this," Erwin said. "I will."

"Much appreciated." Mr. Moffett turned abruptly away.

Erwin grabbed a couple of slices of brown bread and butter before heading to the classroom—the last one there.

He'd planned a full lesson on "resolution" as an appropriate subject for the closing day—suitable for fiction, nonfiction, and even poetry: how to end a creative project. Epiphany was one possibility, sudden insight, loss of innocence, but more to consider: the necessity of connecting endings to beginnings, the resistance against over-tidy finales (no "happily ever after" in the real world), the delicacy of ambiguous closing images, the possibility of stories without any real resolution.

But as the discussion rolled forward, he felt himself slogging through it, and soon made his own epiphany: He was getting too old to bounce back after a late night.

Meanwhile, Laurel showed no tiredness and not even a stray peek his way that might have betrayed their investigations.

It also seemed that Laurel hadn't told anyone about what had been stolen from them. When they asked Pierce about borrowing paper for the exercises, he had handed a couple of pages across. No one else had batted an eye.

Sarah hadn't mentioned the scarf again. Pierce had shrugged off the glass. Lauren could find fresh paper, find more to write about.

Helena's question echoed. Why *not* let it go?

Feeling a quick wave of exhaustion, Erwin called the mid-morning break early—and gave the class a longer one than usual. He needed some fresh air, a short walk, something to wake him up.

But he'd barely stepped into the back garden before he heard a timid "Professor?"

David came up behind him—but not the David he knew. The timid tone was matched by a timid expression. He tugged at his lip with his fingers. "Do you have a minute? It's . . . personal. "

"Certainly, David. Glad to help however I can."

They sat next to one another on an iron bench amidst a curve of shrubbery. David shook his head a couple of times before he spoke.

"Mathilda and me." He took a deep breath. "These last two weeks . . . It's been intense, man. I mean, it's like me and her *just* met, didn't know each other, and her in this relationship with somebody else . . . and then with me, and . . . " David kept searching for words. "It feels like summer camp somehow, you know? Everybody getting tight quick, everything intense, and then the end comes and everybody's promising to get together and . . . And then poof, separate ways."

David stared at the ground.

"It doesn't have to happen that way," Erwin said. "Separate ways."

"That's what I'm thinking, Professor—hoping. I feel . . . Well, you've read Mathilda's poems. She thinks about relationships, about giving your . . . your *heart*, and what it means and . . . Mathilda, she's *for real*, and I think that . . ." He let out a long sigh. "Maybe I'm kidding myself."

David had been knitting his hands together, was worrying at his knuckles with his thumb. Perhaps they are a match, Erwin thought. Perhaps Mathilda wasn't merely an easy catch on the rebound.

"David, if you're seeking relationship advice, I—"

But already David was shaking his head. "No, no, Professor Conroy, that's not it. I was trying to explain, because . . . well, what I did, what I want to tell you, well, it might seem . . . premature, and I hadn't thought of it at the time, what it *means*, but . . ."

"David." Erwin leaned forward. "What's on your mind?"

"Back in Galway, there was this gift shop, and there was a ring—an emerald ring. Not a real one, I mean, but . . . a souvenir. But the green, that green, it was the exact shade of Mathilda's eyes, and it was . . . perfect. So, I bought it, not even thinking . . . . I mean, *ring*—you know—like what a ring means."

"And now you're debating whether to give it to her?"

"No, not that. I mean, I *have* been debating it, was holding it my hand before dinner last night, thinking what I might say and then . . . this morning . . ." Again, a shake of the head. "This morning it's . . . gone."

***

"Shift in our lessons," Erwin announced back in the library. "Small group workshops on final works in progress. Divide up by genre: fiction, nonfiction, poetry. Focus on resolution *and* revision."

Dutifully, the students gathered their things, rearranged themselves. Erwin fretted that Baxter and Sarah were the only fiction writers, feeling again that Baxter might focus better on his own. As Mathilda and Pierce turned toward one another—the lone poets—Mathilda and David exchanged glances, the smallest of losses, this time apart and their last class together. David's comments about summer camp echoed.

"I need to step out for a few minutes," Erwin said. "I'll be back shortly."

"Everything okay, professor?" Sarah asked.

Some disingenuity in the question? Did she know about the missing ring? And if so, how?

Laurel watched too—clearly curious. A detective by nature, ever alert.

Maybe all eyes were on him.

"I'm fine," he said. "I'll be back soon."

After he'd stepped out, he texted Laurel—hoped they had their phone on silent.

`Thief struck again. After our watch. Checking powder.`

`conflict!` Laurel texted back. `rising action!` Texting discreetly, he hoped.

Almost to the staircase, Erwin caught sight of Mr. Moffett at the other end of the Great Hall. His instinct was to update him, but he decided against it quickly. The morning's conversation—confrontation—still echoed in his mind, and then David's closing words too.

"We need to tell Mr. Moffett," Erwin had told David. "Need to call the students together and tell them."

"Tell everybody about the ring?" David had said. "Let Mathilda find out that way? No and no."

A trinket, Erwin he tried to remind himself. A souvenir. That's all this ring was.

And a scarf before that, and a chipped glass.

But whatever David had said, Erwin had seen his face—the emotion, the investment. And then Laurel's notebook, the loss Erwin himself still felt most keenly.

In his room, he clicked the release for the trick door, opened the panel, and flipped on his phone's flashlight. The powder directly outside his room was undisturbed—as expected. No one had come to his door. He stepped carefully through it, making sure not to compromise any actual evidence.

He would find the trail, he would take photos of the footprints, the investigation would make its own steps forward.

Except . . . there was nothing to see.

The powder remained unmarked, start to finish, the entire length of the passage.

***

"So, what does that tell you?" Laurel asked when Erwin explained what he'd found—or hadn't. "Does that mean the theft happened *after* dinner but *before* our stakeout?"

"Unless the thief isn't using the tunnels."

"So how else would the thief have gotten into David's room? And when?"

Erwin hadn't been thinking clearly in any direction, not asking David enough questions, then struggling to concentrate when he'd returned to the classroom after checking the powder. He'd fumbled at best through the final remarks—"our productive weeks together," "the extraordinary progress you've all made," "the great writing in your futures." He'd texted an update to Helena between times—another theft, more drama, but no reply yet, no advice. Still too early with the time difference? And what advice would he have expected?

He'd situated his talk with Laurel in a small seating area toward the back of the castle, adjacent to the Great Hall but away from its busyness. At the corner connecting them, the hotel staff had begun to dismantle the Christmas tree—stepladders on each side, workers at the top gingerly passing ornaments to those at the bottom. More magic seeping away, Mr. Moffett no longer caring to extend the season for the students.

As he and Laurel talked, a middle-aged couple wandered by, new guests oohing and aahing the same as the kids had on their own first day.

Laurel held up the grid from the day before, updated now and tucked inside the pages from the exercise that morning—Laurel's sheet smaller than what Pierce had loaned them, some small camouflage.

"Look. David and Mathilda were in the girls' room—both couples, actually, watching a movie. That went until past midnight. Then David and Mathilda headed back to the boys' room. You heard them, right?"

"Maybe." Erwin remembered the sound of the latch, the distant cough—possibly from inside that room then?

"Sarah and Baxter definitely stayed in the girls' room," Laurel said. "Stayed busy too. And sorry I overheard *that.*"

Erwin tactfully ignored that.

"If all that's right, then yes, the theft of the ring had to happen during the movie," he said. "Which leaves Pierce or the twins, except Pierce was the second victim."

Laurel held up a finger. "Couldn't Pierce have stolen his own glass? But"—a shuffle of pages, the exercises on top—"the problem is that I don't see the tension here rising in a dramatic enough narrative arc."

Erwin was bewildered until he looked down the hallway—Sarah and Baxter nearly upon them.

"Last day, Professor," Sarah said. "You two need to stop working!"

"Lot of sunshine out there," Baxter said.

Erwin smiled. "A professor's work is never done."

They exited a side door.

"As I started to say," Laurel continued, "Pierce could've planted a red herring. But honestly, I can't see it. He's smart, but not that way. And anyway"—Laurel pointed to the grid—"he and the twins were at the bonfire, and that went *past* the time that you and I went upstairs."

"And between us being in the tunnels and the talcum powder, the tunnels were covered from then on." Erwin took a heavy breath. "Which again may mean no one's using the secret passageways at all? They're going through the regular doors?" Again, the sounds he'd heard. David and Mathilda returning to his room, as Laurel suggested? Or someone else breaking in first?

Laurel tapped their thumb on the arm of the chair. "If there's a hidden passage *and* a series of thefts, it's a big loss to the story if they're *not* connected."

"You're workshopping this?" Erwin laughed. "If only this *were* a story."

Laurel idly circled the names of the couples. "So maybe one of the rabbits stepped out and went to the other room the regular way. They probably share each other's keys pretty loosely."

"Are you certain about Pierce and the twins being together the entire time?"

"I can ask," Laurel said. "You'll ask David if anyone left the movie?"

"Already told him I wanted to talk again," Erwin said. "But I keep thinking, there's more than *logistics* to consider. The scarf, the glass, your books—these were all very . . . public things, things that people saw regularly. But the ring was a private thing. Who would have known about it?"

Laurel's eyes lit up, their smile broadened.

"Sherlock! That's genius! *Who knew about the ring?* That'll narrow down our suspects!"

"David didn't mention telling anyone, said he'd kept it hidden ever since Galway, and—"

"Wait wait wait," Laurel said. "Galway? I don't know why I didn't think of it til now." Laurel leveled their eyes with Erwin's. "If it was Galway, *I might*"—shuffle shuffle—"know something about how the *theme* plays out throughout the entire piece."

Even the second time, Erwin found himself disoriented. David coming up this time, earlier than expected.

"You still need to see me, Professor?" David said.

"I only need a few more minutes here." A glance at Laurel, a nod from them in return. "Five minutes maybe?"

"I'll come back."

David wandered back toward the tree, watched the decorations come down, just out of earshot.

"If the ring is from Galway," Laurel continued, "I might have been there when he bought it! A bunch of us had been walking Shop Street, popping in different stores, different groups, different directions, and I remember now seeing David at the jewelry counter, which I didn't think much of at the time, but now . . ."

"Who else was there?" Erwin asked.

Laurel wrinkled their forehead. "Not Mathilda—that's a given. And not Pierce's kind of store, all clothes and jewelry and stuff. Sarah and Baxter were definitely there, but I can't remember if they left before David looked at the jewelry. Maybe? I seem to remember Ainsley or Carson—but seems like not both of them, which is strange."

The twins again, always on the edges of things.

"But who knows. Maybe what I'm remembering wasn't the day he bought it." Laurel turned their palms up, a gesture of surrender. "Guess you need to ask David."

"And you'll confirm with Pierce about the bonfire? If everyone stayed together?"

"Game's afoot," Laurel said. "I'll go tell David he's up."

"You know so much more about this than I do," Erwin said. "All of this, all of them. I wish there was some way for you to sit in on the conversation."

"Sherlock and Watson." Laurel's expression beamed. "Well . . . if you're serious . . ."

***

Sherlock and Watson, Erwin thought. Hercule Poirot and Hastings. An English manor house mystery.

Irish, he corrected, and *castle*.

Still, sitting in the armchair as David approached, Erwin felt briefly like the great detective meeting one of the principals for a tête-à-tête.

But a real detective would have taken time for *each* of the principals. Should Erwin have summoned everyone for brief interrogations? Not a possibility, not easily. Those old-time sleuths wouldn't have had to deal with his GEO contact or FERPA.

And with Laurel's new strategy, he was dealing with similar questions. What would FERPA say about recording a student without their knowledge? Did it matter if they were overseas? And what were the local laws?

It wasn't a recording, Erwin reminded himself—but even that was likely distinction without difference.

As David pulled up his chair, Erwin tucked his phone even more tightly against his leg, hoping he hadn't muffled the speaker.

Laurel was on the other end, muted, listening. An extra set of ears. His Watson.

"Sorry to interrupt before." David clasped his hands. "I know Laurel's got real stuff to talk about. Class stuff, I mean."

"I take this seriously too, David. Theft and"—cards on the table from the start—"the probability that one of the other students is the thief."

David let out a long breath. "I don't want to go there, gotta tell you."

"I *have* to go there, David," Erwin said. "The theft last night must have taken place between dinner and when you returned to your room, right? I saw you and Mathilda by the fireplace for a while."

"Yeah, and then we went up, hung out with Baxter and Sarah. Watched some *Game of Thrones*."

"Did anyone leave at any point?"

David leveled his eyes at Erwin. "Oh, man. I don't want to think like that either." Erwin pictured Laurel listening to the silence from wherever they were sitting. "But no, we were all there, a bottle of wine, a couple of beers. Maybe someone went to the bathroom, but you know, that was right there in the room."

"Which would give those three alibis," Erwin said.

"Alibis." David shook his head. "Yeah, I guess. For them."

"And at least for that time frame," Erwin said. "Then there are the other students. And there's also the night Sarah's scarf disappeared, and then whatever time Pierce's glass and Laurel's notebook were stolen."

"Laurel's missing something too?" Genuine surprise, clearly the first he'd heard of it—and did his surprise serve as some evidence of its own? "She never said nothing about that."

"And you didn't either—about what was stolen from you."

"True that, but I had reasons. No call to let everybody know about the ring."

"That's another question," Erwin went on. "Who *did* know about it? Had you talked with anyone about the ring, or was anyone with you when . . . ?"

Even before Erwin had finished, David had started nodding, a nod morphing into a shake. "I see you, Professor, yeah, I do, but . . . no, that's not it either."

"What?"

"No way that Ainsley's involved."

At least that clarified one question—which twin had been in the gift shop. Erwin could almost hear Laurel on the other end, checking off more boxes on their grid.

"Ainsley knew about the ring? You talked to her about it . . . or . . . ?"

"She . . . *advised* me, I guess . . . There I was at the counter, and then here's Ainsley over my shoulder, what you got there? Like that. I was, no lie, embarrassed, especially . . ." A wave of the hand. "But that don't matter."

"You were going to say something."

"Ainsley and me . . ." David tapped his thumb on his knee. "Well, she and I were in class before, her and Carson too—back home, I mean. We got grouped together in advanced comp, all of us English majors, and . . . well, Ainsley seemed to be sparking toward me some, you know how you feel it?"

Erwin said nothing. Honestly, he couldn't see Ainsley sparking at all.

"Nothing ever said straight out," David continued. "Just a feeling, but she's not my type, you know? Which meant showing her this *ring* for somebody *else*—awkward. She was cool with it, though. No reason she would take it."

And yet, once again: the person you least expect.

"Jealousy could be a powerful motive," Erwin said.

"Maybe so, but . . . Ainsley . . . no way."

An idea popped into Erwin's head. "Would Ainsley have told her sister about it?"

David laughed. "Maybe, maybe not. What's funny is they seem like the same person, but very different. Carson and me, never any spark there. She always seemed put out whenever Ainsley did anything flirty, you know?"

Another potential layer to the motive—a woman spurned, hurt, and her sister taking action to hurt in return. Erwin could imagine Laurel on the other end, making the same mental notes he was: confirm the twins' whereabouts last night . . . though how this might relate to the other thefts . . .

Erwin's phone buzzed. A text—probably Helena's, finally. He ignored it. No need to risk David seeing the screen.

Then it buzzed again.

David picked up his own phone. "Must be yours, Professor."

"I think so." Erwin felt himself reddening. "Excuse me a moment." Carefully he lifted it, angling the screen away.

Laurel:

`wld d hv given ring 2 m if it hadnt been taken?`

Then the second message spelling it out for him, as if he couldn't read.

`would david have given to mathilda?`

"Sorry." Erwin put it away again. "Nothing important."

"No prob." David stretched his hands out. "But everything we're talking about . . . it reinforces what I said. This doesn't need to go anywhere else. It's not my . . . embarrassment about the ring. But accusing Ainsley . . . accusing anyone, even if . . . Like I said, it's summer camp. Last day. That ring was like, what? Thirty bucks? No way it's worth screwing up everything."

"I understand," Erwin said. "I do, but . . ." Even up to the moment he asked it, he debated whether to, wondered why Laurel asked the question. "I'm curious. It's not my business, of course, but . . . had you decided whether to give Mathilda the ring?"

David pursed his lips together. "I gotta admit, Professor, the second I couldn't find it . . . What's that they say, you don't regret the things you do, just the things you don't?" He inhaled deeply. "But same time, feels like it's a sign that it's gone—like the world, or somebody in it I guess, saving me from something stupid."

I'm not sure the world works like that, David. Those were the words forming in Erwin's mind, but he held them on his tongue.

Better to let David believe whatever he needed to believe.

***

"Ainsley interested in David? Such *drama!*" Laurel said afterwards, sneaking around through the castle's back entrance to avoid David. "Maybe I should hook up with Pierce. He and Carson seem to be the only ones not sniffing out someone else, and frankly, Pierce would be a better match, don't you think?"

Erwin raised an eyebrow. "You're not needing relationship advice too, are you?"

"Everybody wants a little adventure, don't they?"

"Adventure enough here already, I'd think." Erwin pointed to the list of suspects in Laurel's hand. Sitting in the same spot again, using the same camouflage. "But speaking of Pierce, you still need to find out about the twins and last night."

"Millennial in front." Laurel raised their hand. "Multitasking is our nature. Pierce and I texted while you talked to David. The twins were with him all evening, *but* . . . one of them stepped away for some cider and one went to the bathroom and turns out he's not really sure whether each of them stepped away or the same one a couple of times or how long. He only remembers that one or the other or maybe both were with him the whole time."

"I can't keep them straight either," Erwin admitted.

"Maybe that's another clue for the mix." Laurel pointed to their chart. "I lumped them together here because I wasn't always sure which of them was where. Most times they're together, but not always. If one has an alibi, it seems like both do. And meanwhile the other . . . ."

"How did you ask Pierce all this without him being suspicious?"

Laurel huffed. "Pierce is, ultimately, clueless. He'll stare into that whiskey glass for hours, pay no attention to anything out of it."

"But you think he's right on the twins?"

"It gives them opportunity, one of them at least. And now sort of a motive."

"But how did they get into the room if not through the tunnel?" Erwin said. "One thing for the couples to be sharing keys, but the twins wouldn't have access. And what about the earlier thefts? What motive with the scarf and the glass and your notebook and . . . ?"

Laurel didn't seem to be listening. Their gaze was caught in some middle distance.

"Thing is," they said, "it's all academic now anyway, isn't it? David would rather lose the ring than let the news out. *Everyone* would rather let it go than blame another student."

"You feel that way yourself?"

Laurel maintained their same studied nonchalance. "Different situation. But . . . This is actually a good thing. The group here, the friendships . . . They're worth more than the things that were stolen. Would that be an intellectual epiphany? Or an emotional one?"

"Laurel," Erwin said. "Positive spin is one thing, but . . . I can only imagine how you must feel, all the work in that notebook, all the hours, all the ideas."

"Actually, being without my notebook was good for me," they said. "And the book too. I was spending too much time in . . . words. I needed to *live* a little. And maybe . . ."

Another epiphany? A real one? Erwin could see something lighting up in Laurel's eyes.

"You want motive?" Laurel tapped the arm of their chair. "It *is* all about what's *good* for each person. I needed to get out of my writing, out of my books, and Sarah needed to move on from that scarf and see Baxter for a change, and really Baxter could've used a break from all Sarah's drama. He's a good writer, have you noticed? And Pierce . . . " An eye roll. "Well, Pierce needs a *lot* of things."

Erwin shook his head. "Pierce moved to a new glass. You borrowed more paper. And how would that fit with David and the ring? David needed to . . . get rid of the ring? Move away from Mathilda? If anything, that brings us back to Ainsley, potentially. Move away from Mathilda, pay attention to me."

"You don't see it?" Laurel stared at him, disappointment of some kind in their eyes. "Well . . . first draft, right? Maybe the theory needs some fine-tuning."

Erwin laughed. "A writer, no matter what. Taking away your notebook, it doesn't change anything."

Laurel turned their head to the side, seemed to ponder that. "Funny . . . I *feel* changed, feel like something's changed. Perspective maybe."

"A silver lining to the thefts? Does that mean you *are* ready to drop our investigation?"

An arched eyebrow. "Let's not go to extremes, Professor. This has been the most exciting thing to happen the whole trip. And I would like my notebook back—and a book for tomorrow's flight."

***

Laurel headed to their room. Erwin started to head toward his, but Helena finally texted—Good luck on last day!! ♡—so he texted back an update. A saga! she replied, empathy but no new guidance. Sorry can't help, but see you soon!

As they texted, Erwin watched the last of the Christmas ornaments being boxed away, the last of the lights being disentangled and wrapped into tight bundles. The tree itself seemed sad suddenly—one more checkmark against the day.

At the staircase, he spotted the twins on a couch in the Great Hall. Their voices echoed—teasing, laughing. The rest of the room was unexpectedly empty. Mid-afternoon lull.

A sign of some kind? Everything seemed to be pointing their way.

Ainsley and Carson had spread out two laptops and piles of material on the small coffee table: open notebooks, photographs slumping in small piles, a genealogy chart. The cardboard accordion file sat to the side, the file that one of them had kept championing, battered and torn.

"The final project isn't due til a week after we're back," Erwin said. "Shouldn't you be enjoying one last afternoon at the castle?"

"I told Ainsley the same thing." Carson poked her sister's arm. (Easier when they called one another by their names, Erwin thought.)

Ainsley ran her fingers through her bangs. "We *will* keep working at home, but I thought we'd be further along *now*."

"And Ainsley hoped—"

"We *both* hoped."

"Fine. Ainsley *hoped* and *I also think it would be nice* to surprise our parents with . . . *something* when we get home."

"And as Carson keeps saying, we can't give them *that*." Ainsley pointed to the accordion folder.

Carson patted her hand. "It's worked really well, it did."

It was the most Erwin had heard them speak at once. In class and out, the bigger personalities had overshadowed them—and Laurel too, until recently.

"So yeah," Ainsley said. "This." She swept her hand over the table's sprawl.

"You've had some time to enjoy yourselves, though?" Erwin asked. "Spare time?" He tried to formulate how to guide the conversation toward information he needed. What did Ainsley know about the ring? Or either of them? Was there jealousy about David and Mathilda? Where had they been last night? What alibis for other thefts?

"Enjoyed, oh, yeah," Carson said. "Bonfire last night was fun."

"Nothing like marshmallows stuck to your teeth." Ainsley laughed. "And we did get out a lot before. It's been really nice to see family—people even our parents haven't seen for years. The *real* Ireland, and maybe we can bring it back to them."

"The boss here is single-minded," Carson said. "Since we got to the castle, she's kept us working. Even last night back in the room, she was nose-deep in it and—"

"It's *important* work," Ainsley said. "Mom and Dad . . . they're going to be really happy."

The smiles they gave each other, the warmth behind those smiles, the goals and focus, and then all the piles of material . . .

Like Laurel had said, Erwin couldn't picture them as thieves—not at all. The least likely suspects did strike Erwin as just that: least likely.

"Why don't you talk through some of your concerns?" Erwin said. "An outside perspective can help."

As they worked together, more students strolled by, joined in.

"Temperature's dropping quick," Baxter said, rubbing his hands.

Sarah picked up a photograph of a farmhouse. "Where's this?"

"Sligo," Carson said, as Sarah sat down and picked up another one.

David and Mathilda followed soon after. Erwin watched them closely. Not the slightest hint of jealousy. David and Ainsley laughed over some comment Erwin didn't hear. Mathilda helped Carson sort some other photographs into piles. Not only group effort, but group admiration. David and Baxter stayed when Mathilda and Sarah went up to pack and get ready for dinner. Pierce came down with a notebook and settled into a chair near the bar, waiting.

In the middle of it all, Laurel texted:

second draft—or third? and another epiphany. if you COULD write the world maybe people would get what they needed? maybe there would be a happy ending?

Thinking about the group—the group effort, the group admiration—Erwin found himself agreeing with Laurel. Wouldn't it be nice?

***

Dinner that night was a sumptuous affair, set up in the library, their makeshift classroom transformed again. The tables had been laid with purple linens and topped with candles, lending the whole room a regal glow. Gold chargers and a full array of silverware graced each place setting, along with crystal goblets—and another complimentary first pour of wine, thanks to Mr. Moffett who greeted everyone as they came into the room, apparently having put aside any fretfulness. Or maybe just glad to see them all close to leaving?

Soft music had been piped in from somewhere, Celtic melodies, and moonlight drifted in the large window. Snow began to appear just outside the window. Falling faintly. Faintly falling.

A glistening turkey—Christmas-worthy—was wheeled out on a serving cart and carved at the table. An array of side dishes graced the buffet: roasted potatoes, browned Brussels sprouts, honeyed carrots, and more.

"Vegetarian-approved accompaniments," Laurel said.

No one mentioned any thefts—old or new.

Instead, all seemed mirth and merriment—Baxter and Sarah even more picture-perfect than usual, David back to his boisterous self, and Mathilda gazing on admiringly. After the midday group work, even the twins seemed more animated than usual, talking and toasting—though honestly the toasting could've contributed to their new liveliness. They'd never been big drinkers.

Was one of them the thief? Not just the twins, but any of them?

Had everyone let it go *because* of that knowledge?

And if they've let it go, why can't you?

More of David's words echoed: *You don't regret the things you did, just the things you didn't do.*

Or that you *couldn't* do—like solve the mystery of the castle thief.

As the dessert course was brought in—Irish whiskey bread pudding—Erwin stood and tried to give a farewell talk, farewell toast, echoes of the sentiments he'd struggled through earlier in the afternoon: gratitude for the hard work, assurances that they were all great students and fine writers, best wishes for more success and accomplishment ahead. His words seemed both heartfelt and hollow in equal measure.

"And to you, Professor." Pierce stood unsteadily, raised his glass.

Everyone rose with him. A fresh glass was passed Erwin's way—"A taste of the Green Spot for yourself," Pierce said.

Erwin raised it to his lips as they thanked him. The whiskey's mix of sweetness and bitterness seemed apt.

Later, as he went up to his room, leaving the students to the end of their revelry, he paused at the top of the stairs to take in the Great Hall. Bare of its ornaments, the tree seemed lonely and out of place, and the garlands were all gone too, but the majestic room still glistened with a kind of holiday wonder, the scene still shimmered with a sense of magic, fairytale magic, romance in the older sense of the word. From the classroom turned dining hall, he heard happy murmurs, merriment.

Something about the light and the sound held a new promise, perching Erwin on the edge of his own epiphany.

But whatever it was, it remained out of his grasp.

I am no Sherlock, he texted Helena. The saga ends with no ending. Home tomorrow at least.

A happy ending for me, having you back!

Can't wait. See you soon.

***

The final morning of the trip dawned without any fresh illumination—and no light on the physical horizon either. Through the small window, the day seemed all gray—thin light, an oppressive cloudiness.

Not the ending Erwin had hoped for.

He shaved, showered, dressed—suiting up mentally as well, girding himself for disappointment, everyone else's on top of his own.

With a deep breath, he opened the door—

And saw an envelope taped to the other side, directly at eye level.

A message was handwritten on the front, precise lettering: *Season's Greetings, Professor Erwin.* And on the inside a crisp sheet of paper with another short message: *Your present is under the tree. No peeking until time to open!*

No signature.

He fingered the edge of the paper, reading it again.

Downstairs, all was quiet. After the previous night's celebrations—final night in the fairy tale—the kids had slept late. A few staff members bustled about their duties. The new couple Erwin had seen the day before were sipping coffees with Irish brown bread and butter, having a quiet conversation.

Erwin approached the Christmas tree, bereft of its lights and ornaments and with all the festive boxes removed and the tree skirt too, but now with an array of new presents arranged beneath—brightly colored wrappings, intricate bows.

Despite the warning not to peek, Erwin peered at the tags—a present for each of the students and, yes, one for Erwin himself.

But then no, no present for David, as it turned out, though his name did appear on another tag: "To Mathilda, Love, David." And the twins had one present between them—both names on a single tag.

It didn't count as epiphany for Erwin to know what was in the present for Mathilda—and in at least several of the others. But what about the rest?

"These presents," Erwin said to a maid, passing by with a stack of sheets in her hand. "Did you see the person putting them here?"

"They were here when I arrived, sir," she said. "Overnight sometime. A mystery."

A mystery indeed, Erwin thought—but no longer about the identity of the castle thief. The summons had clarified—clarified and confused in equal measure. The bigger mystery was . . . why?

***

Soon the students came down to the Great Hall—almost en masse. Erwin had heard voices and movement echoing through the atrium, seen one of the twins peeking over the edge of the balcony, but he wondered how coordinated it was—who had seen the envelopes first, who had knocked on whose door next, what role the person behind it all had played in getting people moving.

Some of the students were readier for the day than others—readied for whatever ceremony was unfolding, for the trip homeward. Sarah looked, as ever, smartly put together—her hair done, an elegant traveling outfit, with Baxter like an accessory himself beside her. The twins carried their bags with them, dressed and ready to go. Pierce, at the other extreme, seemed as if he'd literally rolled out of bed—still in pajama bottoms and pushed forward only by the momentum of Laurel, Mathilda, and David behind him.

Each of them held an envelope—even the one who'd written the notes. A mix of puzzlement and curiosity and—yes—happiness on their faces, almost like that giddy first day at the castle.

"Are you playing Santa Claus, Professor?" Sarah asked. "You really shouldn't have."

"I didn't." Erwin held up his envelope. "My own note said no peeking, so I've been waiting."

"We've been slow getting down, that what you're saying?" David smiled.

Erwin watched him closely, pondering what still lay ahead.

Curious looks all around, it seemed. Laurel had glanced Erwin's way a couple of times as well—questions in their eyes that he wasn't sure about and couldn't answer. His Watson, he'd thought—now having to put their trust in him in a new way.

"So," Erwin said, "should we open our presents at the same time or . . . ?"

"Maybe there are numbers on them or something—an order." Mathilda knelt down by the tree, turning the tags. "No, there's . . . Wait"—she turned to David—"this one's from you. Did you do all this?"

"From me?" David squatted beside her. "No," he said, picking up the present. "I . . . I don't know what this is."

But he did know, of course, and Erwin caught a glimpse of fresh nervousness, more urgent. No second thoughts now, though. No going back.

"Only one way to find out," Erwin said, rising from his seat. "Merry Christmas, everyone."

"That makes it sounds like Sarah was right," Carson said—or Ainsley. Despite himself, he once more couldn't tell. "*Are* you Santa Claus?"

"A season's greeting, that's all," he said. "No one could be more surprised than me by all this."

Already by the tree, Mathilda and David handed out the presents. From their spots on the chairs or sitting cross-legged on the floor, the students began to open them, all except Mathilda. David had tucked that small box under his leg and then motioned for her to step away from the others. As they'd been distributing the presents, several staff members had passed by, clearly curious, but not yet inquiring what was going on.

"My scarf!" Sarah pulled it from the box, stretched it out in front of her. "And someone mended the tear! But who—and how—and . . . ?"

"My notebook," said Laurel, holding it up as well as the lost novel. "And I can finally find out how this one ends."

"What?" said Baxter. "I didn't know you'd lost something too. Did everyone—?"

"Cheers." Pierce raised a whiskey glass. "Empty, alas." He stared at it, then poked into the box again—perhaps looking for a bottle?

"Wait," said Baxter. "That one's not cracked."

"But this one is." Pierce pulled out a second glass, the chipped original. "A matching set. Almost."

"What did you get?" Erwin asked the twins, quiet together on the couch.

"A scrapbook," Ainsley said—or Carson.

"It's beautiful," the other said. She ran her fingers over the smooth leather, opened up the pages. "It's perfect—don't you think, Ainsley?" Which corrected that question again about which was who.

"But I don't understand," Ainsley said. "These other things were"—a slight hesitation—"stolen. But nothing of ours was taken."

"Or of Baxter's," Erwin said. "Baxter, what do you have there?"

"It's a pen," Baxter said. "With a note to keep writing."

"You're in good company," Erwin said, holding up a matching pen from his own present. "And it's good advice." But what, he wondered, was the bigger message? Baxter had been distracted from his writing by Sarah. What had kept Erwin from his?

Even before the castle thefts, he'd struggled to write—his heart simply not in it.

"What are they doing?" Sarah tilted her head toward David and Mathilda, sitting on a couch some ways off. Her voice dropped. "David didn't have a present *to* him, only one *from* him. Was he the one who took everything?"

Erwin had been watching that scene play out: Mathilda rushing a hand up to cover her blush, David managing a bashful, understated smile.

"I know it's my job to tell students to avoid clichés," Erwin said, "but sometimes it truly is better to give than to receive."

"That didn't quite answer Sarah's question," Laurel said.

Erwin tried to keep his expression flat.

"You know," he said, "it's also my job to be a leader here, but I think some things are better left to a vote." He took a deep breath. "Everyone who lost something has gotten it back, and some have gotten extra. Is everyone willing to let our . . . mystery stay a mystery?"

Though the Christmas tree had no lights, a quick hint of sunshine through the window gave it a soft glow. The students looked around at one another. Erwin saw again the camaraderie that they'd built up over their time together, the connections that had Sarah suddenly reversing herself that day with Mr. Moffett, the fact that all of them had hidden, and had kept hidden, those secret passages that Laurel had revealed to him.

Sarah held her scarf as if weighing it. "Yes," she said. "I'm fine with that."

"Everyone else?" Erwin asked.

Nods all around.

"Then let's have breakfast and get ready to head home."

***

The shuttle waited outside the castle entrance.

Luxury coach, Erwin thought, staring out the front window—but admiringly this time, this vehicle clearly a step up from the busses and vans earlier. By design on GEO's part? Leave students with good final impressions?

It wasn't a bad approach, and the morning had cooperated too—the gray burning off, the sun climbing high, a feeling of warmth even if the temperatures hadn't budged much.

Erwin felt pleased. Triumphant even—though whatever his

role had been, triumph might not be the word, and the credit was hardly his.

Bit by bit, the students stacked their luggage outside the front entrance, then headed out on the grounds or back inside for one last look, last photo, last memory.

"Take a picture of Mathilda and me, professor?" David asked, after he'd stacked their bags on the pile. "She's over here by the fireplace."

"Glad to," he said. "And everything okay with the . . . present this morning?"

David grinned. "The color matched her eyes—that was the first thing she said."

"No misunderstandings?"

"I tried to say something 'bout it being a ring, knowing what that might seem like, but she shushed me quick. 'I love it,' she told me. 'Plenty of time to see what's next.'"

Inside, David and Mathilda stood in the same spot where David had jumped and waved his hands the first day. The hearth was cold this morning, but still added warmth to the scene, and David more serious, more serene. He took Mathilda's hand in his. Their fingers entwined. Erwin snapped three pictures trying to capture the ring's glint.

Mr. Moffett stood at a distance, watching—with approval, Erwin hoped. He wondered what the hotel staff had told him about the presents that morning.

Laurel was perched in one of the leather armchairs, suitcase and backpack stacked neatly beside them. The returned novel was in their hands—nearing the final pages.

Erwin sat down on the next chair.

"How's the ending working out?"

"About what I expected," Laurel said. "Not sure it was worth four hundred pages of swordplay to get there."

"Actually," Erwin said, "I wasn't talking about the book."

"Oh." Laurel sat up, turned toward him. "This morning, you mean? Well"—a slim smile—"I'd call it a nice surprise, wouldn't you agree?"

Erwin clasped his hands together, tapped his thumbs. "What

I'm not sure about, though, is . . . why?"

"Motive is everything in a mystery, isn't it?" Their smile broadened. "This trip, Ireland, the way it was marketed, all of it—it was supposed to be this magical experience. And for other people it was. Baxter and Sarah, David and Mathilda, these big romantic adventures, and Ainsley and Carson on their own journey, and I was . . . sitting here reading."

"And writing," Erwin said.

"And writing, yes. But not entirely . . . *living*, like I said. And I wanted a little bit of drama—drama somewhere other than a book." They tossed their novel aside. "This story"— sweeping their arms toward the Great Hall, the castle, all of it—"*this* story had crisis and conflict and rising action and not only a resolution but a *happy* ending and . . . along the way, I got to be a detective!"

"And the thief too, don't forget." Erwin said. "More roles than one."

Laurel leaned forward, deepened their voice. "I *do* contain multitudes, Professor." Then more casually: "So when *did* you figure it out?"

"Your notebook paper," Erwin said. "The clean edges of it, the handwriting too. But I missed it before—the grid you'd drawn with everyone on it. It was on your notebook paper, but the notebook had supposedly been stolen. Right there in plain sight. And the chart itself, that had two purposes, of course—tracking everyone's movements."

"It didn't start out that way," Laurel said. "The scarf was just because I heard Baxter and Sarah coming back to the room next door, heard Baxter say something about the scarf, heard them leave again. That scarf was just trouble, so when I knew the room was empty, I snuck quickly through the tunnel. It was only later I made the chart, but if you keep track of where everyone is, you do know when and where they *aren't* too."

"And the powder?"

"I snatched the ring while the rabbits were watching the movie. I kept worrying you'd hear me there at the other end of the tunnel. I was so close!"

"I heard something, didn't know what it was." The latch, the cough. "And then you put the powder down later?"

"Timing is everything," Laurel said. "Are you angry?"

Erwin thought about that—not just his own reaction, which he was still sorting through—but the others as well. Mr. Moffett crossed the Great Hall then, and Erwin wondered if he should tell him the full story at any point.

"You said a happy ending. Do you see it that way?"

"Still too many plot threads up in the air," Laurel said. "But David and Mathilda, they're cute, aren't they? That might well work out nicely, and all he needed was a nudge. And Sarah needed to *see* Baxter, and Baxter *still* needs to see he's a great writer, and—"

"And you needed to *stop* writing? Is that why you stole your own notebook, or was that merely a red herring?"

"Some of both," Laurel said. "Getting me out of my book for a bit, as I said. But I never stopped writing, let's be real."

"And a pen for me? I need to write more?"

"You'd know that better than me, Professor." A mischievous smirk. "But I didn't want anyone left out, you, Baxter, or the twins either. Everyone needed some post-holiday spirit, right? And speaking of spirits . . ."

Erwin turned. Pierce was shambling down the stairs, duffel bag in tow, but he was dressed now, and his hair combed.

"The second glass in his present this morning," Laurel whispered. "I'm hoping to be the one who drinks from it. He's really a fascinating guy beneath all the facade."

***

On the plane, Erwin stowed his carry-on, settled into the aisle seat beside a couple chatting with one another, then took out his phone. Airport Wi-Fi, one last scan through email, one last message to Helena.

```
The mystery of the castle thief is solved. Turns
out your husband is a tolerable . . . Watson. And an
accessory to crime too, as it turns out. On the plane.
Counting the *hours* now!
```

Erwin smiled. The last passengers shuffled down the aisle, searched for seats, buckled in. Erwin's students were scattered throughout in small groups. He couldn't see any of them from where he sat.

A few minutes later, Helena's reply popped up.

Watson? Accessory? Adventure! I'll be waiting to hear more!

Erwin sent a thumbs-up in return and was about to turn off his phone when it pinged again—Laurel this time.

conned a businessman into trading me for a seat beside Pierce—clueless as ever—a new game afoot!

Erwin felt himself smile. Happy endings ahead, he hoped, for everyone.

He tucked his phone into his carry-on, pulled out the green notebook and his new pen.

Another blank page waited.

He stared at it for a while, thinking, and as the plane taxied back from the gate, he finally began to write:

First-Class Coach, he thought, *thrown once more against the armrest, Luxury Seating, as the bus shimmied and shook . . .*

Premonition

In the dream, you wander down an endless hallway in a loose nightgown, glancing in door after door, looking for something, looking *out* for something. Or someone. Your hand clutches a slip of paper, so tightly that your fingernails cut your palm, and on the paper, you can make out a string of blotted numbers.

With a start, you open your eyes and see the clock flash out the time, 2:43 a.m., but you don't hesitate. You throw back the covers of your bed and scramble up to sit on your pillow, the nightgown bunching at your hips. You flick on the light, you grab the phone, you dial the numbers from your dream carefully, one digit at a time. You have indeed been clenching your fist in your sleep, a nail has broken, and the indentations in your palm shine fiery red—blood? No, no, just flecks of polish. Your breath, heavy and wild at the first ring, deepens with the second and the third. *Just a dream*, you think after the fourth ring has steadied your panting, and you start to hang up. *After all, what should I say to . . . whoever answers? A nightmare—something terrible—worry, fear, panic . . .*Then: *Overreaction. Stupidity.* But before you can replace the receiver, you hear a scrambling on the other end of the line. With another glimpse at the clock—2:45— you ready your apology.

"Oh, help me, help me," comes a weak voice, struggling and desperate. "Oh, please, whoever you are, wherever you are, he's—" and the line goes dead.

A cold terror cuts up your spine. Your thoughts race frantically, but your body, for the moment, is paralyzed. Your hand trembles as you struggle to get a new dial tone, and you fumble twice before hitting the right keys.

"Nine-one-one, what's your—"

"Oh, please help," you cry. "I've had a nightmare and when I woke—"

With a start—

You wake.

The covers of the bed are still pulled tight against your chin. The lights of the room are still off. On your nightstand, the clock shows 1:28, and by the glowing redness of those numbers, you see the edges of your phone, the receiver still in place. Thin moonbeams pierce through the gap between your curtains, and your cat, curled into a ball at the end of your bed, stretches in the dappled glow. Something about her calms you. Your breath steadies. Your pulse slows. You glance around the rest of the room to see the reflection of the moonlight in the mirror over your dresser and, in the corner, the outline of your chair.

And suddenly your breath is gone again.

Someone's sitting there—watching you. Waiting.

You see his pale arm in the moonlight, then the shadow of his other arm hanging motionless from a thin torso. *Him.*

You barely manage to keep yourself from crying out. You wonder if you can grab the baseball bat just on the other side of your nightstand. You wish you'd taken your father's advice and gotten a gun.

Then you remember the blouse you'd laid out for tomorrow.

As your eyes focus, the wooziness of sleep finally falling away, you realize that's all it is, hanging limp across the back of the chair.

Overreaction. Stupidity. Again.

Your nerves are just on edge. The nightmare, the darkness . . . and this night itself, of course. Halloween, for Christ's sake. That parade of ghosts and ghouls darting door to door earlier in the evening had gotten to you. And nothing but horror movies on the TV before you went to bed. A chill wind has been rustling and scattering the leaves all night. And then there's that moon looming above the oaks in the yard.

But you'd thought *him.*

And who *was* the him you thought might be sitting there watching you?

Your brother maybe? Drunk again, and stopping by after the bars just to chat, passing out in your chair? It's happened before. Or your ex-boyfriend, still carrying the torch, persistent with his calls and emails and now pushing the boundaries a step too far? You'd always wondered if he'd made a duplicate key. Or were you thinking of . . .

Somewhere in the distance you hear laughter—more than one person. This laughter, you know, is real. But you can't gauge the direction or the distance. Not yet.

Layers of darkness shroud the other side of the room, but you know the door of the closet and the door to the hallway stand closed. Easing back the edge of the covers, you reach up to turn on the lamp. Your cat wakes when the light floods the room. It blinks its eyes and stretches. You rise and, still gaining your balance, find your way across the carpet, picking up that baseball bat and pushing that white blouse down into a ball on the chair. Surely there's nothing behind either door—you *know* this, the laughter wasn't *that* close—but you go through the motions anyway.

Which one to open first? You decide on the closet, raise the bat high, and with a deep breath, fling open the door.

No one jumps out.

And there's no one hiding in the hallway either.

And as you work your way through the house—checking behind the shower curtain and in the hot water heater closet, in the laundry room and the second bedroom—you began to ease your grip on the bat. The front door is still bolted shut, and the second latch remains in place. The door to the patio is locked, and when you glance through the vertical blinds, you find the plastic chairs and table as empty as always in that same moonlight.

And there, just beyond, you find the source of the laughter: the dregs of your neighbor's Halloween party, the one he'd invited you to—a courtesy, you know, an invitation you'd just as courteously declined. A keg sits in the center of his deck, and he's got his feet propped up on it, leaning back on his own plastic chair. Only two others with him, at least two that you can see—two men, one dressed as a pirate, the other a gangster. You see the latter's tommy gun resting on the railing. Wind chimes clink and jingle, a murmur of conversation, more laughter—just a little too loud, after just a little too much to drink. You know how those parties go. Your neighbor himself is in some sort of skeleton costume, a black outfit with white bones, faintly glowing. The thin bones of his forearm rest motionless on the arm of his chair.

And then you see that he's seen you. That he's looking your way.

Quickly, you pull the blinds tight again, press your hands against them to keep them from swinging, look down at what you're wearing—just that thin nightgown, barely hanging to your knees.

The conversation out there, the laughter that you'd heard, stops.

You wait. You don't hear anything more from over there, nothing but those wind chimes and that same rustle of leaves through the small yard that separates your house from his . . . because he's just told them to keep it down, right? . . . because *you've* told him to keep it down before. More than once. The houses aren't so far apart, and the noise carries, and you've tried to smile each time you've explained this to him and tried to accept his own smile as genuine, even though you've felt his impatience, those little hints of disdain. Entitlement, arrogance. Something cold in those eyes, too—something you saw the very first time you met him, when he asked if you were seeing anyone, asked why you weren't, asked if there was any chance . . . Something cold in those eyes when you'd politely declined his interest, something lifeless there.

Those same eyes that just caught you looking at him through the blinds.

You wait. You hear nothing.

When you peek through the window again, the pirate and the gangster have disappeared. The skeleton sits alone, openly staring at your house now. As you watch, he tips back his beer, almost like he's sending a toast your way.

You shut the blinds quickly.

You promise yourself not to dare another look.

When you return to your room, you lay the bat beside you on the bed. It is exactly 2:01 when you pull the covers up to your chin, 2:04 when you look down to find your cat curling up once more into a ball at your feet, and by 2:15 you've successfully resisted the urge to call someone. And who would you call anyway? That brother of yours, long since deep in his Halloween drink and helpless himself? That ex-boyfriend, a mistake in the first place and one you don't need to compound? Your father, asleep himself, and two states away?

Overreaction . . . Stupidity. Of course.

And Halloween, you think again. The spirit of the season. Just something in the air.

But you find yourself unable to sleep. The wind has picked up now, you can hear it in the swish and whisper of those leaves, and in those wind chimes, too, like change in a stranger's pocket. The refrigerator has never seemed to hum so loudly, and the ice falling into its bin sounds like glass breaking somewhere close by. Something in the hallway creaks. You tell yourself it's always made that sound.

But the worst of it isn't the noise at all. It's the clock's calm measure of minutes and the waiting silence of the phone.

You watch them both without blinking, fearful despite yourself of what might happen just before the time comes and the phone rings.

Because the phone number in the dream had, of course, been your own.

Love Me or Leave Me: A Fugue in G Minor

Garrett heard the music the first time moments before sunrise—if *heard* was the right word.

He was caught halfway between sleeping and waking, not quite himself but drifting uncertainly, trying to find some steady path out of the dying echoes of troubled dreams and towards the new day. In the middle of all that: faint music. Ten notes, maybe twelve. An extra one or two sliding around somewhere? Some fragment of a melody.

An earworm, he thought, rousing himself slightly. A song he'd heard on the car radio or a TV commercial or Spotify—stuck in his head, bouncing around. A DJ in his mind, spinning tunes—that's how he'd sometimes imagined it. The song had shown up in his dreams, and the dreams had carried over into waking.

But then it also seemed the notes were outside of him, a kind of . . . humming? Like the hum of an electrical line?

A hidden alarm on his phone maybe? Or Tess's? He fumbled in the darkness to pick his up, tapped the screen, checked for notifications. Nothing.

His girlfriend kept her phone on her nightstand. Sometimes it glowed in the middle of the night, waking him up, but right now that screen was dark too.

Tess slept soundly. In the light creeping around the blackout shades, her hair flashed red, then quickly back to its honey blond.

He shook his head.

The music persisted. Faintly, but . . . there.

Weeks since he'd moved in, but he was still getting used to her apartment. Their apartment. It felt strange wandering around someone else's space, living in it. The paint color kept surprising him. When he sat on the couch, he sometimes felt like a visitor. He still had trouble finding the right tools in the kitchen.

Was the battery dead on the smoke alarm?

"Did you hear that?" He nudged Tess, her back to him. "Music?"

She lifted her head, looked towards the clock. "Do you know what time it is?"

"That's what I'm saying. Why would there be music so early?"

She waited—clearly listening. He listened too.

The notes floated at once near and far away. Maybe something from the neighbor's place? He'd been surprised at how thin the walls were, how sounds carried. Or from the closet, was that it? He remembered the keyboard propped at an angle in the back, some preset tempo playing itself out? But it wasn't plugged in, he realized, with a chill. He'd never liked that keyboard, the way it had been stuck back there.

"You're hearing things." Tess pulled the covers tighter. "Go back to sleep."

Listen! Garrett could feel the word in his throat, and anger behind it now—chill to heat, a sudden blast of it—because if the situation had been reversed, if *she* had heard a noise, he would've been interested, wouldn't he? If she loved him enough, then—

He fought the urge to shake her.

Because he loved her, he did. He'd been feeling this more than ever lately. That was a true thing.

And she loved him too.

And anyway, the music had faded away.

***

Until it came back the next morning. And the next. And the next.

Like a warning. Like it was calling to him.

Like he should answer it.

***

"It was kind of like a *da dum-dum dum-da-da da-dee-dee dee-da-da*," Garrett told Tess at breakfast one of those mornings, trying to bring it up again, moving his fingers up and down to demonstrate the higher and lower notes. "Like that."

Tess stood at the counter, slid her toast from oven to plate. He'd already mixed his oatmeal.

"You know those games," she said, sitting down with him, "where you have to hum a song and your teammates have to guess what the song is?"

"Yeah," even though he didn't.

"You wouldn't be good at it."

She winked at him, flipped the top off the tub of butter, same as if nothing was wrong.

He watched her butter her toast, tried to focus on sipping his coffee, tried not to think about how late it was getting, how he needed to get to the print shop.

"So, you don't recognize it?" he said.

"Okay." She sighed. "Do it again."

He did.

She shook her head.

"And you haven't heard it, not at all?"

She bit into her toast—chewed it. Chewed thoughtfully, it seemed. He didn't look at her, looked instead at her bread plate, the half slice of toast sitting there, cut on the diagonal, the angle of the butter knife perched on the edge. He listened to the room, the silence of it, the sound of her swallowing.

"Remember right after you moved in, that ticking you heard?" she said finally.

Garrett's turn to shake his head. "This isn't like that."

"You searched and searched. Standing in this part of the room, that part of the room, listening to the walls, listening to the floor."

"But I *found* that." He tried to keep his voice steady. "I Googled it, remember? HVAC ducts. They expand and contract."

"Exactly. No big deal in the end."

She raised her hands, a "whatever" gesture, a small shrug. *What matters?* That was one of her phrases, one he'd understood, but hadn't really.

"So?" he asked.

"So, let this go. You'll find it."

"Or I won't."

"In which case. . ." An arch of an eyebrow. *What matters?*

The woman I love—that was how he'd taken to thinking about her, what he reminded himself of again now, even if the idea had left him anxious. And here was one of the things he told himself he'd loved about her from the first, her steadiness, her practicality, how calm she tried to make him feel, even if right now it didn't hit him as something he appreciated.

He ticked through the other things he loved about Tess:

The curve of her smile, and the smell of her hair.

He liked that she worked in the library, that she liked to read, liked to lose herself in a book.

She never judged him for his own work, clerking at the print shop.

And he'd never felt suspicion or jealousy about her, never had to ask about the men she knew or the time she spent with them, or how far things had gone, never had to ask, "Who was—?" or "What the hell were—?"

Because he did. He did love her. This was *the* true thing.

But sometimes, he felt like he didn't know her at all. Sometimes he looked at her and thought, "Who are you?" and not only like he was surprised by something she'd done or said or thought.

Garrett could see what they might look like from the side, from a distance—the happy couple at breakfast, chatting, start of the day, him leaning forward, her leaning back.

But seeing them like that, they seemed like strangers to him—the way you get so used to someone that you don't notice them really, or yourself either. The same way you say a familiar word over and over until suddenly it's just sound—and a sound you don't recognize. Or stare at something ordinary until your focus blurs. And then those things *didn't* seem true anymore.

Sunlight through the window. The fern on the table.

Yesterday's mail. This morning's paper.

Tess chewed her toast, smiled some mysterious smile, tucked a strand of red behind her ear.

He tried to fight the urge to shout, *Why aren't you listening?* To snatch that toast from her hand. To—

No, wait. Not red.

The sunlight again?

Looks deceived.

He hardly recognized himself either.

Who are *you? What am* I *doing here?*

Awareness, Garrett thought, snapping himself back to himself.

But again, the next morning, *What is that music? Where is it coming from?*

***

"Likely a case of auditory pareidolia," Dr. Bitterman told him.

"Sounds serious." Garrett felt a sudden fear grip him. He pictured a brain tumor, growing.

It wasn't an official visit. They were standing in the parking lot at the print shop. Dr. Bitterman was one of their customers, had come in to pick up a new batch of business cards: *Dr. Marvin Bitterman, Psychologist.* Garrett had been the one who'd printed them, serendipity, and he'd already held a card back, planning to call. When Dr. Bitterman had come to pick them up, Garrett had been standing at the printer watching three hundred copies of a concert flyer roll out of the machine. It was only a last-minute impulse that sent him rushing out after him, to talk to him in person. No harm in that, right? Unless it *was* something to worry about.

"I wouldn't say serious,"—Dr. Bitterman glanced at his nametag—"Garrett. It's more like an optical illusion. Let me guess. You use a sound machine at night? White noise?"

"Tess does, yeah. My girlfriend. Helps her sleep. Me too, I guess."

"That's what does it. White noise, the hum of an air-conditioner, running water, that kind of thing. We humans, we like patterns—we're pattern makers, in fact. And if a pattern isn't there, our imagination *makes* one for us to find. It's like a Rorschach test, to use another analogy—random, nothing definitive pictured, but people see things anyway. Some people have heard voices in white noise, conversations even. Hearing music wouldn't be too far-fetched."

"So that's . . . normal?"

A shrug. "It's not entirely uncommon. And if that's it, then nothing to worry about."

"If?"

Dr. Bitterman gestured to the parking lot around them. "Hard to do an official diagnosis here. Other conditions are possible. Hearing damage, brain damage, some forms of epilepsy. . ."

Garrett shook his head at each one.

"Well, if you *are* concerned. . ." Dr. Bitterman handed him one of the cards he'd just picked up.

Now Garrett had two. And he wouldn't need either if Dr. Bitterman's explanation was right.

"Auditory pareidolia," Garrett said aloud, trying to remember it.

"Turn off the noise machine." Dr. Bitterman smiled. "See if that doesn't clear it right up."

But when Garrett did—waiting till Tess was asleep herself before switching it off—he still heard the notes the next morning, same as always.

***

Garrett began to search more purposefully, then earnestly and frantically and desperate to keep Tess from seeing him. This wasn't like the ticking of the vents at all.

He searched the bathroom. The electric toothbrush. The countertop dehumidifier. Inside the cabinets, inside her toiletry case and his too.

He stared out the window, put his ear hard against the shared wall with the next apartment.

He checked the smoke alarm in the hallway, the cable box on top of the dresser, the DVD player too.

He searched around her nightstand too, the mess on top, the pile of magazines on the small shelf beneath, within both drawers, expecting some stray bit of electronica tucked away inside. He searched her phone while she was in the shower, remembering the code he'd glimpsed once before, suddenly certain that the mystery lay within, an alarm she'd set and neglected to turn off, an app that she'd used and forgotten, or maybe messages coming through, text or Facebook or Twitter, something persistent—or someone?

Scrolling through posts and emails, he found himself stung by a jealousy he didn't recognize, overwhelmed by it, certain suddenly that it wasn't the phone but Tess herself hiding something, hiding some*one*, and if he could find the right post or message, he'd find out who it was.

He could hear the song even now, distant, dimly, swelling up as he hunched over her phone. He scrolled fast and furtive, focused on screen after screen of texts and emails. But he stayed on guard in other ways too—suddenly seeing how he would look to her if she stepped out of the bathroom. Paranoid, intrusive. It was as if he could see himself through those eyes, gazing at himself from behind or above, hardly recognizing himself. Then he saw her too, looking down from above at her as she hunched over the same phone, tapping messages, hiding from *him*, some brand of déjà vu in what he was watching, familiar and disorienting. Her red hair glowed, flamed with the same burning rage he felt building inside himself, and—

"Stop it," he said—out loud, jerking himself back to reality, thrusting the phone down. "She's not, she wouldn't." The shower was still running. She was humming, happily. "I love her, I do."

But he could still hear the music. Not her humming. Not the phone. Something elsewhere. Haunting him. Taunting him.

***

No answers then, and the music was coming at other times of the day now too.

It was strongest in the morning, that same dim twilight, that same woozy awakening, that same brief wondering where he was, even who he was, as that same sun peeked around the edges of the blackout blinds, and that same *da dum-dum dum-da-da da-dee-dee dee-da-da* sounded somewhere in the near distance, and he clutched those same sheets beneath his fingers, searching for steadiness.

Until the morning that he woke to himself, walking through a kitchen he didn't recognize, a house he didn't know, with unfamiliar fingers clutched around a knife—a knife that was the one thing that he *had* seen before.

II

1 Bowl (*absence of*)
2 Knife (*presence of*)
3 Car (*absence of*)
4 Messages (*unanswered*)
5 Toothbrush (*dry*)

These were the items Tess ticked through as she gradually realized that something was wrong—that Garrett hadn't merely left but was, indeed, gone.

***

It hadn't been unusual for her to wake up to an empty house. Garrett was an early riser, usually let her sleep late. More unusual for him to wake her up, like he'd done a week or so before with whatever he'd been hearing.

Most days, Garrett liked a morning walk before work. He said he had a wanderer's heart, said it cleared his head.

She'd learned he was a creature of habit, brushing his teeth first thing, weighing himself, then out the door and around the neighborhood. He would come back hungry—a big bowl of oatmeal always, a small coffee with honey, strict in all routines.

He hadn't had his breakfast yet, she saw that morning—the morning he disappeared. No bowl in the sink, rinsed and sitting the way he left it, no spoon at its sharp angle. Only a knife out on the counter, and it looked clean. Not like he'd cut anything, and odd for him to leave it out. He was "fastidious"—his word, some pride there. She slid it back into the block.

A half-hour passed and then forty-five minutes. Had he left for the print shop? She glanced out the window. No car in the driveway, so he must have.

But skipping breakfast. That wasn't like him.

She texted him then, but he didn't respond. Not even a *delivered* notation popping up. Just a blankness at the end of the message chain. No answer when she called either. It didn't ring, just went straight to voicemail. The same things each time she texted, each time she called, each voicemail she left.

She tried the print shop too, something she never did—she

hardly knew anyone there, Garrett rarely talked work. But the woman who answered said he wasn't in yet, they'd expected him, she wasn't sure where he might be.

His wallet was gone from the nightstand where he always kept it. With a sudden worry (irrational, she thought), she checked the closet, but his half was still full of clothes—his suitcase there too. The small shaving kit was there where he'd tucked it under the sink when he moved in. His toothbrush was propped in its stand, but when she touched the bristles, they were dry.

Definitely not the Garrett she knew.

***

Despite first instincts, she didn't call the police.

Not that she hadn't gone halfway in that direction—more, in fact. She'd Googled the non-emergency number, picked up the phone, dialed most of the digits, then held back, hung up. Too many reasons against it.

1   She hadn't heard anything earlier—no shouts, no struggle.
2   The front door and porch door were both locked, no sign of a break-in.
3   The car was gone.

It was mostly the car that stopped her—the absence of it.

If the car had still been there, that might have been one kind of evidence, but the fact that he'd driven it away was another.

Unless someone had forced him into the car, that is—an idea that had her dialing the numbers again, and then hanging up again. She couldn't seriously imagine that.

Garrett had left abruptly, yes, but of his own free will.

Another text—G? Where r u?—before she headed to the library and a long, distracted shift ahead.

***

Had there been a problem between them? Had she done something to drive him away? Sitting at the breakfast table each morning before work, staring at the empty space across from her, she kept revisiting the same questions, kept coming back to them again and again through the day, talked about them sometimes with Carla, her best friend at the library.

It had happened before with previous boyfriends, she'd told Carla—unlucky in love, no doubt about it.

1 She was too independent
2 She was too practical
3 She was too distant

Still, she couldn't remember anything that might have triggered him to run. No arguments over the last few weeks. No friction really. None that she was aware of.

At least nothing that *Tess* had done, Carla clarified—and Carla had heard already all the ways that the relationship had indeed changed even over such a short time.

In the beginning, Garrett had seemed intense and enigmatic—a good thing then, the attraction, the fun. She'd met him in the psychology section at the library, trying to find a book about dreams and what they mean. Tess had helped him locate it, helped him check out. He'd been nervous when he asked her out. But on the date, he'd been focused, interested in her. He asked questions, he leaned in, he listened.

Tell me about your parents, what were they like? What did you dream about as a kid? Did you always want to be a librarian?

She didn't answer that last one at first—only several dates later, a night at her apartment. "The truth is, I always wanted to play piano," she'd told him, showing him the keyboard in her closet, the one she'd gotten as a teenager, put away a long time ago, then salvaged again from her mother's house a couple of years ago. A second attempt to learn—this last time by watching YouTube videos—before she'd stuffed it away again.

The sight of it, the story behind it, seemed to upset him. Empathy for her failed ambitions?

"I wasn't very good," she explained, but his forehead stayed crinkled. Maybe poor talent wasn't any better than failed ambition.

***

These were the positive traits about him—traits she'd written down in her notebook, weighing her attraction.

1 He listens when I talk about my mother, about how I felt like I'm disappointing her
2 He was concerned, empathetic about my piano playing (lack of)
3 The first time he said, "I love you," I could feel the weight of it, the thought behind it
4 His hand in mine feels strong but gentle
5 The mistiness in those blue eyes of his, smokiness even—<u>mysterious</u>! (She'd actually underlined that word, in a good way.)

Honestly, she'd thought it might be the start of something, date after date.

Too soon, of course, to think of marriage, of children (though her clock was indeed ticking, she felt that all too well). But the possibility was there, the possibility of a future—first time she'd felt that, felt it strongly enough that she'd let him move in, after all.

But then same page, column B—counterpoint after counterpoint:

1 He never talks about his own family—what really do I know?
   (a) Mother was a singer (part of his reaction to my piano playing?)
   (b) Stepfather a "hard man" (no elaboration on what that meant)
   (c) Both of them lost in an accident G doesn't want to talk about (had he been in the car too?)
2 Wasn't his reaction to her piano playing a little neurotic?
3 *Every* time he says, "I love you, " I can feel the weight of it, the hesitation behind it
4 His hands always seem to be clenching and

unclenching, like he's squeezing an invisible stress ball (am I the stress?)
5 <u>Mysterious</u>→<u>maddening</u>

Question piled on question:

- Why did he never talk about that family?
- Why didn't he have any friends he kept in touch with?
- Why didn't he get together with anyone from work?
- Were all his strange routines normal? That "fastidi-
ousness" of his?

His OCD-ness, Tess thought, call it what it was. I mean, *she*
liked order too—writing things down, seeing them clearly, mind-
ful, aware—but bowl in this place, spoon at this angle, coffee with
exactly this much honey, hunting the house for that ticking in the
HVAC, and then this new "music" she was supposed to be hearing?
She'd been patient, though, hadn't she?
He couldn't have left because of anything *she* did. Could he?
(No, Carla kept saying, but did Carla really know?)

***

Tess kept coming back to how she'd made fun of him for the
sounds he'd heard, for being out of tune.
But her intentions had been good, hadn't they?

1 Levity can lighten a situation
2 Best to downplay his urgency
3 Other times he'd gotten so wound up he'd lost himself
(example, HVAC)

Still . . . maybe she'd been wrong to dismiss him.
What was the song? And where was he hearing it?
From her closet, she pulled out her old keyboard, set up the
stand, plugged it in—regretting now she didn't do this when he'd
first asked about the notes.
She began to finger the keys, trying to piece together what-

ever he'd hummed. *Da da da dum da da da dee? Da dum da dum da dee dee da?* A higher note or two first before a lower one, that was clear, but what *was* that first note? And how many of them? And what was the jump to the lower one? Had the note after that been the same note or a higher one again? What was the rhythm?

The truth was Garrett *hadn't* been very good at humming it—and even if he had, she'd never been good at naming that tune.

Which circled her back to her own reaction and how that might have driven him away:

1 Mistaken thought: Levity can lighten a situation
2 Incorrect assumption: Downplaying. . .
3 Etc.

But no, that wasn't it. It was just another relationship gone south, another boyfriend walking out. Sometimes things didn't work out—that same old song.

Same old song. She laughed—a good sign, she thought.

She started to shut down the keyboard, but instead began playing the scales she'd memorized so long ago. Even though she missed some of those notes, it felt good, her fingers against the keys.

She pulled out a music book from her old lessons, tried to brush up on reading the notes. Every Good Boy Does Fine—she'd always fumbled through that. FACE had been the easier one. A memory for faces instead of names, that thought flitted through her mind.

She surprised herself by how naturally some of it came back, some motor memory, and other memories too.

1 How much she'd wanted to learn piano, and her mother stressing the cost and how Tess had to stick with it because if she didn't practice practice practice. . . .
2 How she'd wanted to learn "Tiny Dancer," but her teacher, Mrs. Goolrick, said she had to learn "Chopsticks" and "Twinkle

Twinkle" and "Happy Birthday" and "Für
Elise" first.

3 The way Mrs. Goolrick kept her drapes
closed and that small sliver of light
through the crack.

4 The way Mrs. Goolrick smelled—sickly
sweet mothballs, stale coffee, hairspray—
and how her mother had said Tess was
just trying to find a way out of it all.

Despite her fumbles now, Tess had to admit the music
sounded good. Before she knew it, she'd been playing for an
hour—no longer trying to get it right but just enjoying herself.

She ended up leaving the keyboard in the living room, began playing every day.

Maybe she'd take up piano for real. Or those pastels and wa-
tercolors stuffed away in the same closet. Maybe learn to bake
finally.

Maybe she'd go wild. Shake up her style.

1 Take up piano again
2 Cut my hair short like I've always wanted—
dye it red
3 Learn to surf

She'd always wanted to surf, she realized.

No limits really to who she might be.

***

Several weeks later, after Tess had stopped mentioning any
of it to Carla, after she'd stopped noticing the clothes still in the
closet except to think about whether she should box them up
and donate them somewhere, Tess's phone dinged—an incom-
ing message. Garrett.

Got your texts. Saw your name. May be strange to
hear maybe, but not sure who you are anymore. Or this
"us" you said. Or me really. Though I know who you
are, I mean, I saw you that morning, so I remember

that. It made me afraid, all of it—not of you, but of
me. We must have meant something, I know I loved you,
I must have. I don't want to hurt you.
***

Didn't want to hurt her? Tess shook her head.

How many times had she heard that?

- It's not you, it's me.
- I'm not ready for a relationship right now.
- I need some space.
- You'll make someone really happy someday.
- Etc.

All that. More.

Then a second text a few minutes later.

Whatever's happening needs to be with someone I
DON'T love.

She read that one a few times, not sure what to make of it.
But here was the curious thing: she didn't feel disappointed anymore.

After the initial surprise of Garrett's disappearance—the sud-
denness of his absence, the totality of it—a second surprise had
gradually crept up on her:

- I don't actually miss him.

Tess felt relieved by this thought really—lucky now, thinking
back on his quirks and obsessions, like she'd dodged some trouble she didn't need.

III

EXCERPTS: CASE FILE ON GARY BELL, OFFICE OF DR.
SEYMOUR BITTERMAN

[Standalone notation; no heading]

For documentation and insurance compliance, notes will
use Gary's legal given name and surname. In session, patient
has requested use of the name Garth, request with which I have
complied. Both are in contrast to the name by which he was introduced in first unofficial meeting. Variety of names seem not

evidence of schizophrenia or of multiple personality disorder but of serially progressive dissociative fugue.

***

Notes on third session, 27 May 20—

Gary reports some progress since last session, including returning to his workplace, though he has explained that transition as "bumpy." He retains some mechanical memory of how to do his work—the printing software, printers and copying machines—but he does not recognize his co-workers and continues to feel that he is pretending to be someone he is not. This provides further evidence of the dissociative fugue he has been experiencing, conclusions also based on the many instances he's described of watching himself from some distance, as if he is a stranger interacting with co-workers who are also strangers—awkward and alienating, as he himself describes it.

While he claims to be unable to access any memories of who he is, he continues to make efforts to reconstruct elements of his life both from the items in his possession—wallet, identification, credit cards, insurance card, the business card that brought him to me—and from search through his phone—contacts, emails, messages, social media. He also reports that he has reached out to his girlfriend in response to her text messages, which he calls "puzzle pieces with the picture slowly coming into view." Still, he remains reluctant to return in person to see her or to enter the house where he had been living. He is also reluctant to use the word "home" at all. He continues to live in his car.

While I've tried to encourage him in other directions, Gary has continued to focus on the musical notes he claims to hear, not only at sunrise now but increasingly at random throughout the day. Gary has picked up my term "solution to self" from previous sessions, and he has insisted that the song may provide such a solution. He believes that understanding this song will help him "cut through to the truth," even as he has simultaneously resisted discussions of childhood and family relationships which to my mind might identify the trauma that I suspect to be at the root of Gary's fugue state. (My job is to listen and lead, clearly, not discover and explain.)

As in previous sessions, we played the notes as he'd best determined what they were using trial and error and an app on his phone: several notes of higher C, several of lower, then stepping up to three at D and two at E, all played in various rhythms, fast, slow, etc. But today I proposed a new approach—hypnotherapy—and suggested that the combination of hypnosis and playing the notes might help to unlock further clues to counteract the fugue state and help trigger a return to self (though question of self remains layered, e.g. Gary, Garrett, Garth).

Gary agreed to my recommendation, and I induced a hypnotic state, relying on both metronomic ticking (courtesy my own phone app) and verbal repetition to induce. The results were revealing if not entirely complete.

While he was under hypnosis, I asked Gary what he remembered about his time immediately before his first visit to me—the time between first hearing the musical notes and his call to me to make an appointment. No narrative details emerged; Gary returned to images familiar from previous sessions. Darkness and twilight. A woman lying in bed, with her back to him, humming. Himself standing somewhere in relation, but with his own back to himself—perhaps the initial presentation of the fugue state? There was another image of a kitchen, of standing at a kitchen counter, and of a knife stationary before him.

When I played the musical notes, Gary seemed to become anxious, hunching slightly and curving his shoulders inward while drawing his knees closer—fetal, clearly. But some of the images became clearer, both in more definite focus and in terms of content, angle and setting.

The woman he was watching was his mother (childhood memory, as anticipated), a beautiful woman with bright red hair (beauty and hair color emphasized twice). He explained that she was a singer, information he had not related before. In new images, instead of lying down, she either stands facing him or crouches with her back to him. When standing, she holds a microphone close to her mouth, singing into it, words indistinct but the melody Gary has been hearing. When crouching, she hums the same song, but on the other side of a large room encompassing both a kitchen (same kitchen as aforementioned?) and an adjacent living area. According to a skewed angle of perception, Gary sits at a table at some distance from his crouching mother as another figure steps in between them. At first, this seemed to be a second self (himself watching himself), but upon questioning, Gary said that this was his stepfather and explained that the stepfather was humming the same song as his crouching mother.

Gary's posture continued to retract—evidence that we were perhaps tuned into the trauma scene at the source of his fugue. I have recreated a transcript of our discussion—a pivotal moment, in my professional opinion.

Q: What is your stepfather doing?

A: He's humming.

Q: Is he humming the same song as your mother?

A: Yes.

Q: Do you know what the song is now? Can you identify it?

A: No. He's reaching down towards her.

Q: Is this a gesture of warmth and tenderness? Of aggression and anger?

A: Her hair is like fire. Her mouth is open. [Here Gary formed his own mouth into a wide O.]

Q: Is your mother singing? Is she saying something?

A: She's quiet now.

Q: She didn't make any sound?

A: My father is the one talking.

Q: Your father?

A: Stepfather.

Q: What's he saying to her?

A: [Here Gary's voice shifted to more gruff and husky, mimicking stepfather, it seems] "How far. . . ? Who was. . . ? What the hell. . . ?"

Q: What were these questions in reference to? Were these accusations?

A: He's talking to me. [Returning to his normal voice.]

Q: He's asking those questions of you?

A: No.

Q: Okay. What's he saying to you then?

A: "Love 'em and leave 'em." [Gruff and harsh again, followed by a sound that seemed half laughter, half spitting.]

Q: Your stepfather was talking about women?

A: Sluts. [Still the gruff, husky tone.] Redheads the worst. Don't let 'em get in.

Q: Did your mother say anything in response?

A: _____

Q: Garth?

A: "Don't let 'em get in." [Then a return to his own normal tone.] He pointed at his head when he said that.

Q: With his finger?

A: _____

Q: Garth?

A: _____

Q: Gary?

A: No. The knife.

Q: He used the knife on himself?

A: _____

Q: On your mother?

A: It was an accident.

Q: What was an accident? What happened, Gary?

A: _____

Q: Gary?

A: Garth.

Gary didn't answer any further questions after that. It's worth noting that during the course of the questions and answers above, his body relaxed its fetal crouching, and Gary ultimately seemed more at ease.

After Gary emerged from the hypnotic state, I asked what he remembered. He returned to the images which have become common in our sessions: same light and darkness, same red-haired woman crouching then lying down, more of himself watching himself, same bed, kitchen, knife.

I moved then from specific questions about the memory to more general questions. What is love? How do you treat someone you love? How do you expect them to treat you? Do you believe people are innately good or bad? Do you believe in choice? In free will?

Gary became agitated anew at these questions. He wondered aloud if any of this was working. "What matters?" he asked. He ultimately cut the session short, though he accepted the reminder card for our next meeting.

***

[Standalone private addendum: no heading, not for official documentation]

Nagging concerns about discoveries during hypnotherapy. Consulted Dr. Meriweather to discuss. Consult: Focus on sexual and violent imagery (open mouth, microphone and knife as phallic), intensity of watching (stalking?), latent Oedipal fixations (mother as consistent motif), and related obsessiveness about musical notes.

Location of key trauma in Gary's early life seems potential clue to resolving fugue and identity issues. Question persists whether abuse→abuse, witness of violence begets violence? Sudden appearance/persistence of mother's song, visions/revisions of violence witnessed as child, unresolved trauma = potential danger? To Gary? To others? Possible concern that Gary may replicate behavior?

Argument to Meriweather: If Gary can remember/recognize/resolve trauma, then healing can begin, healthy relationships will follow.

Meriweather counterpoint: If traumatic episode remains submerged/repressed, can fester, or perhaps find outlet in further violence, catching Gary unaware.

Q for Meriweather: His honest professional opinion or merely devil's advocate?

Upshot: Concern about Gary's own potential violence—unclear. No explicit suggestion of violent behavior, either past or future from Gary himself—no ticking time bomb, at least no clear evidence to believe so. But Meriweather consult confirms need to document discussion separately—premature perhaps but liability concerns if potential subpoena of notes, God forbid any reason to.

Despite discussion, remain personally confident, however, of Gary's own fear of violence, fear of hurting someone he loves. So long as love is present, love will prevail? Optimistic perhaps. Will explore more fully in future sessions.

***

[Standalone memo; no heading]
Fourth scheduled session—patient did not show, no sufficient cancellation notice.

Bill insurance per office policy.

IV

Psst. Steph?
You up?
Sorry! Early I know!

3 dings
your worse than my alarm

Haha! Sorry x2

sorry not sorry obvs
whassup pheebs?

I am!
Not just awake.
Feeling good, I mean.

u met someone

How'd you know?

again

LOL!

& its love at first sight

This one seems nice.
Different.

> so much in love he already
> whipped out a ring and proposed

Stop it! We just met.
. . .though he's still here.

> so he did whip something out

LOL!!

> whats his name?

Garth? Gareth?

> seriously phoebe?
> u dont know his name??!

LOL! I did ask, but it was loud.
We were at the club.

> obvs
> he couldve written it down
> his name

No paper.
Took me awhile to get it
out of him anyway.
He was like "What's in a name?"

> real romeo
> rose by any other

And I'm like "Well, you have
to have one, yeah?"

                              and its garth

Or Gareth

                         old guy name
                    he married too?

Was.

                  filling my bingo card pheebs

Or maybe just serious relationship?
Either way, not now.

                                   rebound

"Fresh start."

                         and your the fresh

You sound like my mom.

                     u know how guys are
                prolly a thing for redheads
STFU.

                                just sayin

He was nice.
He listened.
He was there.

                                 there?
                       like 🙄 he was there
                        so y not f him?

No.
I mean there like present.
In a real way.
Intense.

so . . . stalker
beware

I'm gonna phone another friend.

ghead

You don't want to hear more?

im here

Seriously.

seriously

I'm saying he paid attention.
He focused.
He was there.

got it
he listened
but u couldnt get his name

Please?

Sorry

It was the club.

k

Electronica. Heavy beat.

                                            got it

They played that song you hate.

                                    the ticky one?

Yeah. That's how I met him.

                            ticky ticky ticky ticky ticky
                                                    awful

Middle of that song, and here's
this guy drifting my way.
Never seen him before,
maybe part of the allure.

                                stranger come to town

Exact.

                                    same old story
                                    like a xerox

Not always.

Anyway, here we are dancing near one
another and then dancing WITH one another.
Then it's like we're in rhythm.
                        ticky song got no rhythm

You just have to listen to it.
And here's the thing. He WAS listening.
First thing he says, he leans in and says,
'Do you hear it? Those notes.'
                        ticky song got no notes

Well HE heard them.

And he was trying to get me to hear them too.
He's moving his hands up and down like he's
IDK
Conducting an orchestra or something.
And like he was humming but I couldn't hear it really.

                                        the club
                                        the ticky

He tried to hum it again later,
last night in bed.
All hmm hm hm hum hm hm hum.
And I'm listening to it, but whatever
he heard
it didn't sound like that to me.
"It's there," he said.
"You have to listen."

                        somebody had too much to drink
                              why didnt you ask him
                                    his name in bed?

Embarrassed I didn't know it by then.

                                        for real

Anyway, we had fun.
I liked him. It felt good.

                              so true love again?

LOL! NO!

                              swept off your feet?
                        dreaming bout happily ever after?

THAT'S NOT WHAT
I'M SAYING!

                                        all caps
                                        ease up

Just saying I had fun.
And different this time.
But different in a different way—
about me, not him.
And trying to share that news
with MY BEST FRIEND.

                        appropriate use of caps lock
                                              finally
                                              and ty

You know how everybody pretends
they're looking for someone?

                                              yeah

The thing is he said straight out
 he just needed someone.
He said he couldn't
love anyone, not then.
But he needed someone.

                              honest at least
                                 on his side
            did he say he needed a redhead in particular?
                     cause fetish on bingo card too

Hush.
That's the thing.
I felt OK with it.

                        you'll still fall hard

Maybe.
Maybe not.

But that's the thing, what we talked about last
night.
He was telling me all about that ex.
Ex–wife, ex–girlfriend, whichever.
She had cheated on him, cheated with many people.
A singer, he said, so you can imagine.
Band, travelling probably,
sleeping around, broke his heart
Left him hurt and angry,
too angry to see straight,
that's what he said,
said he doesn't even know how
he ended things, what he said,
how he got out.
And so he said straight out
that the next woman
in his life needed to be
someone he didn't love—
because he needed to figure out what love is anyway,
what to do next, who to be next.
Deep really.
But here's the trick.
How he said it, it made sense.
Because who knows what's next?
I mean you could find the love of your life tomorrow
or you could find that what you wanted yesterday
isn't what you want any more and you could die
tomorrow, so enjoy today, right?
Let the future take care of itself?
Live in the moment instead of worrying about everything
Like I usually do—I can hear you saying that.
Which is why bringing him home last night felt different
than other times because he was clear about not lov-
ing
me and I was clear about just wanting what felt good
at the time.

No love.
And if it's right tomorrow then it's right and if
it's not it's
not and if I DO decide love that's fine and if I decide to leave
that's fine and if I were to get hit by a bus or whatever
at least I had what I chose in the NOW, you know?

tl;dr

Asshole!
I was saying I was fine
NOT having love at first sight.
Or love at all.
Live for the moment!
It was an EPIPHANNY!

spellcheck

Jerk.

we are who we are

Anyway I'll fill you in more later.
Sounds like he's getting up.

yep
be a good wifey
make him big hungry man breakfast
Bagels and cream cheese.

apron and nothing else

T-shirt and sweats TYVM.

give it a few minutes

He said he'd slice the bagels for us.
A gentleman!

                                         mansplainer

Hush.

And he's humming again!
So cute!

                               happily ever after

Whatev.
L8R?

                                            sure
                 cant wait for all the gory details
                    meet for coffee early pm, k?

                                       pheebs?

Locked Out

I was walking toward the music, this all-day country music thing my buddies and I were going to, when I caught sight of the boy off to the right, leaning into a red Toyota Tacoma. Probably a thousand vehicles out there, stretched across that field-turned-parking-lot, rain-sludged from the night before. The sun was high now, but the humidity was thick. Wet mud had streaked fenders everywhere. Dirt caked the knobby tires of the big four-wheel-drives. A row of porta-potties stood nearby. Ahead, over the next rise of trees, guitars twanged, voices crooned, the crowd rumbled and roared and rumbled again. But for all that, the boy was the only person I could see: a lanky high school kid, T-shirt and ragged jeans, hunkered over the back windows of an extended-cab pickup. He had his hands cupped around his eyes as he tried to peer through the tinted glass.

I'd seen that pose before, that look. Six days a week, all day, some nights, this is the kind of work I do. Keys left in the ignition, keys dropped behind the seat, keys that fell out of the purse somewhere. I got a deal with Triple-A too, on call 24/7, so I always keep my tools with me, even on an off-duty Sunday like today. The boy was lucky that way—twice lucky, I thought, since I'd told my buddies I might not even make the concert. But nothing on the tube, and it was the ex's weekend with our daughter, so what else did I have to do?

The boy let out a little groan—I could hear it even over that dull tangle of music and voices beyond the trees. And that was when I saw that his knees weren't just buckling in frustration but bending and flexing, moving in slow rhythm, and that his hips were pulsing too, forward and back in small circles.

I adjusted my glasses to make sure I was seeing it right.

"I'm next," he said, a slur to the words and louder than he'd meant, like he'd already had way too much to drink. "Don't take it all, I've got her next." He gave another low groan, something like desire, something like anger. "Damn."

He went on like that, talking half to himself, half to whoever was in the back seat of that extended cab, and all the while grinding his groin against the sheet metal, like if he just pressed hard enough, he might get inside.

***

Later, I'd think about the concert I never made it to and about my buddies, half-drunk themselves, all of us in our forties now but not feeling like it, most of us divorced. *Second chance*, we tell one another, and all of us—even the married ones—still talk about the girls who pass by, still admire a nice set of curves under a T-shirt or a tight little skirt, still vie with one another to see who can flirt most with the waitress when we go out. My buddy Bill always seems to have the easiest time getting those waitresses to flirt back.

Later—much later—I'd think about some of the memories already swirling uneasily through my mind. About how Bill stood guard outside the closet at his parents' house when we were eleven years old while Wendy Shannon and I took our turn playing Seven Minutes in Heaven, both of us still and silent in the darkness, barely breathing, hardly touching—just the brush of an elbow and Wendy's pitiful whisper: "Please don't." About fumbling around as a teenager in the backseat of my old Camaro, trying to get the right angle on Rebecca Henderson, trying to coax her bra off. Busty Becky, all of us boys called her, and when a pair of headlights glanced through the back windows, there'd been a sudden panic, a "Don't move," a "Shhh."

Later still, I'd think about more mature loves: my ex-wife, Julie, and my daughter, Susan. I'd think about Sundays long past: family bicycle rides and afternoons at the pool and rainy-day crafts, and then how I'd coached Susan in pee wee soccer, my wife standing beside me on the sidelines. That's where our daughter's nickname had come from—Skipper—taking charge in every game, leading the pack, playing her heart out.

I'd think about that too, and how that nickname stuck even if our marriage didn't. Skipper's seventeen now. Seventeen.

But I didn't think about any of that at the time—not think, not really. Instead, I just felt: shock and then confusion and then an anger that I didn't understand and couldn't articulate. The feelings came first.

***

"Look at that," said the boy, low and guttural, talking to himself, to no one. "Would you look at that?" He had only one hand on the window now, palm flat against it as if to balance himself, while his other hand rubbed distractedly against the front of his jeans. "Yo!"—louder—"Leave some for—"

"Hey," I called out. "Hey, boy," I shouted. "Hey, you."

The wind shifted: a dank smell of urine from the porta-potties behind me, a different edge to that honky-tonk jam over the trees.

The boy looked my way, our eyes met, and then he knocked twice on the window of the truck.

After a moment, he just turned and strolled off as if I wasn't there—aimlessly it seemed, weaving a little as he disappeared into the maze of cars and trucks and vans.

I didn't follow after him—found myself unable to or to move closer to the truck that was facing me now like a challenge. Unable to pull myself away either. Wondering about that knock-knock on the window. A signal to some embarrassed couple in the back of the truck, hurriedly snapping their jeans and tucking in their shirts? A signal just to the *him* inside the cab? Some other boy saying "Don't move" and "Shhh," pressing his hands hard against some girl's mouth?

Rooted to my spot, my mind adrift, I finally pulled out my cell and punched in the numbers. As the call went through, I heard a sort-of stutter ring, an echo of a ring, and I held the phone away from my ear, at arm's length, struggling to block out the hiss and crackle of the concert as I listened hard to that field of cars and trucks and vans.

"Dad?" I heard at a distance, and then louder, "Dad? Hello?"

It took me a couple of seconds to bring the phone back to my ear.

"Hey, Skip," I said, picturing her on that soccer field, her little legs pumping, her ponytail flying. "Hey, Susan," I started again. "It's me, your pop."

"Dad," she said flatly. That duh sound of hers. "Caller ID. Twenty-first century on the line, and it's for you."

I counted to three. I kept my eye on the pickup. I tried again to blot out the music beyond the trees.

"Yeah," I said. "Listen," I said, listening myself, pressing my ear as close to the phone as I could. What was that noise there in the background? The sounds of the mall, of a restaurant? Some music? A stereo somewhere? A car radio? She shifted, she moved. I could hear it. The truck stood still. "I was wondering," I said, fumbling for what to ask, what not to ask. "Your mom and I, are we still taking you up to look at colleges next weekend?"

"Dad. We've planned on that for weeks. You didn't forget, did you?"

"No, no, of course not. I just . . . Is that one of her weekends or . . . ?" But that had never been an issue. *Amicable*—that was the word we'd learned to use.

A muffled sound—the phone held away, her hand over the receiver, or the cell pressed against her chest. A voice somewhere, not hers, and then she was back. "Hey, Dad," she said. "I can't talk. I'm out with a friend."

"The new fella?" I asked. There was the question, struggling to be casual. "Your mom said you're seeing somebody new these days?"

Laughter on the other end — that other voice again. Clearly male this time.

"Dad, I gotta run, okay? I'll call later. Love you." And the phone went dead.

I held my hand on redial as I watched that Toyota a little longer, its silence and stillness.

***

At my own truck, I picked up my toolbox, the little one, and started to close the door. Then I stopped and went into the glove box and grabbed the pistol I keep there. Late night calls, lockouts on the side of some dim road, you can't be too careful. I tucked it into the toolbox now, just in case.

As I walked back toward that other pickup, the crowd beyond the trees burst into another round of applause, and I could almost hear my buddies somewhere in there, getting good and drunk, cracking jokes and laughing and grab-assing.

The Toyota looked the same as before, motionless, defiant. I waited again. With the tools in my hands, I could open that door in seconds. With a wrench, I could shatter the window. Just a movement, just a cry, just some signal, that's all I needed.

But nothing came from that direction. And the phone in my pocket was silent too.

I went up to the door anyway. I knocked like the boy had, two quick ones.

The glass had an impenetrable tint, but I could feel them inside, whoever they were, watching me. I tried the door handle, but it was indeed locked.

"Twenty-first century calling," I said, knocking again — a quiet, singsong voice not my own.

I put a wedge against the weather-stripping at the bottom of the window, but it wasn't until I pulled out the Jiffy-Jak that I heard the locks click, and a young boy seemed to unfold himself onto the muddy field, pushing the door half-closed behind him.

He wore a black T-shirt with a trio of leering faces on it and the word *Gorillaz* at the top. His jeans were buttoned but unzipped and gaping. He seemed to hunch forward a little, shoulders rolled in front of him, a saggy posture like the other boy but bigger, meatier. After just standing there in front of me for a minute, he glanced without interest at the wedge under the weatherstripping, the tool in my hand, the toolbox at my feet.

"Wassup?" he said then, half-stoned, maybe all the way.

Was this the kind of guy my Susan was dating? Was this him? He smelled like about a pony keg of cheap beer. I still had the Jiffy-Jak in my hand and wished I had the wrench.

"Hope I haven't disturbed you and the missus," I said, a calm I didn't feel. I peered into the slight opening of the door. Was someone crouching there in the back? Cowering? She'd been threatened somehow. She'd had too much to drink. The tinted windows left only darkness within. Nothing to see.

"Nope," he said, not exactly looking at me, not exactly looking away. "It's good."

"Mind if I . . . ?" I gestured toward the truck, began moving toward it. He was shaking his head, not a "no" exactly, but something there, some hesitation or trouble.

I reached out, but before I could open the driver's door, the little half-door of the extended cab sprang wide, and the girl inside flew out at me, leaping from that backseat and toppling me backwards. My glasses went flying, the Jiffy-Jak fell from my hand, the toolbox at my feet spilled over. She had landed on top of me, straddling me now, flailing her arms, punching and slapping.

"Hey," I heard the boy say. No enthusiasm. No urgency. And then another one, even duller. "Hey."

Finally, the girl stopped her thrashing and sat back. My glasses were gone, and my eyes were bleary from where she'd beaten at my face. With the sunlight behind her, she seemed a dim shadow above me. Long hair—blond like my daughter's, but stringy it seemed, ragged somehow. About Susan's age too, maybe a year less. Her face was aflame. She panted heavily. A spitfire, my buddy Bill would've called her. A nice set of lungs, he would've said, how that low-cut tank top clung to her breasts. *Princess*, that tank top said. Pink glitter. *Not her*, I thought. *Not her.*

The girl reached past my head then, and I had the fleeting image of Busty Becky from all those years before, hovering over me. I remembered suddenly how I'd never been able to unhook that bra. "Your first one?" Becky had laughed, and then she'd reached back and just flicked her fingers and it was like magic. And it had been Becky who'd said, "Don't move" when those headlights appeared, Becky who'd pressed her fingers lightly against my lips, shushing me, in a way that made my whole body tingle.

And then I looked again at the girl leaning across me, and I thought, no, no, what happened then is nothing like this. Nothing.

Then the girl straightened up above me. She held my pistol in her hand. She pointed it at my face.

"You creep," she said. Her voice was shrill, reedy. She pressed the gun against my cheek. Her finger played unsteadily against the trigger. "You're as bad a perv as Danny is, staring at us through that window. Like nobody can leave us the hell alone." She moved the pistol over, lifted up one of my nostrils with it, then parted my lips, nudged the barrel against my teeth. "This the kind of thing you wanna see. Huh? This the kind of thing Daddy likes?" She wore a grim smile.

"C'mon," said the boy, calmly, as if she was finishing her homework or watching a TV program and they were late for something else.

The smile of hers faded slowly into a sneer, and she moved the pistol again just slightly, arcing it forward, and I could see already the damage that the bullet might do, the hole where my face would have been. I forced myself not to close my eyes. Her own eyes looked empty, her pupils wide and vacant.

"Jesus," she said, then she tossed the gun into a puddle under the truck. Then half to herself, half to that audience of empty cars around us, "Can't a girl get her rocks off in peace these days?"

She stood up awkwardly, slipping a little in the mud, losing her balance. The boy stepped forward and she leaned against him for support, righted herself then released him again. She wore short shorts, flecked now with mud. She wore flip-flops. Her skinny legs looked too weak to hold her up.

"Let's go," she said, pushing past him, back toward the concert. The music had kept on playing even if I'd stopped hearing it.

"Sorry, dude," said the boy, standing above me, the sky behind him, his face in shadow. "She didn't mean anything. She just had a little too much."

The girl twirled to face him. "Let's GO!" she said again. Frustration there. Ferocity.

He shrugged. He shut the doors to the truck. She'd already begun walking on. Soon he shambled along after her. His pants, I'm sure, were still unzipped.

I lay there in the mud a little longer, looking up at the sun and then at the underbelly of the truck—the frame, the exhaust, the barrel of the pistol sticking up out of the dirt, all of it out of focus. The wetness of the ground beneath me had seeped through my shirt. I hadn't noticed before. The doors the boy had closed hadn't latched entirely. I'd need to get my wedge back. I'd need to get my things together. I needed to get up.

When my phone rang, I fished it out of my pocket. SKIPPER, read the caller ID. Twenty-first century calling.

I'll need to change that, I thought.

But I didn't answer. I didn't know yet—still don't—what to say to her.

From beyond the trees, the music soared and fell. A "thank you" echoed through the speakers in the distance. "Thank you, thank you," the singer cried. "Thank you. We love you too."

A Blanket of Snow
(A Fairy Tale Revisited)

After midnight, the snow began to fall more heavily—puffs of white wonder, glistening in the bright night sky.

Lying awake in the bed beside him, she couldn't see the snow, but she could imagine it clinging fast to the roof, burrowing into the shingles' cracks, weighing down the tender branches of the sapling just off the front steps, smothering the yard. The weatherman on the news had promised six to nine inches by morning, nine to twelve by early afternoon, and the drifts, she knew, would be even deeper in the woods surrounding the house. No, she couldn't see the snow, but from the cold air straining through the caulking around the windowsills, she felt certain it was falling faster and that the wind had grown brisker. Their home was no longer tight.

"This means we can get new windows soon," he whispered, as if reading her mind. She wasn't certain whether to be comforted or not by the fact that he too was still awake.

The news had talked about the mounting layoffs as well, the shrinking economy. Construction had already slowed down. Carpenters were hardly in high demand. And she knew he was sometimes careless, never the best worker on the site. Who knew how long it would be before he was hired on again?

The cold air blew accusingly around the window frame by the bed. He had patched it up, but new windows were needed. Sills and sashes didn't come cheap. And turning up the heat didn't help. The old boiler was far from efficient and they couldn't afford to raise the temperature. Putting food on the table came first. The only way to afford the sashes and sills and higher energy bills was to put less food on the table, and there was barely enough bread to go around now.

Tomorrow would be a busy day. At seven, they planned to pull back the bedcovers in the next room, pile them into some crumpled semblance of anguish and loss. Her husband would rush into the snow while she called the neighbors, the nearest of them a mile down the road. The house would soon be filled with people from this remote corner of the county, while police led others in a search of the woods. And what would she say when it was over?

They must have seen the snow from their window, run out to play in it. That's why they were dressed so meagerly, wasn't it?

No, the door wouldn't lock. The key had broken off in it last week.

No one ever comes out here. We didn't see any rush to fix it.

We never heard them leave.

She remembered watching her husband breaking the key in the door when the forecast called for snow. He'd used pliers to arrange the alibi, control where the key broke so that he could fix it himself later. No use buying new parts. "Every penny counts," he'd told her. He'd assumed as well that the neighbors would chip in for the funerals.

The wind stalked once more around the fissured sill, searching out her hair and her neck, crowding against the blanket she was suddenly embarrassed to have wrapped around her.

Had it been only an hour since they'd awakened the twins to see the blizzard? Sleepy eyes had grown wide at the sight of it. Outside after dark? Hide-and-seek in the snow?

A special night!

Their faces were aglow with wonder.

And they were still out there now, hiding behind some fallen tree or huddled in some shallow ditch amongst a flurry of silly giggles as the air thickened with falling flakes and the snow overwhelmed the land. No bread crusts to cover here, only her husband's purposeful, hurrying strides and her own only faintly faltering footprints. But what frigid blasts could muffle the radiance of her children calling after her, perhaps still calling into the emptiness: "We're ready! Come find us! Come find us now!"

Blue Plate Special

The manager of a local hotel called me one day many years ago to help him with a problem. He wanted to explain it in person and asked me to come over that afternoon. Though he seemed a little shifty on the phone, I figured it wouldn't cost me anything to stop by. It was a nice spring day, after all, and the address wasn't far from the office I had downtown back in those days.

I won't tell you the name of the hotel, but I guess with the info I've given, you could probably do a little detective work of your own, find out which one I'm talking about, and discover for yourself what I'm going to tell you. It's still there, same address, maybe the rest of it too.

I wouldn't recommend it.

***

"I have a problem with the men's room," Mr. Wichard, the hotel manager, told me once we'd sat down in his office. He was balding, middle-aged, spread wide through the belly like a pear squeezed up into a brown suit. He raised his left eyebrow at the end of his sentence, a cue of some kind.

"I'm not a plumber," I said flatly. I didn't go in much for theatrics.

"No, no," he said, his brow furrowing. "That's not what I mean at all." He gave a deep sigh, then tried to explain about the small restaurant off the lobby and about the waitresses noticing strange behavior among the patrons, all of them middle-aged businessmen. There had been, in his word, a "preponderance" of furtive glances and anxious expressions, or sometimes just the opposite, a giddiness, a boisterousness. And in most cases, the men took frequent trips to the restroom, spent long stretches in there—long enough that several times the waitresses feared one of them, or all of them, had simply skipped out on the bill. But they always returned eventually, some of them tipping generously, in fact. Ultimately, and despite the tips, the restaurant staff had called the manager to check it out for himself.

"I've seen the behavior of which they've spoken. I've entered the men's room myself, but I haven't witnessed anything . . . substantial." He emphasized that last word but didn't bother raising his eyebrow. "These men, they're just acting oddly, taking longer than necessary with the facilities. I have no proof, but I admit, I fear the worst."

It all seemed obvious to me. "Why don't you just bust these guys on a loitering rap?" I said, but he was shaking his head before I finished the sentence.

"All of them have lunch first," he told me. "As patrons, they have a right to the bathroom." He rubbed hard at that balding head of his. "It's the best lunch business we've had in years."

***

The manager wanted answers and he wanted evidence and he wanted to avoid a scandal. I told him I'd do what I could on all three counts.

The restaurant stood in the corner of the hotel, a half-wall partitioning it from the lobby, tall windows facing the street. This was not a luxury hotel—mid-range at best (another clue, best to avoid)—and the restaurant was little more than a diner prettied up with damask tablecloths. I took a seat that would give me a good view of it all, then waved off the menu and told the waitress to give me a ham and cheese on toast, mustard on the side.

Most of the clientele were businessmen from the downtown area—and *business* did indeed mean *men* in the period I'm talking about: clean-shaven, coat and tie, a fedora perched on the corner of the table. Most of the tables, a man sat alone at a two-top, and I could see it in them, the nervousness Wichard had been talking about. Even where groups of men gathered at a larger table, usually one or two of them seemed wary, distracted. There was a lot of glancing around, a lot of fingers tapping the table. Several of them made startled movements, sudden grins or grimaces. I watched as I ate my sandwich, trying to see who was looking at whom, trying to decipher if there was a code in those sidelong glances or tapping fingers. But none of the men seemed to be looking at one another, and the tapping seemed just restless energy, no pattern to it. No pattern either that I could see about who went when—no pairing up, no one following anyone else. Each man just finished his meal and retired to the restroom. And Wichard was right: Each man who left stayed gone a long time.

The men's room was my own next stop, of course, but I paid my bill first, tipped generously, and got a receipt for the expense account.

The bathroom was nothing remarkable—not that I expected it to be. Two stalls toward the rear, a line of four urinals to the right with a slight partition between each one, and a line of sinks to the left. Even a quick survey told me there was only one man to a stall, and I caught no untoward peeps across the partitions, though another man stood in the center of the room, glancing around a little fitfully before finally taking his spot in a free stall. No one seemed to pay him any attention. In fact, the men there hardly seemed to notice each other and wasted little time about their business, even as I tried to linger over my own.

Staking out a restroom, I should stress, is no easy task. You can't loiter long without seeming conspicuous yourself. But I tried to pace things out best I could and figured I could take a little more time at the sink.

The trouble was, everyone did exactly the same thing I'd planned, each man jostling loose a pile of soap powder and then lathering his hands with an almost clinical attention to detail, washing and washing while the foam rose and fell. All the while, each of them stared at himself in the mirror, intently, as if inspecting some small spot they'd missed shaving, some nick in the armor. A mix of emotions played across their features: those sudden expressions I'd seen in the restaurant or maybe just a tightening around the lips, a crinkle to the eyes.

A line had formed.

"Could you hurry it up?" one man asked. "There's others waiting."

While I finished washing up, I noticed something else. The men beside me weren't actually looking at themselves in the mirror but at a slant, each of them, angling their gaze toward the backs of the men behind them maybe or sometimes at an empty urinal. More codes, I thought, but I still couldn't see who was receiving them.

To buy myself a little more time, I took out a toothbrush from my inside coat pocket. No one could complain about good dental hygiene, could they?

A man a couple of sinks down backed away from the faucet into the center of the room, his wet hands held high in the air, his feet making little shimmy steps, like a dance or a mating call, but no one seemed to respond to it. Another man walked to the towel dispenser and let out muffled sobs as he dried his fingers one by one.

The guy beside me was watching me brush my teeth. When I turned toward him, he didn't look away at first, but just nodded, then smiled grimly. It was a knowing look, like I'd told him something, and then he turned back to his own business.

***

After a couple of days of such scenes, I met with Wichard again.

"You've witnessed it yourself now?" he asked me.

"Yes," I said. "But I can't explain it, not yet."

"But you've found something . . . immoral here, yes? Something that you could . . ."

This time, I was the one already shaking my head. I'd found nothing of the sort.

"Has there been any development at all?" he asked, confusion verging on desperation.

"Some of the men seem to be staying longer now," I said. I hesitated, then told him anyway. "Seems more than a few of them have started brushing their teeth after they eat."

***

This was not my only case, of course. An average week found me hunting up a check kiter or tracking down some petty nobody who'd skipped bail. In those days, though, most of my work was matrimonial. Philandering husbands, wayward wives, deadbeat dads, child support scams. Sad work, really. The bulk of it reminded me of my own parents, the way they'd bristled and accused and eventually just drifted apart, both of them laying the blame my way. There was a reverse custody battle—each wanting the other to take me—and Dad got stuck with me for a while. I finally ran away at sixteen. I don't imagine he noticed my being gone.

In the midst of all that, the time I spent on the hotel case started out feeling like a vacation—or at least a new routine to break the old one. But as the stakeouts, if you could call them stakeouts, turned up little evidence, restful quickly turned restless. Not that the strange behavior had slowed down, but no clue had emerged yet about what was at the root of it. Even though Wichard had been reluctant to have me "accost" any of his paying customers, I'd gone so far as to try striking up a conversation with a couple of them there at the sink. But the only development was that my suspects now treated me like the one looking for a pick-up. "Don't crowd me, buddy," they said, and "Can't you see I'm busy here?" and "Not interested, stick to your own story." Even after just a few days, especially with those free ham sandwiches I was tabbing up, I decided to reduce my daily charge to Wichard and, if nothing developed, to cut my losses soon.

"You ever get a taste for anything different?" the waitress asked me one day, what would become my last official one on the case.

"Sure." I smiled at her, gave her a little wink. "What'd you have in mind?"

She rolled her eyes, handed me the menu. The waitress wasn't my kind of gal anyway, a little too thin, brittle-looking really, and that curve to her lips that told me she'd always be hard to please. Her nametag said *Dorothy*. She cocked her hip as she waited.

I glanced over it, standard diner fare just like I'd expected, and a slip of faded paper tucked in the middle with the daily Blue Plates and a list of sides.

Monday: Meatloaf
Tuesday: Eggplant Parmesan
Wednesday: Meatloaf
Thursday: Oven-Fried Chicken
Friday: Ribeye
Saturday: Yolanda's Pork Chops

Like I said, Dorothy wasn't my type, but I tried to strike up some banter with her anyway. "Is the Wednesday meatloaf left over from Monday? Yolanda taking the day off for golf maybe?"

"Everything's just yesterday's scraps," she said, humorlessly. "But what's the meatloaf matter? Today's Tuesday."

I glanced at the menu again.

"Kind of strange to have eggplant as a Blue Plate, yeah?"

"I like eggplant," she said.

"Oh, sure, me too. But what good's a meat and three with no meat?"

"No one else seems to be complaining." She gave a sweep of her hand, and I noticed for the first time that nearly everyone was having the special, the spasmic, nervous lot of them. Was that somehow the code?

"You won me over," I said. "Blue Plate it is." I glanced at the list of sides. "And I'll take the mashed, the tossed, and a few of those green beans if there's bacon in them."

"And there's your meat," she said with those curved-down lips of hers, and then she was gone.

The eggplant wasn't bad, and there was indeed a sprinkle of bacon on top of the green beans. Even now, after everything, I still like to think it was Dorothy's way of flirting back.

If the order was indeed a signal of some kind, I failed to see what it meant. I ate and watched and waited, but no one paid attention to what I was eating. Slowly, the futility of it all came back, and a sense of loneliness started to grow. I was struck by the image that I was sitting in front of a television, a TV dinner on a tray table, watching that same strange drama unfolding in front of me like a daily soap, one I watched out of habit but didn't really care about. I'd had more than a few days on that routine, more than a few nights, and suddenly I lost the taste for the food and for the case. In that moment, I decided to tell Wichard after lunch that I needed to move on.

A boy passed in front of my table then, wearing a red sweater. He was a tow-headed kid, probably eight or nine, and out of place amongst all the business lunchers. But it was the sweater that caught my eye first, the fact that it too was out of place in so many ways. Spring outside, sun high in the sky, hints already in the air of summer heat ahead—that was part of it. But it was an older style too. Out of season and outdated both.

The boy glanced at me as he passed, lingered just a second by my table, a second too long. He looked a little familiar, like one of the child actors that used to be so popular back then. But really, all kids look the same, don't they? That's what I told myself at least.

He dropped his eyes, continued out into the lobby. At the men's room, he gave a backward glance my way before pushing open the door and going in.

While I waited for him to come back out, I looked around for the family he must have been with, but I didn't see one. Minutes passed, and then many minutes. Many men coming in and out of that same door. Still nothing.

I thought about that look of his, that backward glance.

I felt sick to my stomach, and I didn't think it was just the eggplant.

***

I went into the men's room myself. Business as usual, if you could call it that. No sight of the boy at first, but I knew he had to be in there. I waited as each stall emptied and then went in to check it out for myself, even patting the side wall on the furthest one for a trick panel, a hidden room. Nothing. I thought about how the men at the sink had stared aslant into their mirrors at the urinals behind them, and so I checked the wall around each of them in turn for switches or hollow spots. Still nothing.

I stood and watched the other men in there, looking for anything out of the ordinary—or rather, even more out of the ordinary. They, in turn, watched me—equally suspicious, I'm sure, though none of them seemed entirely fazed.

"You see a boy come this way?" I asked one of the guys waiting for a sink. "Kid in a red sweater?"

He shook his head nervously, not meeting my eye.

"You're always asking questions," said another man further up the line, a short, plump gent in a pinstriped suit. He'd cautioned me off once before.

I moved up toward him. "What's it to you what questions I ask?" I was angry suddenly, itching for trouble, getting in his fat, jowly face. "Do you know something about what's going on here?"

He had a smug expression, raised a bushy eyebrow, didn't answer me. After a few moments' standoff, he glanced over my shoulder, squinted his eyes as if looking at something at a great distance, then pointed his chin that way. His lips curved up into half a grin. "There. I think that one may be yours."

I turned and saw the boy in the sweater standing by the far sink. A tall, thin man was just walking away from him.

"You!" I called as the man pulled a few towels to dry his hand. "You, what'd you do with him?"

The thin man glanced at the floor near where the boy stood. He shook his head. "Must be yours."

The boy stood by the sink, watching both of us. His sweater had been pulled askew, and his face was flushed, his cheeks rosy—shame, embarrassment, what?

"He hurt you?" I asked, kneeling down toward him. "Someone else did?"

The boy didn't answer, just kept staring at me.

"Your family," I said. "Where are they? I want to talk to them, I need to talk to them now."

The boy gave no response, made little change in expression. He only cocked his head slightly to the side, as if I was speaking some foreign language and he was trying to latch on to the words, to tune into the frequency. There was a hole in his sweater I hadn't seen before, and I felt sweat beading on my forehead, the sickness in my gut deepening. I turned back to accuse the man again, but he'd left.

Despite the line waiting, no one had made a move to help us, and the sink where the boy and I stood remained empty. Looking up, I saw now that the mirror above it had begun to fog a little, like someone was breathing on it or like the bathroom itself had suddenly heated up, a burst of humidity from a hot faucet maybe, except that the faucet wasn't on. I stood up to wipe it clean and saw then that it wasn't fog but frost really, icy tendrils of it thickening at the edge of the glass. When I leaned in closer, I saw that there were two boys in the mirror, the one who'd been standing beside me and another one, similar features but maybe a year older, wearing the same patterned sweater but in blue.

The two of them were tussling, poking and prodding, pulling at one another's sweater for leverage in their horseplay, laughing all through it. The boy in red reached down and threw a handful of powder at the other one—snow it looked like, but it must have been soap from the dispenser. Those soap flakes coated the other boy's face.

That one, the boy in blue, had ringlets of blond hair, curling almost like a girl's, and a little chub to his cheeks, the cheeks reddening just like the other's had, rosy circles along the plumpness of his face, even more rosy as he tried to brush the soap away. He had blue eyes, like his sweater, and a smile I remember that . . .

But no, I'm not telling this right.

That boy in blue . . . Well, I'd never known that a child could be so beautiful. No, even that's not right. He was, this boy, the most beautiful sight of all sights I'd ever encountered. My heart's desire, a desire that I'd tried to forget. There are no other words for it.

Breathless now, I turned to look at the two of them straight on, to reach out and—everything I wanted—to touch the boy in blue, to bend down and grab him and pull him toward me.

But it was still just the other one there beside me in the bathroom, staring at me with that same expressionless gaze. A knowing gaze, I saw now. He knew what I wanted, better than anyone, of course—had known all along. *And how couldn't he?* I told myself. Because I knew then too.

I straightened up as best I could. I looked back at the mirror in front of me, one last glimpse at the boy in blue, at all of it, like there might be answers. Then I turned to see the whole wall of mirrors standing over the sinks, a frail little world opening up, the line of anxious and excited men and everyone surrounding them. I caught my breath, or tried to at least, then came back to myself.

"I don't know where he went," I told the boy in red, feeling my throat tighten. "Quit looking at me. I just don't know."

***

Wichard's secretary said he was busy, but I pushed right past her, burst through his office door. Something in my face must have scared him. He blanched, shooed away a couple of employees he'd been talking with, closed the door and turned to me.

"It's something terrible, isn't it?" he asked. "I can see it in your face. Is it what we feared? Is it—?"

"What we feared?" I said, and I could feel my fists clenching. "Yes. Terrible, truly terrible."

"I knew it. You've found something, I can see it. Evidence. Tell me what you've found."

"You already know, don't you? You've known all along, I'll bet."

He furrowed that bald forehead of his. "What can you mean by that? I hired you. If I had known what was happening, why would I have hired you?"

"The restaurant then," I said. "Either you know or someone there does. Dorothy. Or another of the waitresses. Or . . ." I scanned my memory of the menu. "Yolanda. She's the cook, right? She's putting something in the food. That must be how it works."

"Poison?" Wichard paled. "Poison in the food? These men are sick then? Is that what you're saying? But I saw no evidence of sickness, I saw no . . . Oh, this will ruin us. You have proof of this? We'll have to handle this without the police, without the press. Is it possible?"

Proof? The police? What was the next step? I'd rushed to

his office so quickly, I hadn't thought about it. Should I tell him to round all the men up? The waitresses? The cook? Would the poison be detectable? Was it a poison at all? And what was the connection to the restroom, to the mirror? Whatever answers I'd found, they only introduced more questions.

"You just need to shut it down," I told him finally.

"Yes, shut down the men's room." He picked up his phone, dialing a number. "Of course, of course. We'll say it's being cleaned, closed temporarily for renovation or—"

"No," I said, suddenly seeing what had to be done. "All of it. The men's room, the restaurant, all of it. Padlock it. Bulldoze it. Burn it."

He looked at me, panic turning into its own suspicion. He returned the receiver to its cradle.

"What . . . what *exactly* have you found?"

"There was a boy," I told him, honestly. "He . . ."

"He what?" asked Wichard. "He was hurt? He was poisoned too? Where is he now?"

"No, no," I said. "That's not it, not at all."

"So what crime are you coming to tell me about? What evidence have you brought me?"

I saw myself then how it looked, how I looked.

"You have to trust me," I said. "Close it down or I'll call the police on all of this."

I left with the threat hanging in the air.

"You won't get paid for this," he screamed after me as I left his office. "Not a penny, not a dime."

It didn't matter. I was long past billing him.

***

I didn't go back to my office after that but just walked the city instead. It was spring, as I said, and the sun stood high and bright, not a cloud in the sky. The sidewalk wasn't baking yet, too early in the season, but the heat was coming, I could feel it. I tried to drag that heat into my lungs and the pollen too, thick in the air even in the middle of downtown. I turned my face upward, trying to pull the sunlight into my skin.

Answers? There hadn't been any really—just some dim shading of the truth, empty in its own way. The distant echoes of laughter and tears, the muted sounds of celebration and re-crimination, the delicate shapes of mothers or fathers, of brothers or sisters, of husbands, wives, lovers, children. I'd glimpsed them there, fuzzy indistinct scenes, a messy lot of them suddenly along that wall of mirrors, still vivid enough to make out what was going on—people putting a puzzle together around a kitchen table, a couple making love in the backseat of a car, a boy washing the sheets after wetting the bed, another stumbling over the alphabet, a middle-aged man having one drink too many, another watching a wedding, another a funeral, another baiting a fishing hook, another flying a kite. . . On and on and on, multiplied crazily right down the line.

It hadn't been a mating call, I thought then, remembering one of the men I'd seen the first day, the one who'd shimmied into the middle of the room. He'd been dancing with some-one—a wife, a mistress? Someone long gone certainly, lost then found. They'd been on a beach maybe, sand on their feet, a sunny day, a moonlit night. Or somewhere else, someone else—who knew how it worked?

I would go back again the next day and many days after that, trying to uncover the truth. I badgered Wichard about what he was going to do. I interrogated Dorothy and the other waitress-es about what they knew. I forced my way into the kitchen and confronted Yolanda herself, who fled from me, racing around a metal table piled high with food, not just bewildered but ter-rified. I went down the line in the men's room asking each of them what they'd seen, why they'd come here in the first place—no longer shy, no longer caring about how I looked or about any of the consequences. How had they heard about this? How did the word get around? Did everyone see the same thing? Where was the overlap? Was it the same image each time?

I could answer that last one myself; I had the Blue Plate a couple more times, obsessed with the idea of seeing the little boy in blue again, looking past him, watching and rewatching, picking at a scab. But no one wanted to talk about their secrets any more than I wanted to talk about mine. Their private dramas were their own, of course.

As for the police, I never called them myself. What would I have told them? What proof did I have? But they did get involved before it was over. Wichard called them himself—to take care of a trespasser, a nuisance, a lunatic who was harassing his customers, frightening his staff.

But all that was later—things I eventually did that I never would've imagined when I left that first day, took that long hot walk, tried to shake the frost lingering in my memory, the chill clinging so heavily to me.

***

It had been winter in that men's room, I had no doubt of it. A snow day and school called off early, two boys home alone, playing in the front yard. What could be better? And then a car pulling up, a man driving, an urgent message. Boys shouldn't be home alone, not on a cold day like that. The parents had sent him. They were waiting. Climb in already.

One didn't, one did—frustration on both sides, accusations too.

"Mom and Dad are going to be so mad at you. Just wait. You'll see. You'll be sorry."

His words, my brother's, the last any of us would ever hear from him. And then that final image, the driver's hand laid gently across my brother's shoulder.

He was right. They had been mad. I had been sorry.

I remember them now, the way they yelled at me, the way they cried. My father threatened me, thinking I knew more than I'd told. My mother pled and wept, pulling on that new red sweater of mine, half of the matching set they'd just bought us, finally tearing a hole in its side.

"I don't know," I told them again and again. "I don't know who he was, I don't know where they went."

My first case, the only one that mattered, coming back to taunt me, still unsolved, unsolved again.

All Tomorrow's Parties

There's Shayla flitting past as a young girl: eight, maybe nine years old. Darkness beyond the window, autumn outside, but the aura of some summer day drifting around her. Laughter plays across her cheeks and eyes. Her blond hair is in ringlets.

Shayla first catches sight of her younger self at the far wall of the sprawling condo that belongs to one of the account managers—an all-staff soirée, everyone invited. Candlelight in the corners, a saxophone on the stereo, coworkers and friends of coworkers shifting into small circles as Friday evening shimmies free from the week. Then out of nowhere, there's the girl, this vision of the girl Shayla once was. Young Shayla eases between those clusters of beer bottles and wine glasses and cocktail coupes. Young Shayla slips behind the doll-faced receptionist, who's traded her sensible office wear for a low-cut black dress and who's right now tipping her head coquettishly toward one of the junior partners. Somewhere near the window, Young Shayla darts completely out of view—a white dress vanishing.

Shayla—Shayla today—rubs her eyes, blinks out the blurriness. She did see this, didn't she?

Conversations echo numbly on all sides, words and voices doubling somehow, and the shadows near the wall have begun to deepen and blur.

Fuck. She's already had too much to drink.

But before she can turn down another, Elaine, her new friend at the office, new best friend, has taken her hand and begun guiding her toward the kitchen and a butcher's block thick with wine and liquor bottles.

***

Here's Shayla today: mid-thirties and feeling older, recently divorced, newly childless in a way, fresh on the market again—even if that *again* makes her feel not entirely fresh at all.

Here's what Shayla used to call her Cinderella story: love at first touch at a crowded frat party, Richard (boyfriend-to-be, husband-to-be, ex-husband-to-be) with that shock of red hair

and that devilish grin, beaming with confidence, ripe to be someone's prince. He'd been a business major—summer internship
on Wall Street, a job promised after graduation, a career path
paved with gold. BMOC, his reputation preceding him. Shayla
had been a communications major, not sure she'd made the right
choice, student loans piling up, no prospects yet, no place to go
except tonight's party and tomorrow's and next weekend's and—
and then Richard put his hand on her waist as he passed her
at the Kappa Sig house, the slightest sparks at the small of her
back, shivers accelerating up her spine, and she turned toward
that red hair and that grin and into the swirl of his cologne and
knew at once where she wanted to go.

Rags to riches. Cinderella and her prince. A courtship and
engagement. A wedding, a honeymoon, a happily ever after.

And when the honeymoon was over? *After* the happily ever
after?

"Do we have to be late every time, Shayla? Do you have any
idea how much these clients are worth? How much they're worth
to me? Can you not just put on a smile for a couple of hours?"

"Didn't you tell me you wanted a family too, Shayla? And if
not now, then when?"

"Ever think of taking up an exercise program, Shayla? Ever
want to work off that baby weight?"

"What kind of example does that attitude set for our daughter?"

"Can't you have dinner ready on time? Can't you keep this
mess of a house presentable? Can't you understand that a man
has needs?"

"What do you do all day anyway—besides letting yourself fall
apart? Are you listening to me, Shayla? Shayla?"

Happily ever after meant perfect wife, perfect family. Who
could live up to that?

***

Shayla stumbles in the heels she's borrowed from Elaine.
She's wearing one of Elaine's dresses as well—an ill fit.

"You can't wear *that*," Elaine had blurted out about Shayla's
own dress earlier, Shayla mere seconds through Elaine's door.

"It felt sleek." Shayla had smoothed her hands along her hips. "It felt stylish." Wasn't that the way with little black dresses?

"It's last season's style." Elaine picked at a small fray, dismissed the dress as mousy, as motherly. "Haven't you seen the poster back at the office? *Marketing is a contest for people's attention.* And this"—a gesture toward the dress, or toward Shayla herself?—"is gonna need some attention."

Fixing Shayla up was the first step toward fixing her up *with* someone. This is something Elaine has said more than once. *A new you*—another of Elaine's phrases. But Shayla has learned it the hard way: You can never really get away from yourself.

"Try this little fit and flare instead." Elaine handed across a tropical print, too much white for Shayla's taste, and she didn't like the halter top, but Elaine insisted. "It'll show a little cleavage. And you want to bet who'll appreciate that?" A knowing look, an eyebrow raised.

Dylan, she meant, Dylan from the office, but Shayla was thinking instead about her ex-husband—how he'd nagged that she hadn't been taking care of herself anymore, that she hadn't been taking care of him.

So, Shayla had suited up in Elaine's dress and let Elaine freshen her makeup, camouflaging the crow's-feet and the dark circles, hiding the puffiness from where she'd been crying before in her own apartment.

"Your decision if a glass is half-empty or half-full," Elaine said a few minutes later, and it took Shayla a moment to recognize that she wasn't talking specifically about the bottle of Tanqueray in her hand. "I know you miss seeing your kid. It's heartbreaking, I know—I mean, I can imagine. Divorce is never easy. But think about it this way. You don't have to find a babysitter tonight. You don't have to get home at a certain time. You're footloose, fancy-free."

"The evening's young," Shayla said. "And so are we"—something Richard used to say back when that's what they were.

"Exactly." Elaine topped the glasses with a couple of splashes of tonic. "A little pre-gaming?" She held a glass toward Shayla. "A little liquid courage?"

Footloose, Shayla thought. *Fancy-free.* She felt the foundation on her cheeks tighten as she forced a smile.

She took the glass.

***

A drink at the end of a long day, that's how it had started back in her marriage—just to ease her nerves. Then two drinks. Then why not one midafternoon? Or even with lunch? And after the separation, who was there to care when she started?

Life of the party.

Party for one.

The officer who pulled her over—he'd cared. "Have you been drinking, ma'am?" and "A little early in the day, isn't it?" and peering past her, "That your daughter in the car with you?"

Care maybe, but not sympathy, not understanding, no matter how clearly Shayla tried to explain. *No, I only had one drink. No, I certainly wouldn't get behind the wheel if I'd had too much. No, I would never put my daughter at risk, never ever, no, no, no.*

No sympathy from her husband either or from the judge at the hearing or from the other judge, further down the line, at the custody challenge. And the lawyer's bills mounting in the meantime, and her with no job to pay for them.

Rags to riches to rags to . . . what next?

Shayla has set a deadline, Cinderella in reverse. Some magic by midnight tonight, or else she'll draw this story to a close herself.

***

Keeping her balance behind Elaine, Shayla latches onto the real reason Elaine is dragging her toward the kitchen. Behind those bottles of Maker's Mark and Plymouth and Grey Goose huddled together on the butcher's block, Dylan is playing bartender—Dylan the destination, not the drinks themselves.

Shayla adjusts her halter top. She hugs her purse against her side, the weight of it steadying her.

Dylan catches sight of her as he clasps the cap on a cocktail shaker. He raises it over his shoulder—biceps bulging against the sleeves of his black polo as he swings it back and forth in a slow motion that's almost dizzying. His hair is slicked back, his face partly in shadow, a halo around his head, a radiance, a . . . Shayla ferrets around in her mind for the word. How drunk is she that she can't find it? Can't even see straight? Then Dylan turns toward the light. Half a grin tugs at the corner of his lips.

Dylan is (Shayla understands this) a younger version of her ex-husband. A different career—marketing instead of investment—and nothing similar about them physically, Richard's red hair to Dylan's blond, Richard's stockiness to Dylan's leaner athleticism. But the confidence, the ambition, the potential. Dylan will be junior partner before long. Everyone feels sure of it, just like the man that the doll-faced receptionist had been chatting up before. Dylan has potential. He has possibilities ahead of him.

Possibilities for Shayla too—at a time when she needs them most. She is still amazed that Dylan approached her in the break room one morning soon after she started work, asked how she liked the job, where she was from, glanced down at her bare ring finger. He friended her on Facebook that same night, sent her a couple of instant messages. Interest, flirtation. More?

"Glad you made it." Dylan leans toward her, but even so, she can hardly hear him above the music and the chatter and the laughter. "Get a glass."

He grabs one himself before she can, thrusts it into her hand, and tips the cocktail shaker toward her—but just as he starts to pour, Shayla catches another glimpse of Young Shayla with her head tilted to one side, curiosity in her expression. Shayla tilts with her, leaning, listing, and some of the clear liquid sloshes from the glass onto the floor.

"Party foul," someone calls out, Shayla can't see who. She's searching instead for the girl, gone again, seems like, fading away into the blur.

***

Parties—and Shayla has seen her share—have a sound, a throb and thrum, echoes and undercurrents. All of them the same, she thinks, no matter the little details.

Grunge bands and Miller High Life at high school keggers, electronica in college and everyone tossing back shots of tequila, and then the jazz streaming out of the speakers here and everyone leaning into their craft cocktails. There was a world of difference between playing beer pong with Billy Prescott before they hooked up in the bathroom (everything so much easier then, wasn't it?) and clinking champagne glasses with Richard at their wedding reception, but in each moment she'd felt like she'd never been happier (the new ring glistening as she raised her toast, not yet weighing her down). And then . . . what exactly does the night ahead promise with Dylan?

But the voices are the same, that's what she means, and the people somehow, and then Shayla herself here in the middle.

Always someone being too loud, like the man shouting behind her at this very moment, creative director at the agency, even louder drunk than not. Other voices always piling against you too, gripes and grumbles about one unhappiness or another (love, family, work), or whispers in some cozy corner and little fireworks of flirtation. Then some burst of laughter on the other side of the room, or a yelp when this person bumps into that one (always alcohol sloshing somewhere). Or a cold silence, the lonely girl left unexpectedly adrift along the edges.

There's a rhythm, some variation of that same rhythm party after party. Sometimes in the middle of a room, Shayla closes her eyes and listens for the patterns—steady, relentless, pulsing, jangling. Sometimes she hears the beat inside her own head, like her pulse is trying to become one with it.

"You okay?" Dylan says, and Shayla realizes she's closed her eyes just now, that she's been standing very, very still.

"Sorry." She needs a moment to get her bearings.

***

For Shayla today, everything is new: the admin job at Turner & Blount and even having a job at all, the one-bedroom apartment that feels bigger and emptier than its 750 square feet, the fact of being suddenly single, suddenly free to do whatever she wants, like whatever she's doing with Dylan tonight, her hand clasped in his.

Here are some other things that are new for Shayla: checking messages on Match.com and swiping through Tinder (or being swiped past herself—she doesn't like to think about it, feels too old for Tinder, understands it was desperation driving her that way). Even Facebook has become unfamiliar territory. Months ago, it was a wall of moms sharing stories about their kids, parenting tips, recipes. These days it's a place for meeting and matchmaking, hopes and (she's already felt this) heartbreak. She's been chatting with Dylan these last few weeks, something sparking to life there, she feels sure, even if his IMs sometimes stop out of nowhere, leaving the apartment feeling even larger.

Here's more that's new: condoms in her purse—the first time in many years, and a weight of anxieties with them. Whatever her faults, her husband could never accuse her of cheating. She's not used to thinking about protection.

She carries another kind of protection as well—a gun she bought soon after moving into her new place. Single woman living alone, putting herself out on the market again, walking herself home late at night, not as nice a neighborhood as her home with Richard. The weight of it gives her strength, confidence.

She told Richard about it after she bought it—trying to stir up some sympathy (she would admit that), to get him to sigh and say, "Come home, Shay." But Richard offered only dismissal, disdain. "Protection?" he said, a bitter laugh. "Only danger to you is yourself."

Sometimes, in the quiet of some midnight, the quiet of that lonely apartment, Dylan's IMs gone quiet, Shayla has understood that Richard was right.

She has held the gun to her head, she's held it in her mouth. Seconds have passed, then minutes, before she tucked it into her nightstand drawer, tucked herself alone in that bed, a nightcap easing her into sleep.

***

Has Shayla maneuvered Dylan to this corner? Or has he maneuvered her? Honestly, she doesn't feel steady enough to have managed any of this so smoothly, so quickly.

"I've been thinking," she tells Dylan, hearing the slur in her own voice, the stumble: *think–ing*. "All those flirty messages of yours." She shakes her head, wags a finger at him. "Do you chat like this with all the girls?"

"Women, you mean?" As Shayla nods, she feels her eyelids drooping, then jolts awake. Was he making a joke about her age? "All the time," he says. "Sometimes I can barely keep track of which woman's in which chat window."

Shayla steadies herself against the wall, remembering the poster about competing for people's attention, remembering what Elaine had said—Elaine there on the other side of the room, laughing at something, a haze of action and noise between them. "You just need to find the right one," she slurs. "The one who'll take care of you."

Dylan leans in. Shayla can smell his cologne. "And are you the woman who's gonna take care of me?"

They are close. Things are cozy. Again: who cornered who?

"Haven't you noticed how our names fit together?" Shayla holds a finger up, writes her name in the air. "The 'yla'—right there in the middle." She nods. It really is a coincidence, she thinks, profound even. "I was doodling our names one night, couldn't help but notice."

He squints at her. "How old are you again?"

She waits for a smile, can't tell if it's a serious question or just more flirtation. Finally, she shrugs, waves a hand nonchalantly, like she doesn't care one way or another—and there's Young Shayla hovering again, dancing to the music but not dancing with anyone. She's alone, a world away, world of her own, as people drift around her—through her? Shayla can't tell, doesn't care. She's puzzled by something else, because she's not sure now that this girl looks entirely like her. A resemblance there, certainly, but something different, something off. *Her* but *not* her.

Shayla turns back to Dylan. "Do you know what my mother told me? I think it was when I was about ten years old."

"What?"

"She said—and I remember her tucking my hair behind my ear as she said it—she said, 'You're such a beautiful girl, Shayla, you'll charm all the boys, have your pick of them, a girl as pretty as you.'"

"And was she right?" Dylan reaches up himself and tucks a bit of Shayla's hair behind her ear. When his fingers graze against her, she feels the ground shift slightly, her feet losing their grip on the floor.

"Always some boy or another chasing after me." *Don't seem too available*, this is something Elaine told her earlier, but Shayla can't resist trying out a seductive grin. "Did you know I can tie a cherry stem with my tongue?" The corners of her mouth ache.

Dylan laughs. "Haven't heard that line since high school," he says. "If only we had a cherry stem for you to prove your skills, but . . ."

Their eyes meet, and Shayla is reminded of the way Billy Prescott stared at her when she won beer pong and he had to chug down that last Miller High Life. "The champagne of beers," he'd said, tipping a toast her way. He hadn't broken eye contact, just watched her around the rim of that red plastic cup, playfulness and challenge and desire.

"You're a very interesting woman, Shayla," Dylan says.

"You should find out." She gives what she hopes is a come-hither look.

"When are you going to let me find out?"

Young Shayla—or whoever the girl is—has stopped dancing. She's watching them again, the same curiosity from before and . . . judgment? disapproval? displeasure? Shayla can't find the right shade of meaning, and she's struggling with another question: How many years' difference between her age and Dylan's? How many years' difference between Dylan and that young girl there? Where do the years go?

Shayla's head lolls. She tries to shake it, shake away some of the fog inside, shake off the young girl still standing there, still watching.

Finally, Shayla just takes Dylan by the hand and leads him away.

***

Here is Shayla's deal with herself tonight, how this Cinderella story might come to an end, how she might finally put behind her the husband who doesn't care, the daughter she lost, the future that seems so bleak:

The gun is in her purse.

If Prince Charming doesn't come around by midnight, she's going to put it against her head or in her mouth once more.

And this time, she's not going to hesitate.

***

Here's Shayla in the bathroom, Dylan pressing her against the sink—a pedestal sink, no counter to prop herself up on—the porcelain cold against her rump, panties around her legs, just below her knees.

Did Dylan lure her in here? Taking advantage of the drunk girl? No, she did the leading, she remembers this, the weight of him behind her as she weaved and wobbled through the crowded apartment, even if she doesn't remember planning to lead him here, to this. It must have been on her mind, though—thinking of Billy Prescott earlier, that sly grin of his all those years ago, how she'd won him.

"You meant what you said about taking care of me," Dylan said when she slipped her dress up around her waist, eased one of those condoms from her purse. Noise through the door, the party outside, and Shayla knew how . . . out of step? crazy? ridiculous? . . . what she was doing here was. This was what you did at a high school party or at some frat house, not at some account manager's condominium. But you did have to get the other person's attention, that was the job, wasn't it? And she had Dylan's, surely she did.

"No time like the present," she said—hearing the slurring deeper this time, sloppier.

Her glass stands empty beside her purse on the back of the toilet. She'd downed the rest of her drink before they began.

She closes her eyes and then opens them again, tries to focus on Dylan, searches for that halo around him here under these lights, but it's just hard cheekbones and his cologne sharp against her and his five-o'clock shadow scraping against her cheeks and neck. One arm presses down on her shoulder, one hand cups her ass, and he's picking up speed inside her, and yet somehow he feels further away than ever, or maybe she's the one who's far away, not here at all, as if she's watching this from above, from some great distance, the rhythm he's building that she can't catch up to, the pounding that she feels and doesn't feel.

A pounding on the door too, and then an open door and a burst of music and the guy from the mailroom, wide-eyed, red-faced, grinning. "Hey, hey" and "I didn't—" and someone beyond shouting "Get a room." Sudden music, sudden laughter, all eyes on them, *on her* she recognizes, but Dylan doesn't slow down except to slam that door.

Shayla tries to focus on the moment, feels herself flattening out, disappearing as Dylan finishes.

He grunts in her ear, an explosion of little grunts. Somewhere below there are other explosions, a fury of fireworks, she knows, but these feel far away as well.

***

Here's Shayla readjusting her dress afterward, glancing at the reflection of Dylan behind her, zipping up his pants, not looking her way. She remembers Billy Prescott all those years ago, her whispering into his ear "I love you I love you I love you" and—

While the door was open, Shayla caught another glimpse of Young Shayla, young whoever she is. She doesn't know how much the girl saw, what she must have been thinking. Curiosity? Condemnation?

Shayla adjusts herself in the mirror. Dylan is half circling in place behind her. She wants him to turn her around, to kiss her.

He takes a deep breath, glances nervously at the door, doesn't glance her way—a different Dylan under the fluorescent glare, stark and somber.

"Ready?"

Time to return to the party.

Time for another drink.

***

"Did you seriously get caught in the bathroom with Dylan?" Elaine is as wide-eyed as the guy from the mailroom. "My god, everyone's talking about it. Can you just imagine Monday morning?" Elaine is giggling. She's holding a drink, and then it's in Shayla's hand. The one that Dylan said he was going to get her? She can't see him from the corner Elaine has pulled them into, can't make out any of the faces at all.

"It was like Billy," she says.

"Billy?" Someone laughs nearby, and Shayla wonders if they're laughing at her. "I thought your husband's name was Richard."

"It is. Billy was before. But it's not going *to be* like Billy." Because . . .

Because, staring at Dylan's reflection in the bathroom, Shayla remembered what happened with Billy Prescott the weekend after they'd hooked up, the other girl he'd ended up with, and Shayla simply moving on.

Except it hadn't been that simple, she knew. Had she ever even spoken to Billy after that? She'd written him, yes, that's it. "Do you know how much I . . . ? Do you know how much . . . ? Do you know how . . . Do you . . . ?" She can't remember if she ever sent it.

Elaine rests the tips of her fingers on each of Shayla's cheeks, turns her head so they're face to face. "Who's Billy?"

"It's not going to be like Richard either," she says, and then, "But where'd he go? Dylan?"

Elaine shrugs. "Over there somewhere. He's catching merry hell for you and him in the bathroom, I gotta tell you."

Shayla waves her hand. This has become her gesture, she's suddenly self-conscious about it, suddenly deeply curious about it. What does it mean? She's waving that it doesn't matter to her. She's waving that the other person shouldn't care. She's waving that she doesn't know herself what she means, can't articulate, can't recall.

"Is it midnight yet?" Shayla asks. "But I guess it doesn't matter anymore does it, because my prince, he already came, didn't he?" And then she laughs at the image, the words, her prince coming, giggles like she can't stop.

Elaine tilts her head the way the young girl did, squints at Shayla.

"Honey, you are *drunk*," Elaine says, laughing along with her, because this is how parties go.

***

But where has Elaine gone now? And shouldn't Dylan be back with that drink? Be here *with* her? And whose elbow is this Shayla is standing next to? She concentrates on the elbow to steady herself, resisting the urge to rest her hand against it. Words blip past. Who's talking? What are they talking about? Shayla nods occasionally, she's paying attention, she is. She can sense the sidelong glances at her, the furrowed brows, the smirks. The elbow bends, a shoulder turning, blocking. She's losing her balance.

She needs to sit down, that's all it is. She needs to stop swaying, stop the room from swaying. She eases around a couple of people—from the accounting department she thinks, or no, maybe these two aren't from the office at all but just friends of friends? She reaches the sofa, steadies herself, slumps.

The young girl is sitting beside her. They glance at one another, then Shayla turns away, stares ahead into the room, seeing, not seeing.

She thinks she recognizes the girl more clearly, but . . .

How could her daughter have grown so much in the months since Shayla last saw her? This girl seems years older. But isn't that the same curve of cheekbone that Shayla knows so well? And those eyes, just a shade off from Shayla's own, the color that made Shayla feel each time like she was looking at herself in some special mirror, the past reflected back into the present.

What is her daughter doing here?

"Mia?" Shayla says her daughter's name softly, then again louder. "Mia." The girl's head bobs up and down as if to the music, but Shayla notices that the rhythm is off, the nodding out of beat. One of those ringlets has fallen slack. She doesn't seem to hear Shayla.

Shayla reaches out to smooth the girl's hair back in place, then stops. The girl seems so beautiful, so fragile, and Shayla is reminded again of her mother tucking her own hair back, of Dylan making that same move, of that prediction, that promise, of charming all the boys.

Shayla remembers tucking Mia's hair back the same way another time, another day when she was overwhelmed by how beautiful her daughter was—a tea party they were having at the time. "Sit with me, Mama. I'll pour your tea." And Shayla smiled and said, "I brought my own," and the two of them toasted one another, an empty wooden teacup in her daughter's hand and a half-drunk gimlet in Shayla's, and Shayla was filled with happiness, thinking even then, this is the way it should be, life as a party, a constant stream of them, smiles and happiness and warmth, because if it wasn't, then why would life be worth living anyway?

And then Richard had walked in on that tea party, his face flushing red—anger? shame?—and even though he spoke only one small word this time—her name—it had said enough.

***

Here's Shayla opening her eyes. Has she fallen asleep on the sofa? How long has she slept?

The young girl beside her—her daughter, herself, whoever—is gone. Shayla can't find her out there or Elaine either, and Dylan hasn't returned—and won't, she recognizes. Came, yes, but won't come back. No giggles.

Time for her to go too, she thinks—and then she remembers her plan, her commitment to herself, presses her hand against her purse, feels the weight there again, grounding her own weightlessness. Time to go, but is it really time? Has her midnight arrived?

Shayla stands, tries to get her balance. Crowds of faces, distorted, elongated, that same throb and thrum, a wall of sound, deafening now, but a wall between her and the sound too, and Shayla dodging through the edges of it, an emptiness deep inside her that the noise won't reach.

She can't focus enough to see exactly where she's going, much less find a clock, but she's squeezing behind people, between people. "Hey, watch it!" "Are you okay?" "I don't think she's okay."

Noise, noise, noise, everywhere, pulsing and pushing and shoving, jostling her, jolting her—and how big can this condo be anyway?

The kitchen, the kitchen will have a clock, don't they always? She heads toward the butcher's block, picks up a glass of wine from the corner—a muffled "Hey, that's mine" behind her—and sees the clock, a black cat with a dial in its belly, its pupils darting back and forth, its tail swinging. She stares at the dial, can't tell which is the big hand and which the small, they're so similar.

Both are past the 11.

Close enough.

She studies the glass in her hand, then tips back the wine. Last call.

She'll go home, back to the small apartment. She'll lay herself in the bed where she's sat alone with this gun on other nights. She won't hesitate, she won't—

She tells herself this as she sets down the empty glass, focuses on making a straight line toward the door. But people are blocking her way, and she's staggering—this is the only word—despite herself.

And then she catches sight of Dylan, and he catches sight of her, and is that a blush? He turns away quickly, turns red-faced toward the woman he's been talking with.

The doll-faced receptionist. She's captured his attention now, and Shayla feels her own face redden at the sight of the other woman's sly, knowing smirk.

***

Here's Shayla deciding that she won't wait until she gets home after all. She'll do it here.

Here's the end of the Cinderella story Shayla no longer believes in: No Prince Charming, no glass slipper, but just some shutting down of the storm of expectations and humiliations, of anger and regret, just some laying of those regrets at Richard's own doorstep, so he can see what he's done, finally feel sorry for her like he should've before.

And Dylan will see too, she thinks, as she forces her way toward him, up close and personal. He won't be able to look away like he had afterward in the bathroom, like he's still doing, trying to duck into the shadows. Red-faced definitely, shamed about Shayla or about being caught here with his doll-faced friend, and that girl flushed and flustered too. Red-faced just like Richard always was, and Shayla flushed and flustered herself, and fumbling still in her purse, fumbling to make sense of any of this, Richard, and Billy, and Dylan. Because how could you get inside someone like that, inside her head, inside her body, and then take yourself so far away and . . .

And then the gun is finally in her hand. It's firing even before she has her hand firmly around it. It's like fireworks going off around her, closer this time, real this time, red and white and hot and bursting through all that noise, that throb and thrum, that silence.

***

The party is winding down, Shayla can feel it.

People making sudden exits, rush rush rush, like a clock has indeed struck somewhere, maybe midnight arrived after all and Shayla simply didn't hear the chimes.

Shayla has been here before, overstaying her welcome, that desperate feeling you get when you're the last one leaving the party, and when did the hosts turn the music off and the lights on? She missed the signals. It happens.

But no, that's not it. The party isn't over. Still, something has changed. Many people have left, but others are still standing around, a blur of them almost in a circle around her—backing away? Leaning toward? Watching her. Maybe pointing. Someone grabbed at her arm, tugged at her, did something—what, she can't really tell.

She's been here before too—the drunk girl, life of the party. And then a quick turn, struggling to laugh along with everyone laughing at her. Slurring that laughter, falling into someone or over someone, spilling some drink on herself more often than not. Blipping out. Blacking out. And then trying to forget it all come Monday morning. Shrug it off, move on.

She has indeed spilled something on herself. Red wine maybe? But hasn't she been drinking clear drinks? That was a lesson she'd learned before. Clear liquor, white wine, anything that wouldn't stain when she started to slur or spill or slip. But there it was, red all over her—you couldn't argue with the evidence.

She should've kept on the black dress she'd planned to wear.

She'll apologize to Elaine about spilling wine on her dress, that's what she tells herself, but she can't see her in that blur of faces. She tries to clear her brain to think about what she's going to say to Dylan about how he treated her, the things she wrote to Billy Prescott, the things she should've said to Richard and didn't, but Dylan has passed out himself from so much alcohol and there's that slutty receptionist draped across him and a couple of people trying to help them up. Fat chance. Dylan had been matching her drink for drink, hadn't he?

And then there's that young girl over in the corner, the lonely girl in the white dress, forgotten, at the edge of it all, her head in her hands, whoever she is.

Shayla shrugs, raises her hands palms up, whatever.

Shayla is footloose again, fancy-free, and come Monday, everyone else will have forgotten about all this too, everyone will have moved on—or at least be too polite to mention it.

Glass half-full—that was the attitude—and like magic, there's a glass beside her.

She lifts it, examines it. She raises it the way she'd raised her glass to Richard at the tea party, raises it to the faces around her and to the person coming toward her, arms outstretched.

A toast to Monday and then to next week's better party, to all tomorrow's parties.

Glass half-full, Shayla guzzles it down in a single gulp.

The White Rose of Memphis

All but one of the rooms at the Hotel Belvedere had been refurbished, a boutique hotel in the phrase they use these days. But we were checking into that other one, a suite, supposedly left just as it had been in 1949. I hoped at least it had air conditioning now.

"Can I help you?" the lady at reception asked. Betsy was her name. Her bright smile seemed sincere.

"Rose Kaufmann," my girlfriend said with an air of polite formality and a measured nod. She's a redhead normally, but she'd dyed her hair blond earlier that day, fashioned it into loose curls, and even lightened her eyebrows to match. She's proud of her attention to detail, obsessive about it sometimes. I didn't point out that it probably would've been the man who'd have handled checking in way back when.

"Oh," Betsy said. Her smile didn't entirely dismantle, but a little of the sincerity seemed to drain. "Good afternoon." She glanced around once, maybe to see if someone else could handle this, but it was just the three of us. I noticed a slight tremble in her fingers as she reached for the reservation book. "We have you right here," she said. "There are some additional forms you're required to sign, and a small package of materials." She laid a stack of paperwork and a thick manila envelope on the counter. "And you'll be paying—"

"Cash," I said.

"Of course," she replied. "A necessary detail." I handed over the wad of bills. They hadn't kept the rate at '49 prices, not by far.

My girlfriend scanned slowly over the paperwork and then quickly signed the last page—her real name, Cheryl Hobson.

"You'll need to sign too, sir," Betsy said, composure regained now.

"Should I read it?" There were several pages, lots of legalese.

"Certainly, sir. If you'd like."

I shook my head, scrawled my signature next to Cheryl's.

"Do you get many folks like us?" I asked.

"Not many," she said flatly, but there was something in her face—accusation, uncertainty, fear? I don't know the word for it, but there it was.

***

Her name had been Rose Kaufmann, his was Melvin Pruitt, and they'd come to Memphis in August of '49 to get married—from somewhere in Arkansas, I remember. Cheryl's read all the books. She would know exactly where.

Their parents had been against the marriage: class differences the core of it, Rose's family from the wrong side of the tracks. But she was beautiful—"ethereal" was the word that kept cropping up in account after account and photograph after photograph. Pale features, delicate skin, a timid little smile. Bright and innocent. Something fragile there that you'd want to take care of, to protect and preserve. Not my type, but I guess you could see what drew Melvin in.

It was his idea that they elope. He'd given her a ring, told her to pack her bags, made a sizeable withdrawal from his bank account, and then they'd slipped away. Later, the newspapers said that there was a copy of *Romeo and Juliet* in his luggage, another detail that helped color the story.

Melvin had chosen the Belvedere because it was off the beaten track. His family would've stayed at the Peabody, of course, what anyone of that society would've chosen, but the family also *knew* people in Memphis, and Melvin didn't want to risk running into that crowd.

"I don't care where we are," Rose said. "As long as we're together." That's what he'd told the police later. Young love, felt like it would last forever. In this case, "forever" would take an unexpected twist.

He'd splurged on the suite at least. The bedroom was hers, while he would sleep on the couch. The ceremony wasn't until the next day, and he felt the official honeymoon could wait. But they'd kissed and they'd cuddled and they'd ordered room service so they wouldn't have to go out. Steaks and french-fried potatoes with gravy on the side. A bottle of Bordeaux.

When the knock came, Rose was still changing—a white silk dressing gown that Melvin had bought her as a present, a preview of what was to come. "Stay there," he'd called into the bedroom as he moved to answer the door.

"Decency," she'd called back in a soft voice—a word that had later been interpreted any number of ways: simple agreement, coquettish flirtation, some weirdly psychic plea.

It hadn't been room service at all.

***

Cheryl began inspecting the suite while I handled the bellman's tip.

"I guess this wouldn't be kosher," I said, fanning through the Monopoly money in the manila envelope from the front desk. "Or this." There was a ring in there too, a little gimcrack like you'd find in a box of Cracker Jack.

The bellman shook his head, unsure how to react. I slipped him a five.

The suite's living room was smaller than I'd expected—suites back then maybe not as opulent as they're pictured now. A sofa and two end tables, a coffee table, a single chair packed tightly together. The leather of the chair was cracking here and there. The sofa's fabric was prickly but worn smooth in a few spots. Two circles of white stained the coffee table. There was a large window, the curtains half-drawn. No TV, preserving the illusion. A pair of French doors led into the bedroom. The air conditioning pulsed strongly—cold, like the place had been kept on ice.

Cheryl examined it all, bit by bit, mesmerized, it seemed. And I found myself mesmerized too by a side of her I hadn't seen before—that quiet concentration as she checked off each of the details. This was the view they'd had. This was the couch where they'd sat and held hands and kissed. In there was the bed, the brocade bedspread already turned down, where . . .

Cheryl paused at the doorway and stared at it, then came back and ran her fingers along the brass lamps on each of the end tables. I saw that one of them was unplugged. She checked the cord of the curtains, tugging on it a little, but all it did was pull the drapes open. She closed them back halfway. She looked at the ceiling—clean and smooth.

"They probably patched it a long time ago," she said, staring at it.

"Seems like they could've fixed it up to look like—"

"No," she said. "It's okay." A meekness in her voice. I misread it as disappointment.

"So what time does all this begin?" I asked.

"5:02," she said, the same subdued tone, and then she began to unpack. She'd brought all those books, dog-eared and highlighted, and a DVD of the documentary the History Channel did a few years back. She'd even found a white dressing gown on the Internet—days of searching to find one that seemed right.

"You think they'll be on schedule?"

She shrugged, and I wondered if she was nervous. Even I was nervous a little, the oddity of it all.

"And you're sure you're okay with the room service? I mean, I know it's part of the package, but . . . you don't want to go out?"

She shook her head, quietly flipping through one of the books, looking for some detail maybe, though I couldn't imagine there were details she didn't already know.

"Are you okay with *all* of this?" I asked, because suddenly I wasn't sure that I was.

"Yes," she said, brightening slightly, and then added a modest, appreciative "of course." Beneath those blond curls, she struck me again as unfamiliar.

Nervousness, sure, that made sense, but this *was* a different side of her, a new dimension I hadn't seen in the nearly eight months we'd been together. Reflective instead of impetuous. Withdrawn instead of passionate. It was hard for me to connect the blonde before me with the feisty redhead who'd wakened me one morning at one-thirty with "a taste for waffles" or at three a.m. another day, both of us bleary-eyed, with a sudden hunger for sex. Hard to reconcile this Cheryl with the one who'd belted out "Rebel Yell" at karaoke one night or who'd stolen French fries from a stranger's plate at a downtown bar back in North Carolina, staring him down, daring him to say anything. (He

had, though. "I dig chicks like you," he'd said. "Wild and free."
And I'd agreed.)

She'd been a stripper a few years before, I'd learned. Only
briefly, but I think that fact says a lot. Both of us had been born
into good families, upper class if not upper crust—at least that's
the impression I'd gotten from what little she'd told me about her
past. But while I'd always walked the straight and narrow, she'd
been fearless about pushing boundaries and crossing lines.

"Life is for the living," she'd told me, more than once, and she
was very much alive. She brought something in me to life too.

***

A masked man had waited behind the door that Melvin
opened. There'd been a gun in his hand. He'd demanded cash.
He'd taken Rose's ring, the ring that Melvin had given her just the
day before, and all that money he'd withdrawn. He'd tied up Melvin with the cord he'd ripped from the curtains—"with strength
and quickness and impunity," Melvin had said. And then the intruder had grabbed the lamp off the table and walloped Melvin
on the side of the head, knocking him out cold.

The gunman had dragged Rose into the bedroom and raped
her. Twice, reports clarified later. Melvin woke in the middle of
the second round. He'd wept but was still tied tightly, helpless to
do anything.

"All yours," the gunman had said when he was done. He'd
shot two bullets into the ceiling before disappearing through the
door.

Rose died from shock—but not until three days later. Melvin
stayed at her bedside the whole time.

"He never let go of her hand," one of the nurses swore. "She
was fragile as a flower."

"She looked like an angel," said another. "So pale, so peace-
ful."

It was a reporter for the *Commercial Appeal* who gave her the
name "The White Rose." There'd been a novel by that name a
century ago, a popular one. Faulkner, or somebody related. That
had helped the name to stick too—a torrid twist, one legend
around another.

Melvin's vow: "I'll devote my life to finding the man who stole her innocence, who stole her life, and to bring him to the justice that he deserves." He'd kept that vow, at least the devotion part of it. Restless, relentless, he'd searched. But he never tracked the masked man down.

***

"So tragic," Cheryl had said when she first told me about it. We had been lying in bed, back in North Carolina. It was still early in our relationship.

"Sad," I'd told her. "Brutal. Seems like Melvin could've done something more."

I had turned on the pillow to look at her, but she had just stared upward, at the ceiling, at the skylight and the moon beyond. "But there's something . . . romantic in him too," she'd said, far away. "Something true about it all."

This weekend at the Belvedere was for her—my chance to be unexpected and unpredictable, just like she'd been for me.

"You *know* me," she'd squealed when I told her about it. "You *love* me." And I did. I'd thought how much I loved her when I made the reservations, even as I'd told the man on the other end, "Pretty weird, huh?" and laughed nervously and listened to his silence stretch out too long. Whatever my own misgivings, I'd been glad to do it for her.

But the ring in my pocket, the ring I was going to give her later over the room-service steak dinner—the real ring, not the knock-off from the front desk—that ring, unexpected, unpredicted, was for us.

***

Rose's story had taken on a life of its own—a perverse crime story, then a tragedy, then a legend. The beautiful bride-to-be, her smitten fiancé, the cruel twist, and then his decades of postmortem piety. The hotel had closed down within a year, and while a few businesses had intermittently taken up shop on the lower level, the upper floors had remained empty for years, tainted and abandoned. Then, as the entire area went into decline, the building had become subsidy housing—all but that single room, which stayed locked away.

Maybe because of that room's singularity, the building eventually became a macabre attraction of sorts. People visited it as a curiosity, then later as a shrine, and many would continue the pilgrimage over to her grave. There had been talk of her being buried in her hometown, but as the gruesome details emerged, her parents had shunned any association. Ultimately, the city had claimed her, in more ways than one.

Melvin had turned his back on that family—and on his own as well. Rose was all that mattered. A marble obelisk marked the gravesite—the tallest in the cemetery, no expense spared. And he'd even borrowed the name the newspapers had picked up— THE WHITE ROSE engraved at the top, BELOVED, NEVER FORGOTTEN just beneath. The granite is scrubbed regularly, pristine even to this day.

The *Commercial Appeal* revisited the case on the twenty-fifth anniversary and again on the fiftieth. A book followed, and then more than one. These days you can even find postcards here and there picturing the hotel or the grave or that image of doomed, ethereal Rose herself.

Gradually, that area of the city revitalized—reclaimed first by a younger, hipper crowd, artists and musicians and their friends who liked the cheap rent—and then made trendy chic by quirky coffee houses, a couple of galleries, and ragtag studio space, even an off-Beale jazz club.

When the hotel reopened about five years ago—revitalization turned gentrification—the new owners decided to capitalize on the history, not just preserving the room but, in a controversial twist, offering couples the "White Rose of Memphis Experience."

"History reenactments taken to a new level," one of the owners told the newspaper, but others who were interviewed had less favorable things to say.

"A tasteless publicity stunt," one resident of the area said.

"Disgusting," said another.

The Memphis Flyer quoted one member of the Convention and Visitors Bureau, on condition of anonymity, as saying she was physically sickened by the idea of having to represent the whole thing: "I've gotten nauseous, literally nauseous, in our meetings."

Descendants of the Pruitts and the Kaufmanns had together sought a court order to prevent it, but the story simply wasn't theirs anymore.

***

The actor was on time, right to the minute, three taps just like it had been all those years before.

"Stay there," I called into the bedroom, and Cheryl called back, "Decency," just as we'd rehearsed.

I opened the door, and there he stood, jeans and a white button-down shirt and a ski mask with just the eyes showing.

"You're skinnier than I'd have pictured," I told him.

"I'm the understudy." He shrugged. He had a twangy accent, higher-pitched than I'd expected.

"Was it actually a ski mask back in 1949? I mean, not a bandanna or . . ."

"I'm the talent," he said. "I don't handle the costumes." I couldn't see his expression, but even with us keeping our voices low, I caught a hint of irritation in his voice.

"That real?" I said, motioning down to the gun hanging loosely in his right hand.

"Blanks," he said. "It'll sound really loud. They've even got it rigged to leave a couple of smudges on the ceiling."

"Doesn't that disturb the neighbors?"

"I think they put some extra insulation in the walls," he said. "I really don't know."

"Just the talent," I said.

He nodded.

"You gonna hit me with the lamp?" I asked him. "Pull the cord from the curtains?"

"I've got some rope in my pocket," he said. "They can't be fixing the curtains each time."

"Makes sense," I said.

"And I'll just hit you with the shade part of the lamp. I've practiced it a lot."

"Safety first," I said.

He looked at his watch.

"And what happens in the bedroom?" I asked, even though

I'd read up on it in the brochure.

"We answer whatever questions the women have," he says. "A little bit of history, a little bit of background on the city. They train us in all that, make us take an exam on the story. I got a B-plus."

"Okay," I told him, satisfied. "Let's do this."

He shrugged again, and then adjusted his shoulders, raised them a little higher like he was trying to grow into his role. After a deep breath, he reached out and pushed me into the room—harder than I would've liked.

"Money," he said gruffly. "Whatever you've got."

I thrust the wad of Monopoly money at him.

"Take it and leave," I said, dramatically. "Whatever you want of it. It's all we have, all that I've saved."

As he stuffed the money in his pocket, Cheryl appeared at the doorway of the bedroom. She was wearing the white dressing gown. It fell loosely around her hips but was so sheer that you could nearly see through it. I saw the darkness of her nipples and the outline of her panties. Her expression was panicked and nervous. She was playing her part well.

"Your ring," the actor growled.

Cheryl shook her head, clasped her hands close to her breasts. She was wearing the gimcrack ring now.

"Give it to him," I told her. "We can get you another." Thinking, of course, about the real ring in my pocket, the one for later, when all this was done. And then to the actor, "Just don't hurt us."

Reluctantly, Cheryl handed that Cracker Jack prize across to him. He looked at it, examining it intently. The moment stretched on so long, I half-expected him to pull out a jeweler's loupe or to cry "Fake!" And then I looked over and saw that my girlfriend was weeping and remembered that everyone was waiting for my line.

"Don't despair, my darling," I said. "You are the true treasure." It sounded stagy, unrealistic, but that was what Melvin claimed he'd said. Maybe he'd been overdramatizing it too. Then I turned to the gunman again: "Please take what you have and leave us in peace." (Melvin had "beseeched" the intruder, that was the word the reporters used, and I tried to work a beseeched tone into my voice.)

"Shut up," the actor snarled. "I'll take what I want."

He pushed me onto the couch and then, keeping the gun on me, reached behind the curtain and gave a quick yank. His sleight of hand was better than his acting. When he turned around, a length of cord lay tightly in his grip.

"Hands behind you."

I did as I was told. He tied me up, turned me around, and pushed me again onto the couch.

"I've had enough of you," he said. "It's her I want now." And he reached over and grabbed the lamp, swung it around so that the shade swiped against my head.

I played my role too. I fell backward, flat against the rough fabric. Parting my eyelids just slightly, I saw him grab Cheryl by the arm and thrust her in front of him into the bedroom. He closed the door behind them. I could hear voices then, but no words.

He wasn't any more of a knotsman than he was an actor, thank goodness. Once I was loose, I sat back on the couch more comfortably again. No TV to watch, and the only thing to read in the room was the Bible on the dresser or the books Cheryl had brought. *And I don't need to read those*, I thought. *I'm living it.* I laughed a little to myself about that one.

It was a non-smoking room, but I had a cigarette anyway. I moved over to the window before lighting up, opening it just a crack to let the smoke out. The heat from outside felt good, seeping into the room's cold. From eight stories below came the sounds of the street. Cars passing, pedestrians walking, a horn, a shout, everyone going on about their lives with no thought to the little drama unfolding up here, no knowledge that we were up here at all. No one back in North Carolina knew about the trip either or about that ring in my pocket, though I could picture my parents' reaction when I told them the news. "Not your type," Dad had already told me the first time I'd brought Cheryl home, so we'd stopped going there much. And we'd never been to see her folks. "My dad and I," she'd said with a shake of her head. "We don't see eye to eye." Sometimes pushing ahead meant pushing the past behind.

After the cigarette was done, I moved over toward the bedroom. The French doors were closed, a small crack between them, the voices clearer now.

"Who are you?" my girlfriend asked. "Why are you doing this to Melvin and to me?"

If the actor said anything in response, I couldn't hear it. Wasn't it his job to answer the questions? The whole point of all this? B-plus, I remembered. Maybe he was just bewildered by how Cheryl was still pretending to stay in character.

"Do I know you?" she asked. "Why me? Why us? What do you want? Why are you treating me that way?"

Silence again. I put my eye to the crack between the doors, a sliver of perspective. Movement there of some kind, and then a glimpse of a bare foot at the end of the bed. Down on the floor, the panties that I'd seen outlined beneath Cheryl's dressing gown. A pair of jeans beside them.

***

Cheryl had told me all about the investigation—both the police investigation immediately after the crime and then all the speculation later by historians revisiting the story. They'd unofficially reopened the case in the 1990s, a retired policeman and a mystery writer teaming up to uncover the truth once and for all.

Rumors had arisen from the start that the attack hadn't been random. Someone from the bank in Arkansas, someone who'd known about Melvin's withdrawal—thousands of dollars—and seen an opportunity he couldn't resist. Others said the intruder had been another of Rose's suitors. She was marrying Melvin for his money and had turned aside the man she truly loved, so the other fellow had struck back, leaving his mark, sullying the goods. Darker possibilities emerged later. Melvin's father had tracked them down and hired someone to stop the marriage, whatever it took, and then seen that intervention take an unexpected turn. Some said it was even the father himself who'd done it—a controlling man, ill-tempered, full of lust. The worst was that it might have been someone from Rose's own family, a brother, it was hinted, and a history of abuse, a sordid story there on the other side of those tracks. The '90s investigation was inconclusive on all counts.

***

I pushed the French doors open and saw it all. The Monopoly money and the gun in a pile beside her panties and his jeans, the bedcovers loose around the hips of the actor, his shirt hanging loosely around his slender frame, and Cheryl's dressing gown pushed up toward her neck. He still had the ski mask on, but in the moment before the panic struck, I saw this look in his eyes, a ravenousness there that even I hadn't seen before, bewilderment mixed inside of it. Craven, craving.

"What the fuck!" I screamed. "Get off of her!"

The actor scrambled quickly off the bed and fell backward toward the window, the shirt just barely covering his nakedness. Cheryl pulled up the brocade spread to hide herself. She looked at me in confusion, as if she didn't entirely recognize me.

"What the hell's going on here?" I said and then to the actor, "What the hell do you think you're doing?" My fists were clenched. I could barely see straight.

"He raped me," Cheryl said softly. "He took things too far."

"She's lying," the actor stammered through the ski mask. He was stooped over, trying to pull down the edges of his shirt. "Dude, she pulled me onto her, you gotta believe me. She said you knew."

"I knew?"

"She kept saying that." His breath was heavy. He yanked off the ski mask—just a kid beneath it, blond hair, acne-scarred, a punk. "She said it a couple of times: 'He knows. I haven't told him but he knows. He knows what happened. He accepts me.' I don't know, man. I thought it was something you'd worked out. I was just going with the scene, and—"

"There's no fucking scene," I said.

"I know you," said Cheryl then, reaching one hand toward me. "And you know me. You know it all, you must." One side of the spread fell down. The dressing gown was still tangled over her bare breasts. "And you *love* me." Her voice was almost a whisper—a voice not her own. She dropped her hand back to her side. She wasn't speaking directly to me. "You would've saved me if you could."

"Please, buddy," the actor said, pleading. "You gotta believe me."

"Shut up." I held up a fist. "Just shut up." At who, I wasn't sure.

"I know what you did later," Cheryl went on. Her eyes turned my way again, pleading there too. "I'd been used, but you remembered me better. I'd been defiled, but you saved me. But you could've stopped him in the beginning, couldn't you? And why didn't you?"

"I'm not Melvin," I said. "This isn't real, Cheryl. For God's sake—"

"You'd have used it, wouldn't you?" she said, as if the idea had suddenly crossed her mind. "The gun. If you'd had it then, you would've used it."

"I'm not Melvin," I said again, sterner, teeth clenched. "Melvin was unconscious out there. He was tied up. How the hell could he have gotten to the gun?" I picked it up off the actor's jeans. It felt heavy in my hand. I felt the weight of the ring in my pocket too. "He had no way of using it."

"I need to go," said the actor suddenly. "I need to get out of here."

I swung the gun at him. "Stay," I said.

"It's fake, dude." He laughed bitterly. But he stopped.

Cheryl shook her head. "There *are* ways," she said. "We could go away. You're taking me away. You've already taken me away." A moment of clarity, a quick laugh. "Like those waffles," she told me. "You made me waffles just because I wanted them. No one had ever done that for me . . . You would've known what I wanted back then too, and you would've known I didn't want *him*."

"Waffles?" the actor asked. "What is she talking about? What's this all about?"

Cheryl didn't seem to hear him. "Oh, but you're not Melvin," she told me, her face crumpling, her eyes slowly focusing and then unfocusing once more. "I didn't know *you* then. So, you couldn't have stopped it, could you?"

"Stopped what?" I asked, beginning to see something else in all this. "Stopped who?"

"*Him*," she said suddenly. She pointed at the actor. "*He* did this. He *defiled* me. He *lied*. It wasn't me. It never was."

"She's crazy, man," said the boy. "I'm leaving. I'm—"

"Stay," I said again, loudly. "Stay. Right. There." He obeyed. "What do you need me to do, Cheryl?" I asked. Because I did love her, I did.

"Rose," she said. "Save me."

"Is that what it's going to take? You just want me to make things right here?" I still had the gun aimed toward the actor—useless, but I raised it higher, pointed it with more purpose.

"Dude," he said. "Just let me go. You gotta understand. She *asked* for it. I thought it was part of the gig."

"It's a new gig," I said to him, a stage whisper. "They're blanks, for God's sake."

"Love me," Cheryl said.

"I was doing what she wanted," said the boy. "I was just acting. I was—"

"Act this," I told him, and then louder: "You scoundrel, you fiend. You'll pay for this." I fired twice. He was right. The sound was deafening.

"There," I said, turning back to Cheryl. "Are you satisfied? I've rewritten history. You're saved. It's done."

I expected to see release in her eyes, gratitude that he was dead, symbolically at least, whoever that intruder had been—some small payment for old sins I'd had nothing to do with, had known nothing about.

But she wasn't looking at me. She was looking past me. She was looking at the actor.

I turned and saw that acne-scarred face then, shock there but relief too that it was over, a little smirk brewing beneath it.

"It's not," said Cheryl softly. "Not yet." And then she pulled a gun I hadn't seen, something she must have smuggled in with all those books and DVDs and that shimmery negligee. She fired twice more, and the boy recoiled, his smirk replaced by a desperate sort of look. Then the red spot at the center of his shirt began to spread slowly, like a flower in bloom.

***

We've been in a lot of hotels since then, a lot of different names. Sometimes she uses Rose, and I cringe each time she does.

The police know our real names by now, of course. Our pictures were in the papers and on TV, and on those Wanted posters too, I'd imagine. Cheryl dyes her hair often, eyebrows too, and she's changed the arch of them. She's a master with makeup. All I did was shave my head. I didn't think it would make much of a change, but when I look in the mirror now, I don't see my own self anymore.

Wherever we go, we pay for everything in cash. I pawned that ring one morning while she slept in and that tided us over for a while. Don't ask how we've made our cash since then.

And what are we looking for? Some answer to what happened, some scrap of what we had? Another release? Another recompense? Some punishment? Each other?

We're bound together by what happened—that part's for sure, as sure as Melvin was bound to Rose.

"You would've," she tells me sometimes, when she tries to touch me to get back to what we once had. "You tried."

Most nights, though, we sleep in separate beds, as if on the eve of a honeymoon that might never arrive.

Hard Return

The man and the woman had reached that stage where the relationship would either turn more serious or slowly begin to dissolve. The seriousness wasn't about sex, a threshold they'd already crossed, but a step into some deeper, more emotional intimacy.

It was the woman who made the first move, but it was one the man had been asking for, hoping for, nudging toward.

Tell me something about yourself, he'd said, more than once. *Something special, something not many people know.*

Shared experiences brought people together. He believed this. Sharing them in the moment or a shared story, either one.

They'd been out to a nice dinner, had come back to her place. She kicked off her heels, lit a couple of candles, turned down the lights. They settled down in the living room—her plush couch, two glasses of red wine on a mahogany coffee table, the rim of hers already smudged with lipstick. A photograph on the end table caught a glint from the candle's flicker, caught his eye at the same time. A photo he'd been drawn toward before—her when she was younger, laughing, her head thrown back, her long blond hair falling.

A side of her he hadn't seen. With him, she'd always been more measured, more serious, melancholy even. Her hair was cropped close now.

"I had a boyfriend who . . . hurt me," she said.

"Broken hearts." The man made a motion with his hand, a throwaway kind of gesture. *Been there, done that.* A little laugh with it.

"Broken something else," she said. "Several things." She touched her arm in two places, touched her cheek, returned her hand to her chest—like she was trying to catch her breath, except she hadn't lost it right then. She wore a necklace, and she touched that instead, like an afterthought.

She began to tell him more about this ex: the bickering between them, the accusations and arguments, endless arguments after a while, the first time he knocked her around, the many times after.

"Then this one evening, the evening that *it* happened"—despite his curiosity, he felt a pang of distress, the way she inflected the *it*—"we were already broken up by then. Or I'd tried to break up with him at least. Actually, I had another guy at my place that night—nothing serious yet, but wondering where things might go, you know?"

"Like us," the man said.

The woman twirled a pendant at the end of her necklace, a small prism—catching the light from the candles as well.

"I was young and dumb," she said. "Living in a cheap rental house, not hardly the best part of town. Cheap furniture I'd picked up from Goodwill back in college, dragged along with me. Concrete steps on the front had a crack running down the center of them. Sometimes my life felt just as cracked."

"My grandparents had cinder block steps," the man said. "A stack of them piled up, not even connected together." But the woman didn't seem to hear him.

"So that's where I was, this house I'd rented, sitting here with the new guy I was beginning to see, trying not to think about the ex that everything had gone wrong with. Then he called. You can't put some things behind you."

"Nothing's easy. So, you screened him out? Ignored the call?"

"It was a house phone, this was back in the nineties, before everyone had a phone in their pocket, before everyone had caller ID. I didn't know who was calling until I answered, and then he was . . . yelling at me, calling me names, ugly names. I know the new guy could hear. I should've just hung up. But I was trying to emphasize that it was over, trying to tell him not to call anymore—trying to reason with him, to be reasonable with someone who . . .wasn't." She took a deep breath. "And then he said something about how not only was he going to keep calling, and not only was I going to keep talking to him, but if I hung up, then he was going to come over there in person, and then . . . ."

The man looked at the photo of her. She'd been happier once, and then this *it* had happened. It was coming together now—and who knew? Maybe talking with him about it would be a step toward healing.

"And then?" he said softly, urging without rushing.

She only shook her head.

"Did you hang up?"

"I did. And I regretted it almost instantly. I could feel it, in my bones suddenly, how it had been the wrong thing to do, how it was probably going to cost me. And cost the new boyfriend too, him thinking he was in for just a fun night. Don't they all?" She toyed with the necklace again, insistently now—*compulsively*, he thought. "But even if I hadn't hung up, would that have changed anything? In the long run, I mean? At the time, I felt like if I was clear with my ex, if I stayed firm, if I just made the right decisions . . . But looking back . . . Some things maybe you can't avoid. That's what I've learned."

The candles flickered as she said it—startling him. Was there a window open somewhere? It couldn't have been her talking that had done it, her breath or his either. The candles were on the coffee table, too far away.

"I guess this ex, he came over anyway?" The man shifted on the couch, turned more fully toward her. Attentive. Concerned. "The way he'd threatened?"

She nodded slowly, then shook her head. "We should've called the police," she said. "I see that now, saw that too late, or maybe that wouldn't have made a difference either. But instead we left. The guy I was with, I told him, let's just get out, go somewhere. And we left. Locked up the house, even though my ex, he may have made a key. I knew that. We went down the steps and started walking up the street. No hurry, it was a nice night, cool air, crisp, so we were . . . strolling—until I turned and saw my ex about a block behind us, coming around the corner of my house.

"Had he been watching us, me and this new guy? Had he been right there the whole time? Calling from the pay phone on the corner? But he would've seen us leave, I remember thinking that, because he was walking up the steps, he was banging on the door, and then—suddenly—he turned. Like he sensed me. Like he was an animal or something, smelling his prey, even that far away. I saw him see me.

"It was a cool night, like I said—cold really. I'd felt chilly step-ping out. But suddenly I was raging hot. Anger and frustration and . . . fear most of all, no other way to say it. The way he looked at me, that hatred, something deep and dark and . . . *lunging* about his expression. And everything else on the street, it was like it began to go out of focus, to spin and swirl, like the ground underneath me was shifting somehow.

"I don't know if I said it or not. *Go. Let's go. Now!* But saying it, thinking it, I *went.* Up the street. Fast, but not running—no. I remember what I'd been told about hiking. If you see a bear or a wolf or . . . don't run, because if you run, they'll *know* you're prey. But going, *going* was necessary, getting away, getting any-where but there . . ."

Listening to her, the man knew that this was the moment he should reach out his hand, should take her hand in his, say something like *I know what you mean* or *I feel like I'm there with you* or *I'm here with you now, you're safe now.* Relatability builds connection, he believed that. Shared experiences. Talking. Lis-tening.

But when he did reach out, did take her hand . . .

The flickering candles, the glint of light off the picture and the prism, the sound of her voice too, hypnotic in its flatness, and the story itself—as he took her hand, so very cold it seemed, stunningly cold, everything changed.

He was there.

Not only *felt* like he was there—her storytelling drawing him in—but actually there. Some physical step back in time, into her time—seeing her there on the street ahead of him, seeing it as if through the eyes of that new man she'd been telling him about, feeling the crisp night air she'd described, and feeling too the *smack smack smack* of his feet against the sidewalk, his own feet rushing after her. Away from the house she'd described? Away from that ex?

"Wait," he called out. "Wait, stop."

She slowed, turned—surprised. "We can't stop. He'll get us sooner." Her face was the same, he recognized, but not the same—younger than herself but the same woman still, and the same solemnity about her. She wore low-slung pants, a top too thin for the weather, black with a silver sundial, a pair of Skechers. "We need to *go*." She started ahead again.

Could this be the same woman whose hand he'd taken on the couch? The same but transformed? Had he somehow traveled here with her? Or had he been transported here alone, to step into that other man's experience, to see firsthand this younger version of her? Someone who had no memory of—

Of what? Past? Future? Present? Where were they?

The street was two-lane, a small neighborhood—low-rent like she'd described it. Squat houses, small porches out front, folding chairs, clunky swing sets, some lawns tended, others overgrown. It was well past dusk, streetlights on overhead, TV screens shining from living room windows, the glow from each giving all of it the feel of a dreamscape.

Keeping up with her brisk walk, he touched his chest, his face. He was real.

A police car came barreling down the street, siren wailing. The man had the feeling the police might be coming because of them. But the car kept going—emergencies elsewhere, no knowledge of what the woman with him was facing, and him too.

"They didn't stop," he called out.

"They won't," she said. Her certainty confirmed it: she was a younger version on the outside, but haunted like the older one, the future one.

"You know what's ahead."

She nodded grimly.

He heard another siren, spotted more lights coming toward them. "But it could be different this time. We're here—*I'm* here."

He glanced at her. Her expression held something pitying in it, the way her lips turned down, that crinkling at the corner of her eyes, the sense of collapsing—that was the only way to describe it—inside the eyes themselves. "I don't think there's any way to avoid *it*," she said—that same emphasis again on the *it*.

But he felt sure that things could change, felt determined to prove it. The police car sped toward them. He stepped into the street, waved his hands wildly. The officer veered to avoid him, pulled to a stop.

"See. Have a little faith." But again her look, again that shaking of her head.

The officer got out, started toward them. But at that moment a door burst open at one of the houses on the street, two men spilled out onto the sidewalk between them. One of them had a knife.

The cop rushed toward the men, dancing around one another, the knife swinging. "Hey, hey, hey!" He pulled out his gun, pointed it at them.

"He thinks you signaled him to stop because of the fight." She pointed to the men, the knife making contact, the policeman leaping forward. "The cut isn't bad. You'll be a hero for saving his life."

Beyond the policeman and the fight, the man caught sight of the ex, walking at his same steady pace, coming at them relentlessly.

Like the Terminator, the man thought. Like Yul Brynner in *Westworld*—two of his favorite movies. He was surprised by the solace he felt thinking that—that whatever was happening here, he was still who he was in the middle of it. His favorites, his memories.

"Let's go." The woman tugged at his arm.

She quickened her pace. He struggled to match it—to keep up but not run ahead. To nudge her forward. To not look back.

"Where are we going?" he asked.

"There," she said—a corner convenience store, perched at the intersection of three roads, a corner slimmed to a point. Neon beer signs shone along a row of windows. Cigarette ads covered the door they pushed to get in. A peeling sticker carried the picture of a camera, announcing that the premises were under surveillance. The man took small comfort from it.

"Are we safe here?" he asked as the bell chimed over the door. The inside was only a few short aisles, with refrigerated cases lining the back wall of the store. A magazine rack equal parts comic books and pornography. A row of chips and candy. Stacks of canned vegetables and tinned meat. Were they going to hide behind the Spam? He looked for a restroom sign, some back room, someplace to hide.

"He's come back," the woman said—talking not to him but to the clerk behind the counter, the bulk of a wrestler, a thick beard on him. "Can you stall him a little?"

The clerk seemed to know her, knew the story, gave a firm nod—"I'll do what I can"—before he reached under the counter.

"This way," the woman said before the man could see what the clerk was after. Another entrance on the far side of the store, and another bell tinkling as they pushed through it. And was it an echo of that same sound from the first doors as theirs closed behind them? How far behind was that ex? How long could he be stalled?

"Now we run," the woman said. She took off ahead of him, sprinting along the new street back in the direction they'd come from. He hustled to keep up.

"Where are we going now?"

"Back to the house."

"To your house? Where you just left?" It had the logic—the *il-logic*—of a dream, of a nightmare. No sense to it at all. What was her strategy? Was there a plan at all? "Why didn't you just stay there?" Frustration in his voice, disbelief—he heard it himself, couldn't keep it out.

"Because that wasn't what I did," she said.

"Whoa, whoa, whoa." He reached forward, grabbed her arm, pulled her to a stop. "You're just repeating the same thing that happened that night? What good is that going to do?"

She tugged her arm from his hand.

"What good is anything else?" She threw up her arms, dropped them to her side. "You saw what happened when you stopped the police car."

"Did that happen the first time too?"

She shrugged. "Nothing changes."

"And the clerk at the store back there," he said. "Look at me. The clerk—how long does he stall your ex?"

She wouldn't meet his eyes.

"He's not that lucky," she said. "Every time, he—" She cut herself off, defeated, ashamed. "I'm telling you. We need to run. Now."

From back at the convenience store, a gunshot.

The man's head flicked toward it. When he turned back, she was running again. He took off after her.

Another two-lane street, parallel to the first, an echo of it. More houses, more porches, a deeper darkness now, one of the streetlights struggling to cut through.

She turned abruptly down a small alleyway, then angled through a yard. Soon they were back at her house—the aluminum siding she'd described, the crack in the concrete steps, up to the front door. She didn't seem to fumble with her key but dropped it anyway—in her hand one second, then on the ground. "Every time," she said, half under her breath.

The living room was just as she'd described it too—cheap furniture, threadbare, dorm castoffs, and a smell like a dorm too, thick with memories of late nights drinking and smoking. A stack of paperback books beside a worn leather chair, a crocheted blanket draped across it. A fireplace with a pile of ashes, and above it a mantel lined with photos—groups of college students, the woman in a glamour shot wearing a seductive smile, an older couple who might have been her parents. Among them stood the same photo of her from back in the present, loose and laughing, that long blond hair, but in a different frame now, the edges dinged, the glass on this one cracked.

He heard the deadbolt click on the door, turned to see her hand raising to link a chain lock as well.

"He's coming this way," she said. "He knows we're here."

"We need to do something," he said. "Do you have a gun? Or a bat or—?" She was shaking her head, slowly. "The phone," he said. "The phone that he called you on. Where—?" He caught sight of it as he was asking—on the wall just inside a small kitchen. "We'll call the police. We'll—"

Still she shook her head.

"He cut the lines," she said—not with suspicion but certainty, even before he got the receiver to his ear, before he heard the emptiness there. She'd known. "The guy at the convenience store, he called the police already. They'll get here, but it'll be too late."

She was closing the blinds now, uneven venetians, a couple of slats broken, but she didn't hurry about it, easing them down slowly, swiveling them shut. *Going through the motions,* he thought. She began to push an end table in front of the door but without energy or urgency.

"You don't seem very distressed about all this," he said, and that did stop her short. She stood up from the table, still sitting short of the door. She seemed to puzzle over his comment.

"You can't change what's already happened," she said finally. "Happened over and over." She reached toward her neck, her fingers playing at nothing. He thought of the prism that had been hanging there—back in the present. "I feel like I'm reliving *it* constantly"—her same emphasis on the word *it*, rousing that same tremble of fear inside him. "Eventually you get numb."

He didn't feel numb. He felt everything—sharply. His body tensing for fight. The thrum of his blood. Pulses of adrenaline.

He watched her hands, the absence of that prism, the image of a sundial on her shirt. What was the switch to get them out of this? Take them back? Away from the broken blinds and the glaring streetlight and back to those warm candles she'd lit. Away from the worn sofa and back to that plush couch where they'd been having wine. Out of the past and into some future.

"Your hand," he said. "Give me your hand." Another puzzled look, but she stepped toward him, reached out, palm up. He took her hand in his, felt the warmth where there had been coldness before. He waited . . . but nothing happened.

He sighed, dropped her hand. As he leaned against the kitchen counter, he saw a knife block against the wall. He pulled out the biggest of the blades. Whatever was ahead, he needed to be ready.

"The guy," he said, remembering suddenly. "You told me there was a guy with you, a new guy you were seeing. What happened to him?"

She wouldn't meet his eyes at first—same as when he'd asked about the clerk. In her silence, he heard some dim echo of the gunshot from the convenience store.

Then another sound outside—a real one, something scraping the edge of the house. Feet on the steps and a pounding on the front door, pulsing with each blow.

The deadbolt struggled. The chain on the door swung and jangled. The ex's voice seethed and bellowed. "You let me in— You don't know what— You'll pay, you'll pay, both of you—"

"I'm sorry," the woman said finally, but the man could barely hear her over the raging outside. She turned toward him—the wilt of her lips, the vacancy in her eyes.

He thought about the night air, the way it whipped at him as he ran, the feel of his feet slapping against the pavement. *His* feet. He touched the frame of the doorway where he stood—solid, firm. The photo on the mantel—he could run his fingers across that too, he knew, feel the spiderweb of the cracked glass.

The pounding at the door grew louder. The Terminator, come back with a vengeance.

His favorites, his memories. All of him here.

The man lifted the knife in his hand, tested its heft, the actuality of it.

Without thinking, he ran his thumb down the edge of the blade.

He felt the sting, saw the blood begin to flow, brought his thumb to his lips—reflex.

He had just tasted it—that metallic tang—when the hinges gave and the front door burst inward.

***

"I'm so, so sorry," she said. "But you . . . you wanted to know."

Restoration

"So basically, this is just cloning, right?" The husband set the brochure on the coffee table between us. He'd glanced at it more than read it, despite the fact that I'd customized it specifically for their circumstances. He perched on the edge of his couch, elbows on his knees—perched somewhere between hesitation and . . . hostility maybe? This early in a pitch, it was sometimes hard to tell.

The wife sat at the other end of the couch, too much distance separating them. She glanced at the husband over the top of her own brochure. The wife was the one who'd contacted me.

Not hostility, I thought, looking back at him. *Just feeling hassled. By the wife. By me too maybe.* That was part of it.

Suddenly, none of it seemed promising for a sale. But you had to be ready for opposition, for situations like that.

"We're relying on that technology, yes," I said. "But the conventional portrait of cloning, the controversy . . . that would be a misconception. There would never be two of you. The technology is only activated in the"—I paused briefly—"most unfortunate of circumstances."

"Victim replacement," the husband said, picking up on the media tagline—the worst slant on the industry's work. But his nod wasn't disagreeable.

"We prefer the word *restoration*," I told him. "A restoration of the family. A reestablishment of the norm in the unlikely event—"

He sighed. "In the unlikely event that some thug shoots one of us on the street or breaks in here and—"

"Please, honey," the wife said. "Little ears." She gave a quick nod toward the floor. A child, three or four years old, was stacking blocks into towers on the rug. Beside him, a younger child gnawed at a stuffed sheep.

The husband shook his head.

"Think of it as insurance," I said. "If someone—a careless driver, a drunk driver—were to run into your car, insurance would cover the repairs. And if the car proved to be a total loss, you would be provided a new car, just like the one you had before. In that same manner, you keep insurance on your house, and if there were"—I lowered my voice, for the children—"if there were a fire, insurance would help you to rebuild, to get your life in order again."

A clock stood on the mantel above the fireplace—ornate, antique, clearly expensive. I'd noticed it already, had planned to bring it into the discussion. Something about time, about the value of time, our most valuable commodity. But that's the thing about a pitch: You shift as needed.

"That clock, for example," I said. "Something of that worth, I'm sure you have it itemized in your insurance, part of the premium you pay?"

The husband shook his head again, waved a hand toward the clock. "A gift from her parents," he said. "We couldn't afford anything like that ourselves." He mumbled that last part.

Money was at the heart of it, that was clear—his hesitation. And a small misstep on my part, but how could I have known?

"My point," I said, "my point is that your life—existence itself—is far more valuable, far more precious. Conventional life insurance only provides compensation, but we now have the technology to restore, to fully restore, an existence cut short by injustice."

"But it's not like regular insurance, is it, Mr. Blackston?" the wife said. "I mean, a heart attack, it says here that's not covered."

I shook my head. "Only lives cut short unjustly, *unnaturally*." I emphasized that last word. "Cut short by someone else's actions."

Malice on the part of another—that was part of the phrasing in the brochure. An accident or death from illness, even at a young age—those wouldn't activate the policy. Homicide, manslaughter—only these would. And these were the news stories—of violence, of senseless violence—that had likely prompted the wife to call about our services. Those pervasive fears.

But you never mentioned that in the presentation. Discretion was key. And indirection. Euphemisms helped. You didn't talk about death at all, didn't even use the word, much less talk explicitly about the man who was shot in the eye while walking to lunch, or the woman who was tortured for hours before she was killed, or the children who . . .

No. Let the prospective clients put it all together on their own. Trust that they'd seen the news themselves—that the news had likely prompted the invitation. Laying on the pathos too thickly could backfire.

"The scientific community advising on these new procedures has been insistent about respecting the natural cycles of life," I continued. "Indiscriminate replacement, unregulated *cloning*—to use that word—such options and choices would be fraught with trouble. But in this case . . . well, this is one way, finally approved, *rightly* approved, to afford justice in specific instances of criminal injustice. There's an ethics at the core of these decisions. We adhere very tightly to government regulations with all contracts."

"But the odds are in your favor on that, aren't they?" the husband asked. "You're the one who compared this to insurance, and it's the same here as there, isn't it? Premiums paid year after year, but only a few times you actually pay out. A lot of profit you're bringing in."

Money at the core of it for him—yes, clearly. Setting up to negotiate. You see this move frequently.

Out of the corner of my eye, I saw a blur of white—the younger of the children on the floor swinging the sheep he'd been holding. The older child let out a yelp of panic. His towers fell, the wood blocks clattered. The younger child giggled.

The wife was up from the couch in an instant, playing referee, soothing tempers. She hoisted the younger child onto her hip. She knelt down to caress the other child's hair. "It's fine, little man," she said. "You can build it again."

The husband hadn't moved.

I smiled at him, crossed my legs. "The service is meant to provide peace of mind," I said. "Most of our clients would consider themselves fortunate never to be involved in the kinds of incidents that would require them to collect, neither themselves nor . . ." I glanced at the children, only the smallest glance. "The restored body—the replacement, if you'd prefer to call it that—

wouldn't recall the trauma the original body had endured, but if any family members were to witness the incident or to be injured themselves . . . Clearly such experiences, such images, can be difficult to put aside." I shook my head. "The hope, for everyone's sake, is that you'd never need to collect on your investment."

"You're talking about the odds," the wife said, standing up, turning toward us, the baby still perched on her cocked hip. "But honey, you remember what the other salesman told us. The man who talked to us about a G-U-N." Even spelling the word, she lowered her voice, whispering above the forehead of the child she held. "About the crime rates, about—"

"A gun might be cheaper." The husband shrugged, made a gesture of helplessness toward the brochure he hadn't fully read. The wife grimaced at the word.

I nodded. "There are many options available. For protection, for defense." I could've pointed more explicitly to the children then, mentioned the danger of having a weapon in a house—curious minds, curious hands. There were statistics for that too. But gun rights remained a touchy subject, and such an approach could turn ugly fast. Better to open up possibilities rather than close down others. "Restoration services can—should—be part of a comprehensive strategy to address long-term concerns about the safety of your family."

"How does it work?" the wife asked. "The replace—I mean, the restoration."

I liked her, I did. In closing any sort of sale, you had to look for allies, for ways of leveraging your position. Clearly, she was on my side.

"We keep each client's DNA on file," I said. "That's the first part, the most basic in many ways. But personhood is more than biological. In the unlikely event that one of you becomes"—I nodded toward the child on her hip, the one on the floor, emphasizing again that I was choosing my own words with care—"that one of you becomes the unfortunate victim of today's increasingly dangerous conditions, we want to be able to restore not just the body but also the memories and experiences, as updated as possible to the time of the . . . event. To that end, we schedule periodic brain scans. Think of it as downloads, a regular backup of information." I pointed to the brochure. "All of this is included with the premium. There's no additional charge."

The child in the wife's arms began to fuss, reaching toward the necklace she was wearing, a string of pearls, and then got upset when she swatted at his hands.

"Honestly," she said.

"Just put him down again if he's bothering you." The husband rolled his eyes.

The wife gave him a look. I was the only one who saw it.

"But in that . . . unlikely event"—the wife bounced the child on her hip, trying to settle him—"how long does it take for the, um, restoration?"

"We accelerate the growth, of course," I said. "Two weeks, three tops. The technology has been advancing rapidly."

"And when it . . . I mean *he* was delivered," she asked, then seemed to realize she'd fumbled a second time, "I mean either of us—we'd be full-grown? That two weeks is on your end, right? Because I couldn't handle a third child right now." She laughed a little, pushing away insistent hands.

"Our goal is to make any such transition as easy as possible." I held up my own hand—not quite in the motion of taking an oath but echoing such a move. Reassurance in any case.

"Like the man said." The husband smiled at me. "It's like insurance. You total your car, and within a couple of weeks, they'll wheel out another just like it."

Sometimes in the past, when I've used that analogy of the car, one spouse or another has made a joke about it. *No more dings or scratches on the new one, right?* Or: *Any chance to improve the options on the next model?* A nervous laugh after it—sometimes a mirthless one.

I waited for the wife here to make the joke, but she didn't.

The husband pointed toward the brochure I'd customized for them, the rates I'd quoted. "How much leeway do we have here?" he said. "On the premiums, I mean? With the profits you're making, surely . . ."

The same move as before, the same glimmer of hope for him. Shortsighted, all of it—the dollar spent, the dollar saved. But you had to stay firm, let him come around.

"The premiums are based strictly on actuarial tables customized for age, demographics, and location—all factors considered."

"But this part of town should help with that, right?" he said. "I mean, as much as we're paying on our mortgage to live in this neighborhood. The school district and the zoning laws and—"

"The tables were updated recently, I assure you. They reflect accurately the probabilities for your circumstances, for . . ."

Probabilities of what, I didn't need to tell him.

He chewed the bottom of his lip, picked up the brochure again and opened it, but still not reading it, I could tell. His eyes simply scanned the page.

A minute passed in silence before he laid the brochure on the coffee table again, pushed it my way. "In that case," he said, "there's no way we could do this."

A card player, I imagined—once-a-month poker games. Usually left the table with less than he came in with.

"Honey," the wife said, shifting the child from one hip to the other as he reached again for those pearls. "Let's talk about it before we make a decision, okay?"

Another sigh. "There you go again, *honey*," he said, mimicking the way she'd said the word. "But where's the money coming from? You going to your parents again? *We* can't afford it, and that's final."

Which was another of my cues, of course.

"Really, you can't afford *not* to do it," I began. "In today's society, with this every-man-for-himself mentality—"

"And there *you* go again," the husband said, turning on me. "All you're trying to do is make a sale. You've got leeway, you know it, but—"

"The premiums are set," I repeated, "based on the probability that—"

"The probability that you'll be able to come in here and scare us into paying it, right? You act like you're on our side—"

"I'm doing everything I can for you," I said. "For your family."

"But you're not. You're not on our side, not really. It's just what you said, every man for himself. You're right about that, because it's your goal too."

I held up my hand once more—a hint of oath, a hint of surrender.

"My goal," I said, "is to provide perspective. My goal is to—"

"Pocket that premium." He smirked. "And the bigger the better, right?"

You never let a client get under your skin. It's business. It's not personal. You have to remind yourself of that.

But it's so easy to forget.

"If a criminal breaks into your home," I said, "coming for you or your wife or your children, you think they'll sit around the coffee table with you and let you consider your options? Will you try to come to terms with them? They'd kill you without blinking an eye, and then where are you? My goal—"

Even before the husband interrupted me, I could see my misstep. The way his eyes narrowed and his lips settled into a scowl. The way the wife covered the ears of the child in her arms. The way the older child on the floor stared.

You didn't mention *death*. You didn't mention *killing*. I knew that.

"Is that your message here?" the husband asked then. A snort. "We should deal with you because there's worse down the line—and they won't negotiate like you will." He leaned forward. "But you're not negotiating. It's just take it or leave it, on your terms. Preying on people's anxieties, building big profits on a lot of fear mongering. Seems like that makes you not much better than them, does it? Criminals, all of you."

"Honey," the wife said again, but there wasn't much conviction behind it this time.

In sales, you need to keep your eye on the endgame. You need to know there are many routes to get to your destination. You need to recognize when you've taken a wrong turn.

"Fear mongering," I repeated. "Criminals." I uncrossed my legs, shook my head, rose to leave.

There really wasn't much left to discuss.

***

At the door, I offered my hand to the husband, but he didn't reach out to take it. Over his shoulder, the wife gave me a puzzling tilt of the head, half-apologetic, half-accusatory herself. She'd had hopes.

The child in her arms had won his own battle. He had those pearls in his mouth.

As the door closed, I could hear the older child begin to cry. Maybe he'd knocked over his own blocks this time.

***

I had two other appointments not too far away—two other wives who'd contacted me. Same fears, same concerns motivating them. Probably the same opposition ahead too.

Another joke in our industry: Only a few missteps between an *appointment* and a *disappointment*.

I paused getting into my car, stood there for a moment with the door open, looking across the neighborhood. Two-story colonials dominant. Boxwoods out front, well-groomed yards. Mid-size cars in the driveways—high-end Toyotas and Hondas mostly, a Cadillac, even a Mercedes and a BMW or two. Not entirely affluent but upwardly mobile. Aspiring. They had something to lose, and they wanted to protect it.

I clicked the phone button on the dashboard as I sat in the driveway. "Call the office," I said into the Bluetooth.

When the secretary answered, I asked her to reschedule those two appointments, postpone for the following week. "Tell them I called in sick."

"Certainly, Mr. Blackston," she said.

I stayed in the driveway to make the second call too, the line buzzing slightly as it went through.

"Speak to me," said the voice that answered. That was Walter, gruff as always.

"The couple on Milton Street were a no-go," I said. "The wife was willing—"

"But the husband was weak."

Not the first time for that situation. I stared at the door they'd closed behind me.

"More prospects in the neighborhood?" Walter asked, anticipating. Eager even.

"We're rescheduling for next week, and I'd like them to go more smoothly, of course."

"I'm happy to provide encouragement."

And he was. Sometimes too happy, I knew, but when used sparingly, he served his purpose. "Same as usual? Wait a couple of days? Random house a street or two over?"

I thought of the couple I'd been talking with, the husband's movement from hesitation to hostility, the way he'd refused to shake my hand at the end, and then earlier how he hadn't bothered to help with his own children. That arrogance could use some humbling.

And my own blundering had been an embarrassment.

"A couple of days, yes," I said. You never wanted too much of a coincidence. "But keep it this address."

I looked up at the house, gave him a rundown on the architecture, the placement of the windows and doors, opportunities for entry.

Walter would make a haul of it, help to offset the lost commission, restore some sense of success. That clock, for example, and those pearls. He had an eye for things like that, things of real worth.

It was only a matter of time before someone tumbled into the truth, some enterprising detective finally turning his head away from the gang members and the junkies, those usual depraved. But by then, I'd be out of this business, out of this place entirely.

Majorca, I reminded myself. White sands. Blue seas.

Walter was still on the line when I caught sight of a face in the living room window. The older child's head atop the sill, a tousle of hair framed in the pane, those wide eyes watching me curiously.

In today's society, I'd tried to tell the husband, *with this every-man-for-himself mentality, you do what's necessary, no matter the cost.* That message had become a mantra of sorts, lodging somewhere at my foundation. Hardening there.

"The wife," I began to say to Walter, then hesitated. Then steeled myself anew. "The wife's the target. Leave the children and the husband. The widower who missed his chance. That's the portrait that'll do it, the impact we need."

I hung up. I raised a hand toward the face in the window as I pulled out of the driveway, smiled when the child waved back.

Beyond the neighborhood, I turned toward the bypass, merged into the blur of traffic, all of us homeward bound, calling it a day.

Everyone Talks About the Weather

On Monday it was merely a difference of degrees.

***

"Drive time this afternoon, we'll see highs in the mid-sixties, which is about average for this time of year." Brent Spivey was careful to maintain a broad smile. *The new face has to earn the viewers each day,* he reminded himself. *The new man has an uphill battle but success is at the top of the hill.* He clicked a button on the controls, the remote dwarfed in his palm. "And looking at WTEA's exclusive seven-day forecast"—he glanced at the studio clock, 7:18 a.m., his timing as crisp as the press of his suit—"we'll see some clouds lingering over the next few days and then a *slight* warming trend, bringing in some great weather this weekend, with mostly sunny skies and temps in the mid- to upper-seventies. I know our viewers are glad to hear that. And now back to you, Marva."

"Thanks, Brent." Marva turned her own bright smile to the camera. "Recapping our headlines as we close out this half-hour . . ."

***

"This afternoon's high reached sixty-six and we'll see a repeat of that tomorrow." Jonathan Albritton nodded gently toward the eye of the lens. The camera operator was signaling twenty seconds until the commercial break at 6:17 p.m., and Jonathan stepped off-screen, feeling again that dull ache in his knees, the years catching up. "But expect tomorrow's skies to be cloudier, with WTEA's exclusive seven-day forecast showing the possibility for continued cloudiness, perhaps even a sprinkle or two over the weekend and highs touching the low- to mid-seventies."

The cameraman's fingers counted down three, two, one. "And we're out."

***

"Did you hear that, Judith?" Frank Odom cocked his head, aiming his voice past the edge of his recliner and toward the kitchen.

"What's that?" his wife called, water running in the sink. "I couldn't hear you."

"Channel Seven says rain this weekend." Frank tried to keep his tone flat, waited a moment for her to respond. On the screen, a beer commercial showed women in bikinis crowding around a middle-aged man. Frank glanced down at the empty Coors can on the table beside him. "Wasn't Saturday when you'd set us up for that canoe thing with Roy and Brenda?"

"Well, that's odd." Judith dried her hands as she walked in the room. "This morning that new weatherman said sunny skies." She laughed. "Oh, who knows? I bet it'll change six more times between now and Saturday."

"Likely so." Frank picked up the beer can and peered into the dark opening. The next commercial was for Saturday afternoon's game. He laid down the beer can. *Let it rain, let it rain, let it rain,* his thoughts chanted.

***

Early Tuesday morning, Brent ran the National Weather Service computer models again, both the ETA and the AVN, comparing the trajectory of each forecast. Each time he ran the solution, the clouds cleared, the temperatures rose, the sun came out. He looked back over the synoptic charts, checked the placement of the prevailing front and the current movement of the nearest airstream, examined the upper-air data.

Where had Jonathan come up with precipitation?

Though it had never been officially stated, Jonathan was in many ways Brent's supervisor, and Brent had learned at his last station how difficult it could be to correct your boss. When he'd first approached Jonathan about the conflicting forecasts, he'd had to tread lightly. *I noticed you've been changing my forecasts, wondered where your information had been coming from*—student to mentor, that's how he'd tried to make it sound, explaining the adjustments he'd made to test the impact of various factors on prevailing patterns, walking through NOGAPS and the Canadian models and even the information from the European forecasters, and not one model suggesting rain, so. . . was there something Brent had missed?

Jonathan's office was small, but he had it to himself—one of the few among the on-air team to have earned that perk. On a shelf above the desk sat a row of regional Emmys Jonathan had won over his career. The wall displayed several AMS commendations. Over forty years in the business, Brent remembered, and suddenly the office seemed even smaller.

Jonathan had nodded, had stroked the stubble on his chin. Several people in the station, Brent included, had been talking about Jonathan's thickening facial hair, but to Brent's knowledge, no one had asked Jonathan himself about it.

"Two years ago," Jonathan began, "all the models predicted a snowstorm was going to blanket the viewing area with up to a foot of snow, and I dutifully passed that information along to our viewers. But the days passed, and it never snowed. Then one year ago, the models made the same prediction again, but I noticed that the factors in that case were the same as they'd been the year before with the false prediction. This time, I once more told our viewers what the models were predicting, but I also offered my *own* expectations for the forecast, a forecast which completely contradicted the computer's prediction. Again it didn't snow, but my forecast showed I'd learned well from my mistakes." Jonathan paused. "What we have to avoid is the danger of looking at these models as the gospel. What we have to remember is that it's all fiction until it happens."

Thinking back over it all now, Brent shook his head. All fiction? There was science behind it, there were patterns, there were signs.

He entered his password into the graphics computer. Once the program loaded, he would erase Jonathan's forecast from the previous evening and reconfigure what he himself had predicted yesterday morning. He would change the website graphics next, keeping all his forecasts consistent. And he had already printed up the readouts from the various trajectories — materials which he could use to convince or, if necessary, to defend.

***

"This afternoon's commuters are enjoying clear and sunny skies right now." Jonathan stepped away from the blue backdrop and watched the traffic-cam image spring up on the monitor beside him. He rubbed his chin, realized he'd forgotten to shave. *Need to take care of that before the eleven p.m.*, he thought, then let out a quick snort. *Or who's to say I shouldn't grow a beard? Who's to say whether I comb my hair up front or part it behind?* He pressed a button on the controls in his hand. "But that cloudiness I talked about last night looks like it might actually intensify over the next few days, with the seven-day forecast showing about a forty percent chance of showers by the weekend. We'll be watching this developing pattern closely to—"

***

Shelley sat at the kitchen island, her fractions worksheets spread out before her. Her eyes darted back and forth from the TV to her homework to her mother at the stove. Her mother faced away from her, stirring a bag labeled "Chicken Alfredo" into the shallow pan. Shelley heard the *click-clack* of the frozen ingredients knocking together, the low sizzle of the steam.

"Forty percent isn't definite," her mother said, as if reading her mind was as easy as sliding the top on the pan or turning down the heat.

Shelley curved out her lower lip and crossed her arms. "It's going to rain, you know it is."

"Well, if it *does* rain, we'll just have it inside," her mother said. "Don't worry. We'll make it special no matter what happens. And you can have your party outside next year."

"But I'll *never* turn *ten* again." Shelley watched the gray-haired man on the TV screen, hating the TV, hating him. She let out a low, guttural growl. "Nothing *ever* goes right for me!" She could already see the rain beating against the picnic table in the back yard, and her friends staying home because it was supposed to be an *outside* birthday, and what did it matter since Harrison said he couldn't come that day anyway?

It was her mother's fault. Her mother never planned anything right. All of their food came from bags and boxes in the freezer. Everything in her life tasted the same.

***

Jonathan sat by the weather console before the evening news, the computer models playing themselves out in continuous loops on a screen to his right, jaunting forward sixty hours in time over and over again. Jonathan didn't see them. He was watching the infrared satellite imaging instead and the Weather Tap for current radar conditions across the region. He was looking at the temperature of cloud tops hovering over the Midwest, held there by a slow-moving front. He examined the dew point and the surface barometric pressure for several small airports in Tennessee and Alabama. He remarked on the wind direction in Amarillo, counting the full barbs and half-barbs along the wind shaft symbols at stations along intervals of about fifty miles. A sideways *8* beside the station in Portland, Oregon indicated haze. It was also the symbol for infinity, he knew, and for a moment he imagined, as he had before, the long-term effects of infinite haze. Then in Portland, Maine, Jonathan found slight amounts of freezing rain—a sideways *S* curved around a period. He returned to his desk against the far wall and began jotting notes. Behind him, the computer models continued rotating unnoticed into the future.

***

"And now a brief look at the forecast." Marva beamed Brent's way. "Seems like we have some disagreement in our weather staff these days, Brent. So, are you sticking to sunny skies, or is our *chief* meteorologist right about the rain in our future?"

Brent felt his muscles tighten as she spoke, that word *chief* barbed. She was siding with Jonathan, was that it? And not just behind-the-scenes but on the air as well? Making Brent look bad in front of the viewers? He realized, sadly, that he shouldn't be surprised. She'd been undermining him in little ways ever since he arrived — calling him "kid" as if he was inexperienced, too young to know what he was doing, despite his CV, his work at Penn State, the test project refining the MM5. That modeling system was now being used at more than three hundred institutions—*three hundred*—in places as far away as Chile, China, and New Zealand.

He was proud of that, of being a pioneer in some ways, but to

Marva he was the new kid, the "boy"—another of her words—and just that morning, she'd caught him cursing as he rushed to switch the forecast graphics yet another time.

"Damn, damn," he'd muttered. "Damn that Jonathan." And then there she was in the doorway, watching, reprimanding.

"You need to watch that mouth, kid," she'd said. "Because I am."

A threat of some kind? Was she going to complain about "inappropriate behavior"?

"Well, there may be storms in *our* future with comments like that," Brent said now. He struggled to smile, but felt sure his expression betrayed his irritation, his concern. "But for our viewers, I have nothing but sun and fun ahead."

He clicked the button in his hand, looked toward the monitor to line up his gestures against the blue screen as he pointed toward the seven-day forecast. But the rows of glistening suns that he'd inserted earlier weren't there. In their place were clouds, rain, bolts of lightning.

"Well, that's not the right set of graphics." He blushed. He clicked the button again. Satellite loops, a chart of record highs and lows, current temperature readings around the area. He could have talked about any of them, but where was the page he'd prepared? He looked desperately toward Marva, who met his gaze with a blank smile.

Had she distracted him so much that morning that he'd forgotten to save his changes before the show started? Had that been what she'd meant to do? Or worse, had she gone back in and changed it herself, sabotaging his work to help Jonathan?

Brent stared numbly at the screen, clicking the button in his hand, flipping from image to image until the producer finally cut to commercial.

***

"That didn't go well," Terry said, staring toward the TV high in the corner, the images whisking past—radar, high temps, a blur of colors. "Too much anyway, everything they try to tell us."

He nudged Mack beside him. The two of them sat at the slim counter where they'd eaten most every day since they'd started working together at the site. Some others from the crew sat at their own stools to either side.

"Cold front's coming this way here, high pressure there," Terry went on. "I wish they'd just come out and say, 'Hey, y'all, it's gonna rain tomorrow'—or whatever, you know?" He picked up the first of his hot dogs off the waxed paper in the plastic tray. "Earline, can I get another of those little co-colas?" he asked before the waitress moved away.

"More to it than that." Mack emptied a small bag of sliced banana peppers onto his hot dogs. The lunch counter only served mustard, chili, onions, and slaw; Mack liked mustard and peppers, so he brought his own. "Nature is an awesome, magnificent thing. Weather has a process. Understand the processes and you've unlocked one of the wonders of the world." He sealed the empty bag, the insides slick with the peppers' juice, and tucked it into his shirt pocket.

"Well, I don't doubt it can be awesome," Terry said. "Thunderstorm coming across the field is an awesome sight, anyone who sees it knows that. But do I need all that mumbo-jumbo up there for them to tell me a thunderstorm is on its way—or for them to tell me that it's already here or that the sun's shining? If you want to know the temperature outside now, just walk outside. If I see it's raining other side of the window, why do I need to watch the TV to tell me that?" He swallowed, then took another bite of his hot dog. He ordered his dogs all the way and they were piled high with ingredients. "I don't need to know the how or the why. I just need to know what they say it's going to be like tomorrow and whether I'm gonna need a jacket or an umbrella or my sunscreen, you know?"

"I carry an umbrella with me every day." Earline slid the Coke across the counter.

"That's just responding to the elements, Terry," Mack said. "Any animal can seek shelter from the storm. But cognition separates man from the brutes." He bit into his hot dog, then said, between chews, "It's a gift not to be taken lightly."

"Are you calling Terry here a brute again?" Earline laughed. "Well, I told you *that* the first day you two came in here." Mack heard some of the other men at the counter laughing. Earline wiped the counter, moved along.

"What I'm saying," said Mack, "is that the process of understanding provides an order to the world—a meaning, even."

"Meaning of life." Terry chewed on that along with his next bite. "Meaning of life from the TV weatherman. Now that's a good one!" As he laughed, a speck of chili flew from his mouth onto the counter, but he didn't notice, and Mack didn't point it out.

***

"I need to talk to you." Brent stormed through the doorway into Jonathan's office, not bothering to knock, no long caring about niceties. "Do you give one shit about how you're compromising the integrity of my forecasts? Do you know how stupid you made me look this morning?"

Jonathan swiveled his chair around to face the younger man. "I wasn't here this morning," he said. "I don't know what you mean."

"You know exactly what I mean," Brent said. "You're still changing my forecasts every evening when you come in."

"And you change mine each morning." Jonathan's tone was calm, steady.

"At least my forecast is backed up with evidence." Brent raised his voice. "National Weather Service, Naval model, Canadian model, European model." He ticked off the list on his fingers.

"A regular United Nations of weather agencies allied against me." Jonathan nodded. "But evidence? If you want evidence, then walk outside this Saturday evening and you'll have all the evidence you'll need." He swiveled in his chair, turning his back on Brent. "Just remember your umbrella. I'd hate for you to get rained on."

Brent felt the fury rising in him as he stared at Jonathan's back. To hell with that row of Emmys and that wall of commendations, to hell with the special office and that self-righteous smile, to hell with Jonathan Albritton himself.

"You know what, Albritton?" he said. "I hope it *does* rain. I hope it rains on *you*. I hope your house floods. And I hope a bolt of lightning comes out of the sky and strikes you dead."

***

Jonathan poured himself a bourbon and ginger ale when he got home that night and sat down to reflect on the curses Brent had leveled at him and the way the balance of the day had unfolded. Jonathan's forecast had, in fact, escalated into the severe weather category that evening, with predictions for isolated thunderstorms and the potential for high winds. Jonathan truly felt that he had the high ground on his predictions—in more ways than one—but an unexpected twist had troubled him. Each time he had clicked between graphics during the evening forecasts, he'd felt a small shock in his thumb—a tingle at first, then a pulse of electricity. A short, Jonathan had thought. He'd had this same remote for a long time, too long. But then—

A bolt of lightning? Wasn't that what Brent had wished upon Jonathan? Had Brent perhaps tampered with Jonathan's equipment?

Even on air, Jonathan had lifted the remote and stared at it, lost in thought, until the anchorman had nudged him back into motion.

Sipping the bourbon now, Jonathan listened to the silence around him—listened for some settling of his house, the type of creak that he sometimes pretended was his wife coming around the corner or climbing the stairs for bed. But the silence was complete, and his dread descended once more in advance of another restless night ahead, the memory of his lost love and the children who never called. There was little that held him to this life now except for the job, the old habits of work, those everdimming passions. So much had changed, especially in the last weeks. There had been a time when his co-workers turned to him for advice and guidance. He'd helped Marva to get her job years ago, and she'd once been like a daughter to him, but those days were gone now and now she barely gave him a passing nod. Her loyalties had changed—everyone's had—and what a paltry thing they had chosen to want now: a shallow eagerness, a handsome young face, rash confidence and a quick temper and . . .

And now . . . a bolt of lightning. Not from the sky, but very much earth-bound, man-made.

"I hope the clouds do clear," Jonathan said aloud, raising his bourbon into the air as if in toast. "I hope the sun shines so bright that it burns holes in your hide."

***

Once more, Sam Holbrook walked the well-worn path away from the small house where he had grown up, the small house where his father had lived—or had lived until a month ago. The house was theirs now, they'd already begun staying there some, and inside, Sam's pregnant wife was asleep, exhausted from the latest of their arguments. Ahead of him lay the fields that his father had tilled and planted, tended and harvested, season in and season out—acreage the old man had bartered for, mortgaged against, spared no effort or risk to acquire and maintain . . . a legacy of sweat and blood that was now Sam's own, his burden alone to bear.

He looked up toward the midnight moon for some hint of the gathering clouds that the weatherman had been talking about a half-hour before. He watched the news each morning before he left for the textile factory and each night before he went to bed, hoping for . . . he didn't know exactly what, only that he ultimately felt as addled as the two men who couldn't agree about whether it would rain.

Before he died, Sam's father has turned the soil, but the planting still needed to be done. Sam was already behind on the corn and the soybeans, and next month tobacco season began. Working alone with the help of only a few hired men, his father had held out as other farms consolidated under the control of big landowners. No money to farming at the scale his father did, nothing to earn but the pride of persistence, the right to keep the land and to call it your own. But now his father was gone. The estate would never be able to pay off the mortgage, especially after the meager crop sales from last year's drought. And if the land couldn't pay for itself . . .

Beyond the shadowed yard, Sam headed toward the barn

out back, opened the doors and watched the outline of the John Deere appear in the darkness. He climbed atop the tractor and placed his hand on the steering wheel, trying to adjust to the feeling, preparing for Saturday morning.

"We'll meet you at daybreak," his father's men had told him, "make what headway we can, provided the weather holds and the fields don't wash to mud."

"We can take it off your hands," the McKenna brothers had said, with their fleet of tractors, their steady supply of migrant labor, and all their time to focus on the business. "We'll pay top dollar, just like we offered your daddy."

"You better just sell that land," his wife had told him more than once, and each time he had heard a more powerful bitterness brewing in her voice. "You already have job enough at the plant without spending your weekends on a second one. Think of me, think of the baby, think of . . ."

Sitting in the driver's seat atop the tractor, Sam knew that no matter which path he chose there would be disappointment and regret. But at least he could atone to his wife and child in other ways. There was no way around the disappointment of the dead.

Unless, of course, the decision is taken from me, he considered again. *After all, if the fields* do *turn to mud* . . . But even thinking this seemed a betrayal. Even alone in the silence of the barn, in the dead of night, he still couldn't bring himself to pray for rain—not now, not yet at least—and so he contented himself instead with wondering in vain whether the arguments might not go better next time.

***

"We've still got sixty-four days until summer," Brent said. Despite double-checking all his changes to the graphics this time, he still felt nervous as he clicked the image ahead. His hand itched, his stomach fluttered. "But it's going to feel like mid-July this weekend, with temps touching the low-nineties and fair skies as far as the eye can see. A day to really get out and take advantage of opportunities we don't normally see this time of year."

Facts were facts, and the sun was coming out. But still Brent regretted the way he'd stormed into Jonathan's office, regretted everything he'd said to him, his inability to bring them together.

The camera's red light blipped off. Brent's face settled back into fretfulness. He took a seat in the meteorology center, wringing his hands as his mind went back to Penn State again, thinking about his fascination with the idea of consensus theories in meteorology. To reach consensus, you inserted slightly incorrect factors, fictional factors, into real data to determine their effect on the forecast models—in essence, testing how the end forecast might be changed by shifting factors in current conditions. If the result predicted by the computer stayed the same despite the artificially modified data, then you'd built a consensus and could take greater faith in the forecast offered.

No consensus with Jonathan though—not in the forecast, not in their personal relations. The only times they'd seen one another in the station had been in the break room, Brent giving a curt nod as Jonathan poured his coffee, and Jonathan pouring a second cup for Brent, turning it his way, a façade of hospitality, his expression masked behind that thickening mess of facial hair.

At the anchor desk, Marva was wrapping up the news briefs. Nearly time for Brent's own recap before the top of the hour. He willed himself to be calm, straightened his tie, but his hands still itched, felt twitchy even. He held them in front of him to see if they were trembling, something he'd never want the camera to catch. And it was only then, staring at them, that he noticed the beginnings of a rash on his fingers, the slight bumpiness stretching in a swath across his skin.

***

"Hurricane season, as we all know, ended nearly five months ago," Jonathan reported later that night, trying to feel comfortable in the new suit that he had bought earlier that day. He'd gotten a haircut as well and bought a comb for his beard. "Circumstances this time of year are unable to give rise to the atmospheric conditions necessary for tropical depressions to develop in the Central Atlantic. But over the past few days I've been charting developments in the Midwest that have struck me as, well, frankly peculiar. A mild winter that has left ground temperatures warmer than usual. A lifting of the airstream that can't be explained by geographical terrain. And, in turn, the development of conditions that promise to magnify the kind of vertical instability we're used to seeing about now, anyway."

He grasped the remote, felt the electricity pulse through his fingers as he clicked through the graphics he'd prepared, felt empowered by that shock. He resisted the urge to click again just to feel it one more time.

"All of which is to say that Mother Nature may soon be making up for last fall's mild hurricane season, delivering winds and storms this weekend reminiscent of the worst that this state has ever seen."

***

"Honey," Dolores Fields said, laying down her knitting needles. "Did Jonathan Albritton have a beard earlier this week?"

Her husband peered around the newspaper spread out in his hands. "Well, hon, can't say that I've ever paid him much mind, but sure looks like he has one now."

***

Lying alone in the bed she'd once shared with her husband, Georgia Sandling pulled the covers tighter around her neck. How many years had it been now? And yet even the mention of the word *hurricane* still knocked her insides off-balance.

She remembered the two of them lying on the floor where the air was cooler, the fourth night of the power outage, no air-conditioning, fretful sleep. They'd kept some distance from each other to keep from incubating the heat, the sweat. But she was still surprised when she woke in the middle of the night and he wasn't there. She'd walked through the house, softly calling his name, but no answer. And then she saw the closed door and opened it gently and heard what he was saying into the phone, what he was whispering to the woman on the other end of the line—checking in with her, worried whether she was okay, promising that they'd be together again soon.

His words had kicked the breath from her as surely as the hurricane had torn down the powerlines.

Her own life had been uprooted as quickly and easily as the trees.

***

When Marva and her husband made love, she usually imagined a teleprompter rolling its script just over his shoulder—a series of *oohs* and *ahhs*, a *c'mon, baby* here, a *that's the way* there. It was a performance, just like any other, and she always played her role adequately, adeptly even.

But lately it was Brent's square jaw and muscular shoulders that Marva imagined instead, the words *C'mon, kid, c'mon, big boy* racing through her head, and she knew that her theatrics had suddenly taken on a new vigor.

While her husband grunted and groaned, Marva pictured Brent poised above her in a field somewhere, one of his large hands cupping her breast, the other holding up a bronze lightning rod. The sky trembled in anticipation of what would happen next. A pounding thunder drowned out her cries of pleasure. A bolt of lightning pierced her to her core.

But that wasn't right, she remembered after her husband had finished and begun drifting off to sleep. That image wasn't quite Brent at all. In fact, he'd seemed nervous around her lately, puppyish even—maybe conflicted about his own crush on her, her a married woman and all, and him needing some coaxing?

The weather was wrong too—the thunder and lightning. She should have imagined blue skies instead, a lushly tropical day, the hot sun beating down on her skin. *That* was Brent's forecast. *Jonathan* had predicted the storm. And the word around the station was that the coming weekend's actual weather would cost one of the men his job.

Jonathan had been useful, of course. Marva couldn't deny that. Without him, she wouldn't be at the station today. But she also knew that Brent was the future—younger, snappier, handsome too, virile, virile she felt sure—and she wanted to tie her fortunes to the fastest rising star.

As Marva laid herself into the cradle of her husband's outstretched arm, she wondered whether she would be the one to get Jonathan's office after he was fired, and how long it would take her to lure Brent in there with her.

***

"Your weather forecasters may *both* be right," said the voice on the general inbox of WTEA's voicemail system. A man's voice, deeply toned, with a vague accent. "But they cannot yet fathom what they are really predicting. Do they need help? Very well. Seek out Quatrain Eighty-three of the Ninth Century, when Nostradamus tells us, 'Sun twentieth of Taurus the earth will tremble very mightily, it will ruin the great theater filled: To darken and trouble air, sky and land, then the infidel will call upon God and saints.' They are having trouble predicting the weather because there's more at stake here than weather. Check the prophecies themselves to see how they can mesh their forecasts, hone their omens of all that's yet to come, and finally comprehend the consequences for us all."

***

"What the hell is going on here?" Frederick Barston, WTEA's owner, bald and bespectacled, had corralled the two men near the weather desk. "You're predicting summer sunshine," he said, tapping his finger against Brent's chest before pointing it at Jonathan, "and *your* forecast is just short of a hurricane."

Barston could feel the veins in his temples throbbing. Why hadn't he retired last year like his wife had begged him to? Wouldn't he have been happier at the golf course this afternoon? Or finally re-reading the *Iliad* and the *Odyssey*, Herodotus and Thucydides?

"You know what *my* prediction is? Ratings that'll put us in third place after the other guys—for the first time in my twenty-three years at the helm of this station."

Barston stared down each of the meteorologists in turn, but they didn't speak, didn't blink, their expressions as inscrutable as their voices were silent. The two of them were keeping their distance from one another—Jonathan's arms crossed over his chest, Brent's hands shoved into his pocket.

Barston looked around the room at the TV monitors stacked into their cubbies: various computer-generated maps of the city, the South, the United States. One of them was awash in color: lime greens, bright yellows, hot reds. Another showed clusters of lightning bolts. Here was a series of ridges, a topographical map of fronts and isobars. There was a list of numbers labeled *temperature, humidity, barometric pressure, dewpoint/wet bulb, windchill/heat index, rainfall.* Which of the men had read all the information correctly? Which one had truly deciphered the mystery? Looking at their blank expressions, he thought suddenly of Pythia in her trance, sacred Delphi, towering Parnassus.

"Hell, if I knew how to work this shit, I'd fire you both and do the job myself."

***

Inspiration had struck and Kate Jasper's fingers moved quickly across the keyboard. "Tempest in a TEApot?" the Metro reporter typed into the headline field, then hit return and entered the slug for the body text before starting a new draft of her lead paragraph. "There's a squall brewing over in the WTEA weather room, with dueling Dopplers, fast-changing forecasts, and the makings of a melee that could lead to meteorological mayhem. Are gray skies gonna clear up? Are there darker clouds on the horizon? What's really going on at the eye of this storm? Only one thing seems certain: Local industry analysts agree that this whirlwind of on-air conflict will lead to an even stronger surge in ratings for a station that's already a consistent front-runner in this market."

"Too much figurative language." Kate turned to see her editor, Henry Welbourne, looming over her shoulder. She hadn't heard his footsteps.

"It's not done yet," Kate said, sitting up straight in her chair to help block the screen.

"I hope not," he snorted. "Albritton's got *two* t's. Look down there below."

"I'm still shaping it," she said. "I'll fix those typos once I get the style right. I'm just finding the right tone for the piece."

"Journalism strives for the simplest means of communication," he reminded her, one of his catchphrases, then segued right into another. "An *invisible* style allows the *substance* to be revealed." He turned to walk away. "And you'd better get those so-called 'typos' fixed on this one. The *next* time we have to print a correction on one of your stories will be the *last* time your byline appears in this paper."

"Jackass," Kate said under her breath. "I'm a writer, not a copy editor." She looked around the newsroom to see who else might have heard Welbourne berating her, but everyone seemed preoccupied with their own work. Probably just pretending, she knew. She would overhear someone talking about her soon enough.

She highlighted the paragraph and hit *delete.* She told herself it didn't matter. She was simply biding her time. Someday *she* would be the editor—someplace besides here—and then she would write what she wanted.

***

The headline of Kate Jasper's story, as published on page 3B of the morning paper's final edition: "WTEA Steeped in Weather Controversy."

The paper's own weather forecast, page 8B: A sun partly obscured by clouds, two symbols overlapping, neither predominant, highs in the mid-70s.

***

"Something else wrong, kid? You're not yourself these days." Marva seemed genuinely concerned—a nice surprise, Brent thought. Her smile was reassuring, encouraging. "I get the feeling you've got something to tell me."

"I do," Brent said. "I'm—"

He hesitated. A risk revealing anything, he knew that.

They were sitting at the coffee shop a block from the station— a corner table, some degree of privacy even with the place full, but Brent kept glancing at the door to make sure no one from the station had come in. He was watchful everywhere now, entering and leaving the station, wherever he was inside the building itself but some rooms more than others—bathroom and breakroom especially. And people were watching him, he felt certain. Other people in the station asking the same kinds of questions Marva had. *Are you feeling okay? Everything all right?* And more people not asking but probably wanting to. The bags under his eyes, the paleness of his skin. He'd been adding extra foundation before going on air, extra concealer.

"Don't worry, kid." Marva leaned forward, almost tipping her cortado. "You can tell me anything you need to." She reached toward him, but he kept his hands under the table.

"Well . . . I thought it was just stress, you know, and nervousness and . . ."

Marva smiled, nodded. "You've had a lot going on. The tension with Jonathan, getting dressed down by Barston, and maybe . . . well, I'm sure other things on your mind too. New place, new people. Where do you fit in? Especially being single and all and . . . Look, whenever you need someone to talk to, know I'm here. Friend, confidante . . ." She raised an eyebrow, gave a single-shoulder shrug.

Brent had been watching the window as she spoke—the sunlight falling through it, bright and strong. But each time a cloud passed and the light dimmed, he felt his spirits tremble.

"I . . . I had a . . . a doctor's appointment," Brent said. "Yesterday afternoon." He watched Marva's expression, her body. A tightening at the eyes, a slight lean back.

"A doctor?" she said softly. "I . . . That wasn't what I expected. Is everything okay?"

"Dermatologist. A skin rash, that's what I thought. Just stress, like I said, and . . ." He raised his hand, rested it palms-up on the table. When he was in the station, off air as well as on, he'd been keeping a layer of concealer on his hands too, but he'd wiped them clean before meeting Marva, and now the spots and bumps on his palms and fingertips stood clear.

Marva drew her own hand back, held her fingers to her lips. "Oh," she said. "This . . . this isn't *at all* what I expected. Is it . . . ?"

"Skin cancer? Oh, no, it's—"

"I was going to say contagious?"

"Oh, no, it's much worse than that, Marva, it's—"

Marva had pulled back further into her seat. She crossed her arms. "Honestly, Brent. How could something be worse than contagious?"

He took a deep breath. "It's poison, Marva. That's what the

dermatologist suspects at least. Cyanide maybe—*cyanide*. He's running a test. Said it must have been in some cleaner I used, something around the house, but I think . . . it doesn't make sense, I don't know how he did it, but I think it was on a cup of coffee Jonathan gave me." He leaned forward, another glance around, lowering his voice to a whisper. "I think Jonathan Albritton has been poisoning me."

***

"Well, that's a load of hogwash," Agnes said to Herb as they watched the weather Friday morning in the parlor of the Elysian Fields retirement home. Always the last to their rooms each night after watching the news and the late show, they were still up at 5:30 each morning to watch the early news. The first one to the parlor got the recliner and control of the television. "It's all about *atmospheric lift*"—she curled her forearms slightly, palms up, her right hand gripping the remote—"and lifting leads to rainfall. That young fella there doesn't know what he's saying."

"Makes more sense than what the other one was saying last night," Herb said from the sofa. "I think he's got a pretty good head on his shoulders. And him being younger, I expect his training's more up to date."

Agnes shook her head. "Training or not, he's losing it. Look at him. It's like he's sick or something. His cheeks are sunk in, and he's all twitchy."

Herb shrugged. "Maybe he's having a bad day. What difference does that make to the information he's giving you? Either way, I'm not so positive that you're right about that lifting you talked about."

"You don't believe me?" Agnes shook the remote at him.

"I'm not saying I don't believe you, Ag," Herb said. "I'm just saying some proof would convince me more. Without proof, what have you got?"

"If you want proof, I'll show you proof." Agnes kicked down the footrest of the recliner, slammed the remote down on the arm of the chair. "You'll see, you just wait." And she headed off toward the dog-eared encyclopedias in the room next door.

Herb's plan had worked. He watched until Agnes had round-ed the corner and then moved over to the recliner himself, settling into the soft leather before flipping the channel over to catch a glimpse of the weathergirl on the other station, the blonde with the shining eyes and the dimpled grin and the shapely figure he dreamed about each night.

***

The clerk at City News watched the gangly teen reading *Rolling Stone* and the fat one flipping through *Maxim*. She didn't like the way their jeans were slung low around their ass cracks, and she didn't like the way they cut their eyes at her every few minutes. Shoplifters, she felt sure, and she thought again how she wished the owner would let her keep a gun under the counter, so that she could raise it up for them to see and wink at them slyly and nod. They would stop cutting their eyes at her then, wouldn't they? And after all, a woman her age needed to protect herself, didn't she? Especially after the sun had gone down?

Just beyond the teens, she saw that the middle-aged man in the "Adults Only" section had propped a copy of *Club Confidential* on the shelf and jammed one of his hands fiercely into his pocket.

Two things to worry about now, she thought, and realized she had never wanted to shoot anyone who bought *The New Yorker* or *Martha Stewart Living* or *Travel and Leisure*. Not yet at least.

"I'll take these," said a small man in a brown bowler, laying three magazines on the counter. He seemed to have appeared from nowhere.

The clerk tried to keep her eye on the back of the store as she sought out the prices on the magazines and punched the numbers into the register: *Weatherwise . . . Weather . . . Endtimes.* She laughed at the last one.

"You know what's funny about this magazine?" she said, not waiting for an answer. "It talks about how the end of the world is right around the corner. But when you look at the subscription form"—she flipped through the magazine and pulled out the card, held it up—"they want you to subscribe for two years. You see?"

But before the customer could respond, the clerk heard the

chime of the bells hanging from the door. And when she looked toward the back of the store, the shoplifters were gone.

***

Late Friday evening, Reverend Bertram Tucker struggled to complete the notes for Sunday's sermon, addressing the topic of how the Lord provides for the faithful. His problem was not finding something to say, but rather paring down his many thoughts on the subject, which threatened to overwhelm the twenty minutes he allotted himself each week. He had learned that his parishioners thanked him more warmly at the end of the service when he kept his sermons short.

As he jotted down his outline, he heard from elsewhere in the house a still, small voice. But hadn't his wife gone to bed? And who would she have been speaking with?

He raised himself up gingerly from his desk, fighting the arthritis that had lately seemed to plague his joints even more.

"Martha?" he said, walking down the hallway. He peered into their room and found her already fast asleep, her body curled toward his side of the bed, her right hand pressed against his pillow, softly clutching it close. He smiled, relieved.

And yet still he heard the voice somewhere in the house.

It was the TV, he discovered when he entered the darkened living room and saw its ghostly glow. Martha sometimes had trouble with the remote control, and he suspected she had simply turned down the volume instead of turning it off.

Searching for the control, he caught sight of the TV screen—a map of the U.S. and a bearded man whose visage suddenly gave Tucker pause. Didn't that man look exactly like the image of Elijah that Tucker had carried in his head since his years in seminary? And if Elijah had returned, what did that mean?

***

Jonathan stopped in mid-sentence and stepped in front of the computer model, turning to face the camera head-on. "You know, I began my career as a meteorologist decades before we even had computers in the workplace. In fact, it may surprise some of you to know that even during my career, even recently, meteorologists have relied on Western Union—on teletype—for reports from airports across the country.

"When I first started in this business, we would lay out a blank map of the country each day"—he stretched his arms wide and pretended to flatten out some spread of paper on an imaginary table before him—"and we'd plot by hand the prevailing weather conditions from each of these stations"—an invisible pen made quick marks on the paper—"and bit by bit we'd see the patterns emerge, the truth revealed."

Truth? Jonathan wondered what it was anymore. An empty word maybe—at least the way that Brent had been hurling it at him. *Tell the truth, Albritton, tell them how you've been poisoning me, tell them about the cyanide.* His expression had seemed crazed, deranged. He'd lunged at Jonathan, his hands streaked with white, the fingers like speckled claws.

Several of the cameramen had struggled to hold Brent back. He'd been taken away then—where, Jonathan didn't know. To a hospital? To jail?

The remote had been sitting in Jonathan's pocket throughout the scuffle, and he had considered raising it up as an accusation of his own, evidence of what Brent must have done. But had he? It didn't matter anymore. Jonathan found comfort now in the pulse and surge.

He looked down at his shoes then, suddenly glad that he hadn't bought new ones when he'd bought the suit. The suit, he'd discovered, was too snug under his arms and the fabric itched. But though his shoes were dingy, scarred and faded, his feet felt free and fine.

"Today's meteorologists . . . Everything is state of the art. Computers today can draw on all the laws of physics to calculate thousands, maybe even countless of thousands of numerical forecasts—completing in minutes what would otherwise take us all day to figure out, finishing in hours what it would take us a week to determine."

Jonathan closed his eyes and imagined pressing the clicker and sparking a charge, imagined his worn leather shoes sprouting wings maybe. Maybe his whole body could fly out of the studio then and across the countryside and higher into the air, away from all the turmoil around him, the anger and accusations, the bitterness—rising higher and higher until he could see the entire state, the entire nation in one glance like he was looking at a map: the places where the sun fell unfettered or where storm clouds gathered or where ice crystals formed, the fronts and air masses, the wonders of air damming and of lift—the invisible made visible, everything finally clear at once.

"And yet, I must say," he concluded, opening his eyes, "that there's nothing like the thrill of discovering something for yourself."

He clicked the remote, feeling the sparks piercing his skin, pushing everything forward.

***

Throughout the WTEA viewing area, people planned garden parties or stocked their cellars, bought freesia bulbs to plant in their flower beds or flashlight bulbs to shore up their emergency plans. They lathered themselves with sunscreen or anointed their brows with holy water. They sought out lost loves on the Internet, made last-ditch efforts to save their marriages, or indulged in wanton pleasures with no thought of the consequences. They charted their lusts, gorged their fears, tried in vain to hide from their own loneliness. Some fled for higher ground; others huddled in corners. The brave stayed where they were. The authorities braced for threats and troubles.

Regret did not rule, nor did pettiness, envy, or hatred. But neither did optimism. Instead, a vague anxiety filled the land.

People watched their sets, they watched the horizons, they watched the skies.

The Great Detective Reflects

During the long days, the great detective roams through his old adventures, following again the twists and turns of those most baffling murders and thefts and conspiracies, tracing the endless trails of clues, measuring the accusations and confessions and recriminations, meditating over the surprises that wait in unexpected places.

The cases stand as testimony to a victorious career. The books stand too, like milestones, his old companion's popular accounts of the great detective's genius, of his keen eye and majestic mind. The shelves groan under the weight of those tributes, but the published volumes gather dust these days because the great detective has lost interest in them. It's the trove of manuscripts that draws him in, the marginalia there and the edits, the letters and notes, all of it long since deeded his way—yellowing journals and parcels and scraps of paper that he sorts and sifts through. Some of the pieces crumble under his fingers, and the handwriting has dimmed as the ink ages. But there's pleasure even in the brittleness of the paper, in the faint scent of tobacco on the pages, and the penmanship hardly fails to bring back his old friend, lost so early to illness. The writing itself is now an old friend of sorts, those bold downstrokes, the curving hooks of the *g*s and *j*s, an absence of hesitation in the ligatures, and that prideful flourish in the swoops and stretches of the titles.

"The Adventure of the Apish Forger"
"The Case of the Edinburgh Extortionist"
"The Case of the Purloined Peridots"

His old friend and chronicler had a weakness for alliteration, more pronounced as time went on. The great detective smiles at this memory.

Then he corrects himself: an *affection* for alliteration. Not friend and chronicler but *companion* and chronicler. And not a smile at the memory but a *musing* over it—these small tributes of his own, privately, posthumously paid.

Something selfish at the heart of even this, he recognizes as he pushes ahead. Less tributes than mental exercises. Keeping the acumen agile. Keeping the grey cells smoothly geared. Providing proof of that legendary prowess.

Endlessly exercising.

Exercising.

Exorcising.

***

The great detective's companion these days is a small spaniel—a Cavalier King Charles, loyal and attentive. At least once an afternoon, the spaniel twists her head, pricks up her ears—sudden alertness and guardedness, a scurrying toward the door, a readiness to bark.

Usually it's simply the postman of that small English village (or French village or Swiss village—place hardly matters, the great detective's focus has turned so inward). The postman—a new postman now, Roy or Ray—does not deposit the mail in the chute as the previous one had but always knocks, greets the great detective with a brief hello, bends down to greet the spaniel. "Just wanted to give her a quick scratch behind the ears," Roy or Ray says with an apologetic smile, but the great detective often feels that he's the one being attended to. The daily batch of fan mail has dwindled. Only an occasional letter now among the bills and circulars, the endless waste.

This postman is often his only visitor for weeks on end, but sometimes the scuffing of shoes against the walk strikes an even more unfamiliar rhythm, and as the dog tenses and scurries, the great detective rises from his armchair with a readiness of his own, bracing himself for whatever might be on the other side of the knock—ready for the worst, a vengeful foe, welcoming it perhaps.

But who approaches? Occasionally an admirer. "I'm a great fan. . . It's a pleasure. . . It's an honor. . . I've read of your adventures"—one of those old books in hand usually, praise for his old companion, the dearly departed, and condolences too, admiration for the new companion as well, a rub behind the dog's ear same as the postman's, while the great detective scrawls his own name above his old friend's on the title page of the book—dodging nostalgia, pretending confidence.

***

In bed at night, the darkness closing in and him ever restless, the great detective calls forth with satisfaction some of his most cherished cases and celebrates silently the inevitable dénouements—those moments akin to a worthy opponent conceding a contentious chess match by reaching forward and toppling his, or her, king.

You have bested me, great detective. I was no match. The truth has come out.

He reminisces about the moments before such confessions and concessions too—his discovery of the clues that sealed those fates.

The accountant Farnsworth had been farsighted, not nearsighted, he remembers on this night.

The widow Gurganus had bought the same fish as always that Friday but from a different supplier.

The height of the begonia in Albert Dunstan's garden had shifted inexplicably, and there was meaning in his choice to trim it before it had bloomed.

The overnight train regularly blew its whistle at Coburn Junction at 2:18 a.m., like clockwork, but no one could have known about a cow on the tracks the night of the great robbery—a delay that proved twice costly, first to the train line and then to old Davy Gardner and his crew too, improperly synchronized, scrambling in the aftermath to cover their tracks.

The guilty parade before the great detective's imagination, silhouettes of the past, and so they fall again one by one, all those who matched wits with him—all those who failed to.

***

In the darkness this night as on others, more details rise before him—these unbidden.

Farnsworth, the farsighted accountant, for example—he wasn't an accountant at all, was he? An attorney perhaps? An obstetrician?

The glasses, the lenses—this is what the great detective forces his attention back toward. The important detail, he stresses to himself.

***

Has the bedroom grown chillier?

The great detective forces his attention toward the daylight as well, toward the few times, often on a greying afternoon, when a gaggle of schoolchildren from the neighborhood have arrived with a challenge in hand—a five-minute mystery torn from some magazine and the answer coyly withheld, or some story from the neighborhood itself, some small mystery of their own. Logic challenges usually, exercises for the mind here too, he tells himself. He welcomes such play, even if the answers are often rudimentary.

Like a parrot, a mynah bird can mimic the human voice.

There is only a single place in the world where you can travel one mile due south, one mile due east, and one mile due north and end up at your original destination.

Diamonds can cut glass, but the cutting of glass does not a diamond make.

Trivial bits of knowledge still tucked away in the corners of his ever-greying cells. Basic logic, difficult to forget. But the faces of those schoolchildren, rising before him in the darkness, are tinged with awe.

The great detective dimly recognizes those faces, believes that he recognizes them. Are they always the same ones who've come before? Each time the children visit, they seem familiar, but perhaps they have changed.

***

In the darkest parts of the nights, questions accumulate, the irksome specifics, the unraveling particulars. Unless he can stop it, the great detective's mind summons up other cases, the ones whose endings never fully satisfied: "The Adventure of the Erstwhile Arsonist," "The Adventure of the Bashful Blackmailer," "The Case of the Shimmering Mist." Instinct clicking, intuition humming, clues aligning same as always, all those details, and then an accusation made. Constance Henshaw had set those fires. Shorty Daniels had been forced toward extortion by gambling debts but had ultimately paid a higher price than any of his victims. And Vernon Beck had been the one slowly summoned out of the mists and marked as a killer by clue after clue—a missing mah-jongg tile, a secret affair with the lieutenant's secretary, a diagnosis of diabetes and an extra vial of insulin.

But each of these had declined to tip that king, refused to concede the game. Even as he mounted the gallows, Beck had protested his innocence, protested unwaveringly that "the real crime here is. . . and the true villain is. . . "

***

An undertaker. Farnsworth was an undertaker. Yes?

And that secretary—she hadn't served a lieutenant but a lieutenant colonel, correct? Or perhaps a full colonel?

***

Slowly, the shades of the past merge one with another, shadows and silhouettes dim against the general darkness, a deepening mistiness.

Pulling his counterpane tighter, the great detective listens himself for a train whistle—some signal, some comfort amidst the silence, some resynchronization of his own.

But it's a scuffing of shoes he hears instead, the echo of a scuffing, the echo of a knock. Other afternoons, other visitors, someone occasionally seeking consultation—a real case, a real problem, an urgent need, and couldn't the great detective possibly. . . ?

"I'm retired," the great detective repeats into the emptiness of his bedroom, closing the door in his mind, pushing it shut firmly, sometimes mid-protest. "*Je suis désolé*. Retired. I'm sorry."

Only slowly does sleep finally approach.

***

In the morning, the great detective examines his face in the bathroom mirror: the thinning hair, the sagging flesh. The eye of the hawk, that's how his companion had described him—and he'd regularly written about a glimmer of mischief in the great detective's eye, a glint of triumph. But where is that twinkle now? Where is that upturn at the corner of his lips, that expression that always meant he'd solved the case?

His mouth is a grim slash these days. His eye is jaundiced, quailing. Window to the soul.

Even after he cleans his teeth, some trace of age hovers on his tongue. Decay, rot.

He bares those teeth, he opens his mouth. He stares into his widening maw, the darkness of his gullet, that abyss.

His body, his mind, his past—all of him increasingly a mystery to himself.

***

But no time to linger over such matters. The morning awaits, the notebooks and the yellowing pages, the sorting and the sifting.

Farnsworth was in there—the undertaker, the obstetrician, the accountant—waiting. And the notes, extensive notes, about that lieutenant or colonel, about the length and volume of that vial and the fingerprints on it, about the shape and texture and placement of the mah-jongg tile, a real thing, a tangible, undeniable thing, the proof he needs.

A plethora of it perhaps.

A cornucopia of clues. A cavalcade, a cascade.

An excess, an exigency of evidence.

It's all there, the great detective knows, as the spaniel stares up, tilts her head.

All there, all there.

Acknowledgments

In addition to my gratitude to the editors who originally published so many of the stories in this collection, I also want to thank the friends and fellow writers who at various times helped with drafts of specific stories, especially Donna Andrews, Ellen Crosby, John Gilstrap, Alan Orloff, Kyle Semmel, and Brandon Wicks—and my wife Tara Laskowski, always a generous and keen-eyed first reader for so many of these. Dash is still too young to read many of the stories here, but he's good at generating plot ideas for both Tara and me, and his own creativity and enthusiasm and diligence are an inspiration always.

Thanks also Jeffrey Marks at Crippen & Landru; to my agent, Ellen Geiger of Frances Goldin Literary Agency; and to several people who contributed to the creation of this book: Luke Buchanan for the cover painting; Christina Luboski for the jacket design; and Meredith Phillips for the keen-eyed copyediting (any persistent mistakes are mine, of course).

I'm also grateful to Mystery Writers of America and Sisters in Crime, particularly the Chesapeake Chapter of SinC, and to the Weymouth Center for the Arts and Humanities, where I spent another week-long residency in January 2022.

Sources

Many of the stories in this collection were previously published in other anthologies or journals, as follows:

- "All Tomorrow's Parties" in *Chesapeake Crimes: Invitation to Murder*, Wildside Press, 2020
- "A Blanket of Snow," originally published as "The Blanketing Snow" in *One Paycheck Away* (Main Street Rag Press, 2003) and republished in *Shotgun Honey*, 2016
- "The Great Detective Reflects" in *Ellery Queen's Mystery Magazine*, November 2016
- "Hard Return" in *Crime Travel: Tales of Mystery and Crime Travel*, Wildside Press, 2019
- "Mrs. Marple and the Hit & Run" in *Prick of the Spindle*, Summer 2010
- "Premonition" in *Chesapeake Crimes: Homicidal Holidays*, Wildside Press, 2014
- "Locked Out" in *Plots With Guns*, Fall 2011
- "Love Me or Leave Me" in *Music of the Night: The Crime Writers' Association Anthology*, Flame Tree Press, 2022
- "Restoration" in *Crime Syndicate: A Magazine of Crime Fiction*, January 2016, and republished in "Barb Goffman Presents" for the Black Cat Mystery and Science Fiction eBook Club, 2020
- "The White Rose of Memphis" in *Needle: A Magazine of Noir*, Fall 2011

THE ADVENTURE OF THE CASTLE THIEF

The Adventure of the Castle Thief is printed on 60-pound paper, and is designed by Jeffrey Marks using InDesign. The type is Baskerville, a modern interpretation of the original Baskerville font developed by John Baskerville in 1762. The cover is by Luke Buchanan. The first edition was published in two forms: trade softcover, perfect bound; and one hundred copies sewn in cloth, numbered and signed by the author. Each of the clothbound copies includes a separate pamphlet, "Sunday Morning, Saturday Night," a short story by Art Taylor. *The Adventure of the Castle Thief* was printed by Southern Ohio Printers and bound by Cincinnati Bindery. The book was published in February 2023 by Crippen & Landru Publishers, Inc., Cincinnati, OH.

Crippen & Landru, Publishers
P. O. Box 532057
Cincinnati, OH 45253
Web: www.Crippenlandru.com
E-mail: Orders@crippenlandru.com

Since 1994, Crippen & Landru has published more than 100 first editions of short-story collections by important detective and mystery writers.

This is the best edited, most attractively packaged line of mystery books introduced in this decade. The books are equally valuable to collectors and readers. [Mystery Scene Magazine]

The specialty publisher with the most star-studded list is Crippen & Landru, which has produced short story collections by some of the biggest names in contemporary crime fiction. [Ellery Queen's Mystery Magazine]

God bless Crippen & Landru. [The Strand Magazine]

A monument in the making is appearing year by year from Crippen & Landru, a small press devoted exclusively to publishing the criminous short story. [Alfred Hitchcock's Mystery Magazine]

Crippen & Landru Publications

Challenge the Impossible: The Impossible Files of Dr. Sam Hawthorne by Edward D. Hoch. Full cloth in dust jacket, signed and numbered by the publisher, $45.00. Trade softcover, $19.00.

Nothing Is Impossible: Further Problems of Dr. Sam Hawthorne by Edward D. Hoch.
Dr. Sam Hawthorne, a New England country doctor in the first half of the twentieth century, was constantly faced by murders in locked rooms and impossible disappearances. *Nothing Is Impossible* contains fifteen of Dr. Sam's most extraordinary cases. Full cloth in dust jacket, signed and numbered by the publisher, $45.00. Trade softcover, $19.00.

Chain of Witnesses; The Cases of Miss Phipps by Phyllis Bentley, edited by Marvin Lachman. Lost Classics Series. A critic writes, "stylistically, [Bentley's] stories ... share a quiet humor and misleading simplicity of statement with the works of Christie .... Her work [is] informed and consistent with the classic traditions of the mystery." Full cloth in dust jacket, $29.00. Trade softcover, $19.00.

Swords, Sandals And Sirens by Marilyn Todd.
Murder, conmen, elephants. Who knew ancient times could be such fun? Many of the stories feature Claudia Seferius, the super-bitch heroine of Marilyn Todd's critically acclaimed mystery series set in ancient rome. Others feature Cleopatra, the olympian gods, and high priestess Ilion blackmailed to work with Sparta's feared secret police. Full cloth in dust jacket, signed and numbered by the author, $45.00. Trade softcover, $19.00.

The Puzzles of Peter Duluth by Patrick Quentin. Lost Classics Series.

Anthony Boucher wrote: "Quentin is particularly noted for the enviable polish and grace which make him one of the leading American fabricants of the murderous comedy of manners; but this surface smoothness conceals intricate and meticulous plot construction as faultless as that of Agatha Christie." Full cloth in dust jacket, $29.00. Trade softcover, $19.00.

Hunt in the Dark by Q. Patrick, Lost Classics Series. Full cloth in dust jacket, $29.00. Trade softcover, $19.00.

All But Impossible: The Impossible Files of Dr. Sam Hawthorne by Edward D. Hoch. Full cloth in dust jacket, signed and numbered by the publisher, $45.00. Trade softcover, $19.00.

Sequel to Murder by Anthony Gilbert, edited by John Cooper. Full cloth in dust jacket, $29.00. Trade softcover, $19.00.

Hildegarde Withers: Final Riddles? by Stuart Palmer with an introduction by Steven Saylor. Full cloth in dust jacket, $29.00. Trade softcover, $19.00

Shooting Script by William Link and Richard Levinson, edited by Joseph Goodrich. Full cloth in dust jacket, signed and numbered by the families, $47.00. Trade softcover, $22.00.

Subscriptions

Subscribers agree to purchase each forthcoming publication, either the Regular Series or the Lost Classics or (preferably) both. Collectors can thereby guarantee receiving limited editions, and readers won't miss any favorite stories.

Subscribers receive a discount of 20% off the list price (and the same discount on our backlist) and a specially commissioned short story by a major writer in a deluxe edition as a gift at the end of the year.

The point for us is that, since customers don't pick and choose which books they want, we have a guaranteed sale even before the book is published, and that allows us to be more imaginative in choosing short story collections to issue.

That's worth the 20% discount for us. Sign up now and start saving. Email us at orders@crippenlandru.com or visit our website at www.crippenlandru.com on our subscription page.

CPSIA information can be obtained
at www.ICGtesting.com
Printed in the USA
JSHW020858090523
41434JS00001B/25